Their Forever

TARA CONRAD

HIS ONE HER ONLY PUBLISHING

Contents

Chapter 1   1
Chapter 2   3
Chapter 3   10
Chapter 4   13
Chapter 5   17
Chapter 6   22
Chapter 7   29
Chapter 8   31
Chapter 9   35
Chapter 10   38
Chapter 11   42
Chapter 12   48
Chapter 13   50
Chapter 14   52
Chapter 15   57
Chapter 16   64
Chapter 17   67
Chapter 18   69
Chapter 19   72
Chapter 20   75
Chapter 21   78
Chapter 22   82
Chapter 23   86
Chapter 24   88
Chapter 25   95
Chapter 26   100
Chapter 27   105
Chapter 28   111
Chapter 29   117
Chapter 30   120
Chapter 31   123
Chapter 32   127

Chapter 33 132
Chapter 34 136
Chapter 35 139
Chapter 36 141
Chapter 37 146
Chapter 38 150
Chapter 39 155
Chapter 40 159
Chapter 41 163
Chapter 42 167
Chapter 43 170
Chapter 44 172
Chapter 45 176
Chapter 46 181
Chapter 47 184
Chapter 48 189
Chapter 49 192
Chapter 50 196
Chapter 51 202
Chapter 52 206
Chapter 53 211
Chapter 54 214
Chapter 55 218
Chapter 56 224
Chapter 57 229
Chapter 58 233
Chapter 59 235
Chapter 60 240
Chapter 61 245
Chapter 62 248
Chapter 63 255
Chapter 64 258
Chapter 65 261
Chapter 66 263
Chapter 67 266
Chapter 68 270
Chapter 69 272

Chapter 70	279
Chapter 71	284
Chapter 72	287
Chapter 73	291
Chapter 74	295
Chapter 75	298
Chapter 76	302
Chapter 77	305
Chapter 78	308
Chapter 79	313
Chapter 80	316
Chapter 81	320
Chapter 82	325
Chapter 83	328
Epilogue	335
About Tara	342
Acknowledgments	343
Resources	344

To my husband, my Sir- You have been my rock throughout this entire series. When I was lost, You helped me find my way. i look forward to living our happily ever after.

To the men, women, and children affected by the horrible act of human trafficking. Know that you are not forgotten. We will continue the fight to end trafficking and to bring each and every one of you home.

Chapter One

XAVIER

My plan is genius. Hide in plain sight. New York City is the perfect place to do just that. Here, I'm just another nameless face in a sea of millions. People go about their daily lives without so much as sparing me a second glance. It's taken a shit ton of patience, but my plans are finally coming together.

I pull open the glass door of the historic building and nod at the security guard.

"How are you this morning, Xavier?" the man asks.

"I'm livin' the dream." I smile and head for the staff elevator.

As the basement door chimes, I step inside and head towards the stockroom to gather my supplies. I adjust my olive-green cap, giving it a snug fit, and then push the maintenance cart down the concrete hallway. The cart's wobbly wheels squeak with every step I take. After loading my cart onto the elevator, I ride to the tenth floor, where construction work is in full swing for a new business set to open its doors in January. Everyone's been tight-lipped about the specifics of the project. While the project's details have been kept under wraps, being part of the maintenance crew has perks. People tend to let their guard down around us, thinking they're speaking in private, but we're always listening. Word on the street is that Alexander Montgomery is spearheading the opening of a women's shelter. He's always trying to play the hero.

The doors open, and I step out. "Good morning." I nod to Steve, the foreman, who's standing just outside the elevator.

"About time you got here, X," he jokes. "Do you mind helping my guys get this stuff out to the dumpster?" He points to a pile of drywall pieces.

"Consider it done," I say as I move my cart out of the way and head over to the clean-up crew. Without hesitation, I gather garbage and pile it into boxes to load into the elevator. As we work, we chat about the Giant's game from last week. In this environment, I feel like just one of the guys, and there are no doubts about my place here.

What's better is that no one is aware of my true intentions. And they won't know.

Until I'm ready to strike.

Chapter Two

∞

NATALIE

OUR WEDDING WAS LIKE A DREAM COME TRUE, A REAL-life fairy tale. Although it wasn't exactly what we'd originally envisioned, sometimes even the most carefully crafted plans can be improved with a little bit of change. I don't know how Alex planned a collaring ceremony and a surprise wedding a few weeks later. I'm married to the most wonderful man in the world.

After the wedding, we skipped a traditional honeymoon. Instead, Alex and I chose to spend our first few days as newlyweds nestled away in our cozy lake cottage. Now that we're back in the city, our lives have been a non-stop flurry of activity.

"Keep your eyes closed. No peeking," Alex says as he leads me to what used to be one of our guest rooms. Recently, he converted it into a shared office space. He forbade me from peeking while the room was under construction. The crew finished earlier today, and I'm finally getting the big reveal. Alex holds my hand, leading me into the room. "You can open your eyes now."

The walls have been painted a lovely shade of soft purple, my absolute favorite color. A set of stunning ebony-stained book-shelves is neatly arranged along the back wall. The real showstopper is the custom-made black two-person desk positioned in front of floor-to-ceiling windows that offer breathtaking water views. As I look closer, I notice that Alex's side of the desk features a framed photo of us on our wedding day alongside an ultrasound picture of our baby. "I love everything about this."

"And I'm going to love working side-by-side with my wife." He wraps his arms around me from behind, splaying his hands on my tummy.

Aside from overseeing the work in our home office, Alex's other focus has been on phasing himself out of the day-to-day operations at Montgomery Advertising. That process has been going smoothly. His personal clients have all agreed to stay on with Brandon at the helm. One more week, and the transition will be complete. After that, Alex can focus solely on our Jelena's Hope NYC project.

Getting that off the ground started chaotically, but it's much smoother now that the permits have finally come through. The construction crew is in place and has begun the first stages of demolition. Earlier today, the architect sent over the digital design for the offices and residences. Signing off on the rendering is the last step before the actual construction begins.

Alex peppers my neck with kisses. "Ready to look at the design?"

"Mmm." I tilt my head, giving him more access, and rub against the erection poking my back. "I'd rather we explore this."

"That's very tempting, Mrs. Montgomery, but I told the architect we'd get back to her by this afternoon." He releases me and pulls my chair out. "Let's get to work."

I push out my bottom lip in a pout and lower myself into my black and purple desk chair. Sex with Alex has always been good, but being pregnant has made me insatiable, craving his touch at all hours and leaving me breathless with need every time he's near. The last thing I want to do right now is look at a computer screen. Alex's playful blue eyes glance my way, and he smiles. Then, he gets comfortable in his black chair and fires up the laptop.

With a click, he opens the file, bringing to life a three-dimensional mock-up of the new facility. I lean forward in my seat as Alex begins our virtual tour of the building. I'm enthralled by the images on the screen. The program offers a true-to-life view of the proposed design.

"What's this?" I point to a cluster of rooms.

"It's our education center." Alex clicks the area, and the program zooms in on one of the classrooms. "The children in our care will need to be enrolled in school. Traditional schools don't have the support system they need. Having an in-house school allows us to meet both the therapeutic and educational needs within the safety of our walls." He moves into another room. "There are additional classrooms for adults who wish to complete their education while they're with us."

I didn't stop to consider that we'll recover children, and they'll need schooling in addition to mental health treatment. Thankfully, Alex was looking at the bigger picture. "You've thought of everything."

"I'd love to take the credit, but it wasn't my idea. It's part of the startup plans Max sent us."

The next stop on our virtual tour is the medical, therapy, and job training rooms. Each will be fitted with ultramodern equipment to provide the best care possible to our residents. After we finish the business area, we move up a floor to the residences.

"There will be mental health and medical professionals available around the clock for the residents," Alex explains as we get our first view of the units.

Our facility will consist of three floors with a total of eighteen apartments designed to provide separate living spaces for men, women, and children. The twelve adult apartments will house three individuals per unit and boast identical layouts with a shared kitchen and living area. The designer has carefully selected calming shades of blue and green for the walls. Each resident will have a private bedroom and bathroom with a clean, minimalist aesthetic, furnished with a full-size bed, dresser, desk, and comfortable chair.

The remaining six units are specially designed to cater to the unique needs of children. Each apartment will house four children and a set of vetted and trained house parents who specialize in working with trafficked children. These units have an open floor plan to allow the house parents to keep a watchful eye on the children at all times. In addition to the kitchen and living room, the children's units have fully stocked playrooms filled with games and toys to keep them entertained. Like the adults, each child will have a private bedroom and bathroom to provide a safe and nurturing environment for them to heal and recover.

"I wasn't sure what to expect. Part of me feared the apartments would be sterile and institutional-looking, but they aren't. They're comfortable and homey."

"We're good to sign off on these?" Alex asks.

"We are."

"I found a few houses outside of Manhattan that our realtor is in the process of closing on." Alex opens a web browser to show me the listings. "Since Dad and Maxim are funding these properties, I sent them the links the other day to get their approval."

I'm amazed at the vast amount of progress Alex has made on this project in such a short time. When he sets his mind to something, there's no stopping him. Alex's excitement is contagious as he shows me pictures of the listings. Each house is located in flourishing neighborhoods on tree-lined streets, an idyllic setting for someone transitioning back into society.

My heart aches as I look at the pictures, knowing there are people out there right now suffering. They don't know their rescues are being planned and that they'll be safe very soon. Tears trail down my cheeks.

"What's wrong, baby girl?" Alex turns me to face him.

"Knowing we'll fill up as soon as the doors open." I swallow over a sob. "That the need is so great. The reality is hard to face."

"It's a part of society most people are either unaware of or choose to turn a blind eye to." Alex wipes my tears. "But for those who've experienced it firsthand, it's something they can never forget—never pretend it doesn't exist."

"When I decided to become a therapist, I was sure my future was in Northmeadow and that my purpose was helping other youth from close-minded families like mine. In my wildest dreams, I wouldn't have been able to imagine the path my life would take, that I'd meet you. And that I'd be personally affected by trafficking. But now I know everything I experienced was leading me to this moment."

Alex gently rubs his knuckles along my cheek. "I hate what happened to us—to you. But I wouldn't want to do this with anyone else. You and I, Natalie Montgomery, are an unstoppable team."

He kisses me, and I bask in my Dominant's affection. With only a few simple words, he makes me feel like the most treasured woman on the planet. But as cherished as he makes me feel, it doesn't stop the doubts and questions plaguing me.

Being a mother has always been part of my plan. Yes, I wanted to get my education and have a career, but in my head, I always saw myself being a stay-at-home mom, like my mom was when we were little. It's hard to imagine I'd want to do something the same way as my mom, but it's true. We continue to butt heads, although it's been much less lately.

I always admired Mom for her dedication to raising Michael and me. I can't imagine how she must've felt watching my dad go off to work every day, knowing she'd be alone with two young children for long hours while he was at the store. I smile, remembering the antics Michael and I would get up to. We climbed trees and tore our clothes, made mud pies in the dirt, and then brought them into the house to show our mom the delicious *snacks* we made. Michael and I were a handful, but no matter how messy or loud we were, Mom always remained patient.

She tried to give us as many experiences as possible within a small town. We spent countless afternoons at the park playing with the other children. We spent time at our neighbor's farms, helping with their animals. From the time we were little, Mom would have us at her side in the kitchen, helping her cook.

As we got older, we spent time at the store helping out where we could. And countless art projects. Mom is very artistic and tried desperately to pass that on to Michael and me. She hoped at least one of us would be artistically inclined. Instead of master-pieces, she got finger-painted floors and crayon-colored walls.

Summertime holds some of my very favorite memories. Michael and I spent hours helping Mom meticulously plant flowers and vegetables for the family garden. As we got older, she gave us a tiny patch of our own to plant. It was hard work keeping our young seedlings weed-free and adequately watered. But when fall came, Michael and I were so proud of the vegetables we'd harvested. I've always wanted to pass the love of gardening on to my children one day.

It wasn't until Michael and I were both in school that Mom started working part-time at the pharmacy. She'd wake up before dawn each morning to cook breakfast and get us ready for school. After the bus picked us up, she would get a ride into town to work for a few hours. Mom always made sure she was home before we got home from school. She'd be waiting with snacks and ready to hear our endless chatter about everything that happened at school.

While we did our homework, Mom got dinner started. When Dad came in from work, dinner would be on the table. We sat down and ate as a family every night. After the meal, Michael and I helped with chores while Dad watched the evening news. Then, she'd get us bathed and ready for bed. Each night, Mom read us a bedtime story and then tucked us in. But her night still wasn't over. She'd head back down to the kitchen to pack our lunches for the next day.

Looking back, I don't know how she had the energy to do all that day after day. That's always been the picture I had of my future life, the kind of mother I imagined myself becoming.

Opening Jelena's Hope NYC has changed what my future will look like. I'll be a mother in a few short months, but I won't have the luxury of being a full-time stay-at-home mom. I've committed to working with the women who'll no doubt be at our center. I'm finding myself torn in two directions.

Alex has mentioned possibly hiring a nanny while I work. The thought of letting someone else raise my child is disheartening. I need to share these concerns with Alex, but I'm unsure how to approach the topic. Even though I'm running out of time, I'm not ready to put my thoughts and fears into words yet.

"Earth to Natalie." Alex places his hand on mine, snapping me from my thoughts.

"I'm sorry. I guess I spaced out." I force a smile.

"Are you okay?"

"I am." I point to the screen. "The houses are very nice."

"Mhm." Alex eyes me suspiciously. "I've instructed the real estate agent to put full asking price offers on each one."

"Fingers crossed, we'll get them all."

"Even if we have to go above the asking price, I'll make sure we get them."

Everything's set in motion. We're one step closer to making our dream of Jelena's Hope-NYC a reality.

Chapter Three

∞

ALEX

After sending the last email, I close the laptop and turn to my wife. "Thanksgiving's next month."

"Yes, Sir. I recall that happening every November." Natalie gives me a cheeky grin.

She's feisty today. I like seeing this side of her. "I want to invite your parents for the holiday."

"Like they'd ever come here for Thanksgiving." She raises her eyebrows, possibly questioning my sanity.

"We have plenty of room for them to stay with us. You and your mom can have Pie Day. Maybe we can even convince them to go to the parade."

I know Thanksgiving holds so many special memories for her until the disaster last year. But the holiday is only a few weeks away, and she hasn't mentioned anything about it. I'm sure she's trying to avoid the memories, but that won't help anything. My hope is that if her parents come here, we can start new traditions—make new memories.

Natalie bites her lip. "I don't know, Alex." She stands and walks to the door.

"I want this." It's not a question. Not open for argument, yet she tries anyway.

"You know my parents won't come to the city. Especially for a holiday."

"We'll see about that."

"If you say so."

"I say so."

"Don't be surprised when they say no." Her shoulders slump in defeat. "I'll be in the baby's room if you need me."

Although the relationship with her parents has improved since this time last year, there's still healing to be done. There are things about Charlotte and Stanley that'll never change. Quirks, we have to accept. But New York City is our home. That's a fact that's not going to change. They want to be part of their daughter and soon-to-be granddaughter's lives. That means they'll have to compromise and be willing to travel to the city occasionally.

I give them a call.

"Hello?"

"Hi, Stanley. It's Alex."

"Is everything okay?"

"Everything's great. I'm calling because Natalie and I would like you and Charlotte to spend Thanksgiving with us in the city."

"I see."

"I'd like to fly you both out the week before so we can spend time together before the holiday."

"Well, we've always had Thanksgiving here," Stanley says. "Charlotte and I assumed you and Natalie would come to Northmeadow."

"I understand that. However, with Natalie this far along in her pregnancy, she can't be traveling that far."

"Hang on. Let me get Charlotte."

This isn't going as planned. I thought Charlotte would be the hard sell. But if I can't get past Stanley, I'm not sure how well this is going to go.

"Alex, how are you?" Charlotte asks.

"I'm doing well. I'm trying to convince your husband to agree to spend the holiday with us here."

"Oh, I see," she says, echoing her husband's initial response. "This is very unexpected."

"We'd like to fly you out the week before the holiday. You can stay with us. Maybe you can help Natalie with the nursery?"

"I'd love to be able to help Natalie get the baby's room ready," Charlotte says.

Aha, I found the right angle. I can almost hear the smile on Charlotte's face.

"I suppose it wouldn't hurt to try things a little differently this year."

"Excellent. I'll buy the tickets and email you the information. Natalie's going to be so excited. Oh. And bring that pretty apron for Pie Day."

"Of course," Charlotte chirps. "We can't have Thanksgiving without Pie Day."

What I didn't tell them was that I'd already bought the airline tickets. I don't want to risk them changing their minds, so I email the flight information as soon as we hang up. Then, I shoot a quick text to my father to confirm his and Luna's flight arrangements. Brandon and I spoke last week. He and Lana will be here. My last call is to Maxim, who assures me they can't wait to get here. I sit back and take a deep breath. Everyone I invited has said yes. The holiday is going to be perfect.

Now I get to tell Natalie the good news.

Chapter Four

NATALIE

I'm standing in what will eventually be Rose's nursery if I ever figure out the paint color.

"Still trying to decide?" Alex asks as he comes into the room and stands next to me. Out of the corner of my eye, I see him watching me curiously as I study the paint swatches on the wall.

"I've narrowed it down to these two, but I can't decide if I like this one," -I point to one of the samples- "or this one."

Alex takes a step closer to the wall. "They look the same to me."

The colors are not the same at all. The one on the right is a cool gray with undertones of blue. And the one on the left is a neutral gray.

"I think this is the one." I grab the neutral gray and hand it to Alex. "It'll be perfect with the pink accents we already chose."

"Is this your final answer?" He grins as he dangles the paint swatch in his hand.

Still feeling a bit indecisive, I take a last look between the sample in Alex's hand and the one taped to the wall. "Yes. I'm certain that's the one."

Alex takes me by the hand. "Let's get it mixed."

One of the perks of living in such a big city is the accessibility of almost anything we could ever want. We have a paint store a few blocks away, and since it's a beautiful late-October afternoon, we chose to walk. The fall air is crisp and cool. This time of the year was always my favorite in Missouri. The tree-covered mountains turn into a canvas of reds, oranges, and yellows. Part of me longs to be at our lake house, the fallen leaves crunching under our feet, but the other part is at peace, knowing we're exactly where we're meant to be.

A few blocks into our walk, Alex says, "Looks like we're hosting our first Thanksgiving."

"My parents said yes?"

"They sure did." Alex smiles proudly.

"How did you pull that off?"

"I may have mentioned that your mom could help decorate the nursery. And that she should bring her apron."

"You bribed her?" I laugh.

"It worked." He shrugs before opening the door, holding it for me to go ahead of him. "Anyway, I can't wait to see my sexy submissive in nothing but an apron."

"So, you had ulterior motives, Sir?"

"One could call it motivation. Your parents aren't the only ones coming."

"Who else did you invite?"

Alex goes down the list of everyone who's said yes.

"I can't believe it." I throw my arms around his neck and kiss him.

A salesperson clears their voice, interrupting our public display of affection.

"May I help you?"

Without missing a beat, Alex hands over the paint swatch. While the paint is being mixed, we shop for the rest of the supplies. I suggested we hire a painter, but Alex insisted on doing the work himself. I love that he wants to be hands-on with everything concerning the baby. After the paint is mixed and Alex is confident he has enough rollers and brushes, we pay for our purchases. Then, with bags in hand, we walk back to our apartment.

Alex has been painting for the past few hours. I wanted to help, too, but even though we bought no-VOC paint, his answer was still a firm *no*. I've been on the phone with Lana for quite a while discussing plans for the holiday, but now it's time to get some video of Alex painting.

I tiptoe down the hall, hoping to sneak up on him and get some candid shots. I plan to document every moment of our getting ready for our little girl. Even with the door closed, I can hear his music. I hope it provides enough cover so he doesn't hear me as I slowly turn the handle and push the door open just a crack.

Peeking around with the camera, I hit record. It takes all my self-control not to drool when I lay eyes on a shirtless Alex wearing my favorite pair of jeans that fit in all the right places. His muscles flex as he rolls the paint onto the walls.

"I know you're there." Alex stops painting and turns around. "Are you recording me?"

"I am. One day, I want to be able to show our daughter these videos so she knows how loved she was, even before she was born."

Alex sets the roller down on the tray. "Is that so?" His eyes are now laser-focused on me as he stalks across the room.

"It is." I bite my bottom lip. "I want her to see how much her mommy and daddy love each other and how excited we are about her."

Alex flashes me a sexy grin right before he grabs the camera from my hand. He holds it up to film us as he leans in and kisses me before looking directly into the camera.

"Rose, your mama is my world." He kisses me again. "She's the best thing that ever happened to me." Another kiss. "I'm sure you already know, but she's also going to be the best mommy in the world. We're both lucky to have her."

Then, he turns off the camera and slides my phone into his pocket before wrapping his arms around me and pulling me against him. His hand finds its way through my hair, and he tugs it, making me look up at him.

"I want you naked and waiting for me in our bedroom. I'll be in as soon as I clean up."

"Yes, Sir."

Alex releases me and strides back across the room to complete his task. My feet stay rooted while I watch my sexy Dominant bend over and pick up the paint tray.

"Now, baby girl."

His command is all the encouragement my feet need to start moving. I quickly leave the nursery and head down the hall to our bedroom. My entire body tingles with anticipation, eagerly awaiting whatever surprises Alex has in store for me.

Chapter Five

∞

ALEX

I'M FINISHING UP THE LAST OF THE PAINTING WHEN Natalie tries to sneak up on me. I'm crazy attracted to her on a typical day. But seeing her growing my child, my sexual attraction to her is off the charts. I can't keep my hands or dick to myself. She doesn't seem to mind either. Being pregnant has only increased her already healthy sex drive. After closing the paint can, I head to the guest room for a quick shower, knowing the extended delay will only heighten my sub's anticipation.

After I've showered, I wrap a towel around my waist and stop in the kitchen to grab a glass of ice before heading to our bedroom. When I open the door, I find Natalie gloriously naked and on her knees waiting for me. My body responds immediately, the outline of my erection prominent from under the towel. I put the glass on the dresser and go to Natalie.

"Stand up." I offer her my hand to help her off the floor.

"That's not as easy as it was a few weeks ago," she says with a slight shake of her head.

"Come sit down." I lead her to the bed and have her sit back against the pillows. "Give me your leg."

She places her foot on my lap, and I massage one leg first, then the other.

"Mm..." she groans. "That feels so good."

"No more kneeling while you're pregnant." I finish her mini massage. "Are your legs okay?"

"Yes, Sir. They're much better now."

"Good. Now get on your hands and knees." I arrange a pillow under her stomach to give her support.

She looks over her shoulder and wiggles her ass flirtatiously, earning her a playful slap before I make my way into our closet.

When I return, I set one of my surprises in the glass of ice before stopping to admire how beautiful Natalie looks with her legs spread, baring herself to me. Her breasts are full and begging to be sucked. My erection throbs between my legs as I remove my towel with one hand and let it fall to the floor. In my other hand is her favorite flogger.

Coming up behind her, I knead the globes of her ass, preparing her for what's to come. Natalie moans softly. With a flick of my wrist, the leather tails land gently across her skin. This isn't an impact scene. My plan is to experiment with different sensations. The next hit lands between her legs, and she gasps. I run my finger through her slit before sliding it inside. She rocks against my hand.

"My greedy little sub."

"I am, Sir."

"What's your color?" Checking in has become more important as her pregnancy progresses. Her body reacts differently now than it did even just a week or two ago, and she tires quickly in some positions.

"Green, Sir."

I continue alternating between light strikes with the flogger and teasing her clit. The next gentle lick of the leather tails is followed by dragging my finger through her wetness. Then, I circle her tight entrance before sliding it in. She drops her head as I pump my finger in and out, gently stretching her.

"That feels so good."

I remove my finger, eliciting a groan from her.

"We're nowhere near done yet, baby girl." I set the flogger down on the dresser before grabbing the glass butt plug from the ice and the lube. I apply a generous amount to the cold toy before teasing her, sliding the tip in and out.

"How does it feel?"

"Mmm. So good."

"Touch yourself," I order. "I want you to make yourself come for me."

She slides one hand between her legs, circling her clit while I tease her ass with the plug. The closer she gets to orgasm, the less her body resists. Her pleasure is growing more and more.

"Come for me, now."

I push the plug in all the way as her orgasm washes over her. She drops her head, breathing heavily, but we're far from done. I help Natalie off her knees and onto her back, propping her on pillows so she's not lying flat. Then, I drop to my knees and position her legs over my shoulders. Her pussy is glistening with her arousal. It's an erotic sight. I lean in and lick from one end to the other. "You taste exquisite."

Natalie's eyes flutter open as she watches me drop my head between her legs. My tongue teases her, nipping and sucking her clit before adding my fingers, pumping them in and out. Natalie moans in response, pushing herself against me, seeking more friction.

"Patience, baby girl." I grab her hips, stilling her.

She drops her head. "Please, Sir. I want you." I love hearing her beg for me.

Without wasting time, I return to my ministrations. This time fucking her with my tongue while my hand pumps the plug in and out of her ass. It takes only seconds before she's screaming my name. But my mouth doesn't stop. I intend to take everything she has to offer. Once her orgasm subsides, I stand and fist my cock. Pre-cum drips from the tip. With hooded eyes, she watches my every movement as I line myself up with her opening and enter her slowly, allowing her to adjust to the overwhelming sensations I know she's experiencing by having both holes filled. Once I'm fully sheathed, I stop, savoring how tight she feels wrapped around me. I slide my hand up her body, stopping at her breast. I alternate between palming her soft flesh and rolling her erect nipples. Then I start moving, slow and steady.

"You feel so good." Her voice is breathless. "I need more."

"You need more?" I tease.

"Yes, Sir." She moans. "Harder, please."

That request, I can oblige. My hands hold her hips as I pick up the speed and strength of my thrusts.

"Is this what you want?"

"Mmm..."

Natalie's moans grow louder, her breaths quicken as she approaches another climax. I am poised to join her, eager for the plunge into bliss. Her cries of pleasure fill the room as her body shudders with the force of her orgasm. I'm also overwhelmed with sensation as my release pulses through my body, and I fill her. Though Natalie is starting to tire, my selfish desire pushes me to continue, alternating between gently pumping in and out and circling my hips, each motion grazing her overly sensitive clitoris.

"Oh my God, don't stop."

I continue teasing her until I feel myself getting close. As I approach my climax, I speed up my thrusts. Right as I let go, I pull the plug from her ass. The sensation causes her to orgasm again, and her body shudders beneath mine. Sweat drips from her forehead. She's spent.

"That was mind-blowing, Sir."

"You're incredible, baby girl." I move from between her legs and immediately miss our intimate connection. "Wait here."

I go into the bathroom and wet a washcloth with warm water before returning to my sub. Parting her legs, I clean her before tossing the cloth onto the bedside table. Then, I pull the comforter back and help Natalie to the top of the bed, where I climb next to her. She lays her head on my chest, her arm thrown over my abdomen. My fingers draw lazy circles on her back. At this moment, words aren't needed. Instead, we bask in the connection we share.

I wait until Natalie's body relaxes, and she's snoring softly. Then, I carefully slide my arm from under her and get out of bed. I throw on clean clothes and go to the kitchen to cook dinner. Natalie's going to be hungry when she wakes.

Chapter Six

NATALIE

"I DON'T KNOW HOW YOU HAVE THE PATIENCE FOR this," I say to Viktor, who's driving, or, should I say, sitting at a standstill in traffic.

"If we took the subway, we'd be there already." Viktor shoots Alex a frustrated glance in the rearview. But Alex doesn't seem to notice. He has his head down, engrossed with something on his phone.

"I already told you, no subway," Alex says without looking up. "We have plenty of time to get there."

Alex and Viktor have been engaged in a battle of wills, which has had Alex on a knife's edge all morning. We have to be at Jelena's Hope NYC for a walk-through. Viktor wanted us to take the subway, but Alex has been struggling with being in confined spaces since our ordeal in Mexico. So, he insisted that we drive even though it would take twice the time. The tension between the two men is unsettling. I place my hand on Alex's leg, trying to calm him. He puts his hand over mine and gives it a reassuring squeeze.

We slowly crawl through the streets while the city's iconic

yellow taxis weave in and out of traffic. Each time they zoom by, I cringe at their proximity. I would've much preferred taking the subway, too, but Alex has the last word. Finally, after over an hour, Viktor pulls up outside the Jelena's Hope-NYC building.

"I'll drop you off and meet you upstairs after I park the car."

"Thanks," Alex says curtly as he steps out.

He offers me his hand, helping me to my feet. Standing up grows more difficult as my stomach grows rounder with each passing day. Once in the building, we stop at the security desk to check in.

"Good afternoon, Mr. and Mrs. Montgomery," the guard greets us.

"How's everything today, Leon?" Alex asks. "How's your wife feeling?"

Alex never ceases to amaze me with how he makes a personal connection with everyone he comes in contact with. He has a heart of gold.

"Not well. Her body's no longer responding to the treatments," Leon says, his shoulders sagging in defeat. "The doctors are scrambling to come up with another plan."

"I'm so sorry to hear that. Please let me know if there's anything I can do to help."

"I appreciate the offer, Mr. Montgomery." He looks behind us. "No Viktor today?"

"He's parking the car. He'll be along shortly. We're going upstairs to check in on the progress."

"I'll make a note of that." Leon turns to his computer screen and begins typing.

Alex and I walk hand-in-hand to the elevator, where he presses his finger against a pad on the wall. He wasn't kidding when he told me this building has state-of-the-art security. Alex explains that if someone who isn't programmed into the system enters through the underground parking, the elevator will only take them to the ground floor. "It ensures no one can access any of the upper floors without going through security first. We'll program your fingerprint while we're here."

"What about the steps?"

"They're equipped with the same technology."

"That's amazing."

The elevator ride is fast and smooth as it brings us to our floor. The last time I was here, the demo had just finished, and the place was a blank slate. I'm anxious to see what progress has been made.

Steve, the construction foreman, is waiting for us when we step out. "Good to see you, Mr. Montgomery." The men shake hands. Then he quickly glances my way. "You as well, Mrs. Montgomery."

"It looks so different in here from last time."

"We've been busy," Steve says. "Are you ready for the tour?"

We follow Steve to a sectioned-off area to our right. This will eventually be the reception area. Alex and Steve don't waste a second discussing technical things I don't care to understand.

Touching Alex's arm, I say, "I'm going to look at the design samples." I motion toward a table.

"I'll be over in a minute," he assures me, and then returns to his conversation.

We've already signed off on the paint. This time, the designer has left several options for the hardwood floors. There's also a tablet with digital photos of the furniture that'll be used in the reception area. Although it's commercial-grade, the couches and chairs look plush and inviting. Several fabric swatches are laid out for us to choose from. At first glance, the light gray fabric stands out. It seems to meld with the peaceful aesthetic we're looking to achieve.

"What do you think?" Alex asks, coming up behind me.

"I love the choices. But something's missing." I look around the room. Alex and Steve stand silently, watching me. "The colors are soothing, and I'm sure once the furniture gets here, it'll help, but it feels sterile. When the survivors step in here for the first time, they'll likely be in fight-or-flight mode. This area is going to be their first impression of Jelena's Hope-NYC. It needs to feel safe and comfortable—they need to see life. What would you think about adding some plants and maybe a large aquarium?"

Alex looks around as if he's trying to envision what I've described. "I think that's an excellent idea. Steve, will you contact the architect and put that into action?"

"Yes, sir," he says, although he looks unsure. "How about we continue the tour?"

Alex places his hand on the small of my back as we follow Steve to the offices. While we walk down the spacious hallway, Steve says, "There's someone I'd like you to meet." Steve checks in a few rooms but doesn't seem to find whoever he's looking for. "I was hoping to introduce you to X-man?"

"Excuse me?" Alex asks.

"That's the nickname we've given the guy. He's one of the building's maintenance men who's been helping out." Steve checks in another room. "He was just here. I guess he went on break. The guy's a hard worker. I'm thinking about offering him a permanent position on my crew."

"If you think he's a good fit, I'll trust your judgment. I'm sure we'll catch him next time."

After the tour of the business section, we come to the private elevators that service only the floors belonging to Jelena's Hope-NYC.

"Hey, Steve," one of the men calls. "There's a phone call for you."

"I've been waiting to hear from one of the product suppliers. Do you mind continuing the tour on your own?"

"We'll be fine," Alex assures him as we step into the elevator for the quick ride up to the next floor.

Stepping out into the first of our residential units, no one would ever suspect this was anything more than a high-end apartment building. The hallway has dark floors, but with the bright lighting, it balances well. I'm not sure if it's authentic hardwood or a laminate. Either way, it's beautiful. What steals the show are the hand-painted murals on the walls. We're walking through a jungle with lifelike trees and animals. It's magical.

"Obviously, this is the children's floor," Alex says as he opens the door to the first apartment.

As we step into the open expanse, sunlight pours in through floor-to-ceiling windows, illuminating the entire space. To one side, a cozy living room greets us with plush couches and chairs. They're arranged to face a generously sized flat-screen TV mounted on the wall. Nearby shelves overflow with books and games. Brightly colored bean bag chairs complete the inviting atmosphere.

On the opposite side of the room, a modern kitchen and dining area beckon with gleaming white cabinets and sparkling marble countertops. Top-of-the-line stainless steel appliances add a touch of luxury that the house parents will appreciate. An expansive island with several chairs separates the eating area from the rest of the room, creating the perfect spot for a quick snack. A large dining table sits before the windows, comfortably accommodating at least seven guests for more formal meals.

"This is exactly how I pictured it." I squeeze Alex's hand in excitement. "It feels like a home."

We continue down the hallway until we reach the first door. Alex opens it to reveal one of the children's bedrooms. At first glance, the space appears somewhat generic, eliciting feelings of disappointment. However, I remind myself that the minimal design is intentional. These rooms are designed to provide a haven—a peaceful and unstimulating environment. As the children settle in and become more comfortable, they'll have the opportunity to personalize and decorate the space to their liking.

Two windows fill the room with natural light, but heavy curtains can be drawn to darken the room when needed. Across from the windows sits a cozy twin bed, complete with a fluffy white comforter and an abundance of soft pillows. Much like the play area, the bedroom features a bean bag chair and a small shelf that will eventually be filled with books and toys.

The last wall has two doors.

"Which one should we look behind first?"

"You pick."

I chose the door on the left, which opens to a bathroom complete with a tub and a walk-in shower. The last door leads to a walk-in closet just waiting to be filled with clothes.

"When the kids arrive, they'll have nothing. So how do we know what clothes to buy? What sizes we will need?" I ask Alex.

"Honestly, I have no idea." He pulls his cell from his pocket. "Let's call Max and Irina for some guidance."

"Pardon me for eavesdropping," a dark-haired woman says as she walks into the room. "I can answer that for you."

"Imani, it's so good to finally meet you." We've had many online conferences with our designer, but this is the first time we're getting to meet in person.

I offer Imani my hand, but she surprises me by pulling me in for a hug instead.

"It's great to meet you, too," she says, shaking Alex's hand. "In answer to your question, Irina and I have spoken at length. She's instructed me to buy wardrobe staples—pants, shirts, pajamas, everything a child needs in nearly every size. I've done the same for the adults as well. Each floor has a general closet room to pull from. Once the child or adult is settled, we can get their exact size, and if they'd like, they can help choose their clothes," she explains. "Irina stressed the importance of providing each person freedom with as many choices as possible."

"Given that so much of their freedom has been stolen, that makes perfect sense and answers my question." I smile.

"What do you think about the apartment?" she asks.

"You've done a wonderful job.

"Have you been in the parents' suite yet?"

"Not yet," Alex answers.

As we walk down the hall, Imani explains that the other three children's rooms are identical to the one we were just in. At the end of the hall, we come to a set of double doors. "This is the parents' suite. I've tried very hard to make it a luxurious sanctuary."

I'm speechless as I look around the room that's set up like a loft apartment.

"I've spoken to each of the couples to get their input on the design," she explains.

"Imani, this is exquisite." Alex compliments her work.

A kitchenette and a cozy sitting area with a fireplace are on our left. Opposite that area is a sleeping area with a king-size bed. Like the kids' rooms, there's a spacious walk-in closet and a large bathroom. The walls in this room are cerulean blue, and the floor is covered in a cream-colored carpet.

"This particular couple requested a coastal design," Imani explains. "The linens and décor will arrive later this week."

"I love it." I walk toward the window and look out at the view of Central Park. "This job will be demanding. The couples will need this sanctuary to escape to at the end of the day."

"Then I've accomplished my goal." She smiles proudly.

"You've done an excellent job," Alex adds.

"Thank you, Mr. Montgomery. Shall we go up to the adult floors?"

The three of us do a walkthrough of an apartment on each floor and find them in good order. Imani took our initial vision and ran with it. She far exceeded our expectations.

"Thank you for the tour."

"Don't hesitate to contact us if you need anything," Alex says.

Chapter Seven

XAVIER

I'm going about my daily routine when Steve approaches me.

"Xavier, do you have a minute?"

"Sure thing." I wipe the sweat from my forehead. "What's up?"

"You've proven to be a valuable asset to my crew. I want to talk to Mr. Montgomery about hiring you to help complete this project."

"Oh?" I'm pleasantly surprised at this turn of events.

"It would be a pay raise and the chance to join us permanently if you're interested."

"Can I let you know in a few days?"

"That'll be fine. Mr. Montgomery will be here any minute, and I want to introduce you to him."

Shit. That can't happen. "No problem. I'll be here."

I go back to work and wait until Steve is out of sight. Then, I slip into the stairwell and hurry to the basement. There's no way I can be around while Montgomery's here. I've worked too hard for my plans to be ruined. My plan is complicated, especially with the buildings' tight security. But if you watch and listen, the weak spots always show themselves.

In this building, the weak spot is Leon, the head of security. He has a wife with a terminal illness. The doctors have tried everything to get her out of pain, but it hasn't worked. Leon's desperate to see her pain-free, and I happen to have what he needs. It didn't take too much persuading. In exchange for some product that helps his wife, Leon's agreed to turn a blind eye when I need it. It was like giving candy to a child.

Once I'm in the basement, I head to the employees' locker room and open my locker to double-check that the package I brought is still hidden. There are just a few more pieces I need to get in place. Then, I'll have everything I need to move forward with my plan. I close the door and make sure it's locked securely. I can't risk being careless.

Just a few more weeks...

Chapter Eight

ALEX

Viktor: I'm at the airport now. The Clarkes' flight just landed.

Me: Great. Keep me updated.

"I still can't believe you convinced them to come here."

"What can I say? I can be very persuasive."

"I seem to remember that about you." Natalie grins.

It's taken a few hours, but I'm finally tightening the last screw for my daughter's crib. I stand back and admire my handiwork. "What do you think?"

Natalie pushes herself to stand from the rocking chair and walks over to look at the white canopy crib.

"I love it." She runs her hand along the rail. "And I love you, Sir. May I show you how much?"

"Are you topping from the bottom, baby girl?"

"Maybe." She bats her eyelashes at me.

Other Doms might see that as a problem, but I don't. Natalie knows her place as my submissive, but she's also my wife, and I enjoy this playful, seductive side of her. I love that she's not afraid to initiate sex, so I play along.

"You do remember your parents are on their way?"

"I do, Sir. They haven't left the airport yet, so we have plenty of time." She begins unbuttoning her shirt and starts walking toward the door.

I watch her shirt slide down her arms and flutter to the floor. While Natalie walks, she reaches behind her to unclasp her bra, tossing it to the floor. I trail behind her like a moth attracted to a flame. When she gets to our bedroom door, she stops and looks over her shoulder. "That was all I could manage gracefully." She giggles.

"Go sit on the bed," I order and strip my shirt, tossing it to the side. Once I'm in front of her, I lean in for a long, slow kiss. My hands caress her breasts while I kiss my way down her neck, nipping her skin as I trail my mouth down to her nipples. "Lie back." The phone rings, momentarily distracting me. I don't check who it is before swiping the screen and sending the call to voicemail. Then, I toss my cell to the other side of the bed. "Now, where was I?"

I slide her leggings and panties off before spreading her legs wide. Getting down on my knees, I don't waste any time. I dive in like a starving man, my tongue going right to work. She gasps.

"Do you like that?"

"Yes, Sir. Very much." Her voice drips with need.

I go right back to work and drag my tongue down her pussy and into her wetness. She moans while I fuck her with my tongue, my fingers teasing her clit. Her body is so responsive. She's close already, so I pull back and tease her with my fingers.

Natalie lifts her head. "Please, don't stop."

"Don't stop this?" I run my finger down her wet slit. "Tell me who you belong to?"

"You, Sir. I belong to you.

"Only me," I say and slide two fingers inside her while my mouth attacks her clit. It's only seconds before she's crying out, her body squeezing my fingers. I lick and suck, extending her orgasm until she begs me to stop. Standing, I open the button and zipper on my jeans, freeing my erection. "Do you know how much I love you, baby girl?"

"I do," she says quietly.

Leaning over her, I'm careful to keep my weight on my arms as my lips meet hers. She grants my tongue entrance as I kiss her slowly and deeply, allowing her to taste herself before I roll over and position her on top of me. Using my hands for balance, she lowers herself onto my cock. Her body feels like my personal heaven as she raises and lowers herself in a slow rhythm. Her eyes never lose contact with mine.

My phone rings, and I reach over to silence it. Anyone who's trying to reach me will have to wait.

Her hands go to her breasts, kneading them and rolling her nipples between her fingers.

"Fuck, you're gorgeous."

She smiles seductively.

Seconds later, my phone rings again. Viktor must be getting close. I swipe the phone, ignoring the call one last time. As much as I'd like to spend the rest of the day worshipping Natalie's body, our time alone is almost up.

"Touch yourself. I want you to come with me."

Natalie's hand goes between her legs while I grab her waist and take control.

"Don't stop." She throws her head back. "I'm so close."

A few more thrusts and I explode. Natalie follows right after, her body squeezing my cock, draining every last ounce of myself inside her. She leans forward, her elbows on my chest, leaving room for her tummy. I run my fingers through her long hair, tucking her curls behind her ears.

"Are you okay?"

"I'm better than okay." She pushes on my chest to adjust her position. "Other than your phone ringing, that was perfect."

I reach out and grab my cell. "Viktor has terrible timing." I unlock the screen and see it wasn't Viktor who's been calling. I carefully move Natalie to the bed beside me and sit up to listen to the voicemails. "Shit."

Natalie watches me, concern etching her features.

"There was a fire at the job site." I pull up Steve's contact.

"How bad was it? Did anyone get hurt?" She rapid-fires questions.

"I don't know. Go get cleaned up while I figure out what's going on."

Natalie gets up, gathers her clothes, and heads into the bathroom. I call Steve while I'm getting dressed.

"What the hell happened?"

"I'm sorry to bother you, but we had an issue."

"Tell me everything," Steve explains, saying that one of his crew members was careless while welding and started a small fire. "How much damage was done?"

"Everything was contained to the immediate area." His voice shakes from nerves. "I'll cover the costs of the damage."

"And the employee?"

"He's been let go."

"How far behind schedule will this put us?"

"Not long. A week at most. We'll work overtime to fix the damage and get back on track." He pauses. "I won't let anything like this happen again. You have my word, Mr. Montgomery."

"I trust that it won't." I disconnect the call before I completely lose my cool and fire him. Sitting on the edge of the bed, I run my hands through my hair.

Natalie comes out of the bathroom dressed and freshened up.

"Did you find out what happened?"

"A careless employee is what happened." I blow out a frustrated breath before I stand and kiss her forehead. "It's handled now."

My phone chimes, and I check the text.

"It's Viktor. They're pulling into the garage now."

Together, we make our way to the elevator to greet her parents.

Chapter Nine

NATALIE

"Sweetheart, you look adorable," Mom gushes as she hugs me. "How are you feeling?"

"I feel terrific." I reach out to hug my father. "I'm so glad you guys came."

"Alex offered a deal your mom couldn't resist." Dad winks at me.

"Let me give you a hand with those, Viktor." Alex reaches out and takes a suitcase from him. "Follow me. I'll show you to your room."

Mom links her arm with mine as we walk through the house.

"Natalie, your home is gorgeous. I had no idea." Mom chats about the flight and the constant traffic she hates so much until we walk by the nursery, where she stops dead in her tracks. "Is this my granddaughter's room?"

"It is. Would you like to go in and see it?"

Mom walks into the room ahead of me and looks around silently. I stand next to her and examine her face, trying to figure out what she's thinking, but I'm falling short.

"It's still pretty bare," I explain. "But what do you think so far?"

Mom cups her hands over her mouth, and tears spill down her face. "I think it's perfect."

I'm filled with pride as I tell her how Alex painted it and put the crib together himself. "I have the theme picked out. We need to finish getting everything and decorate the room."

"Let's have a baby shower while we're in town." Mom suggests.

"What?"

"Your friends and Alex's family will all be here, right?"

"Yes. But when are we supposed to find time to plan and actually have a baby shower? No one else is coming until next week, and they're only staying for the holiday." I can't imagine how this could possibly work. "I'll have to ask Alex and get his permission."

"His permission?" Mom looks taken aback.

Think fast, Natalie. "Alex, Sam, and Maxim will be tied up with business." My words come out hurriedly. "Things for Jelena's Hope."

"What's Jelena's Hope?"

The more I say, the worse I'm making things, so I'm glad when Alex and Dad join us in the nursery.

"It looks really good, son."

"Thank you." Alex smiles proudly.

"Alexander, I want to have a baby shower for Natalie while we're all in town, but she says she needs your permission?"

I shrug.

"We always make decisions together, Charlotte. I'm sure you understand."

"So, that's a yes?" Mom asks expectantly.

"Would you like to have a baby shower?"

"I'm not sure when we could pull it off, but yes. I think it would be fun."

"Perfect. That's settled," Mom says.

"Let's head to the kitchen and have a snack while we make plans," Alex suggests.

My parents sit at the table with Alex while I get the Charcuterie tray and drinks. I try to ignore the questioning glances from my mom when I make Alex's plate and set it on the table in front of him before taking my seat. While we enjoy the delicious meats and cheeses, Mom uses her party planning magic to devise the perfect plan. By the time we finish eating, the shower is planned, and Mom's buzzing with excitement. Armed with Lana and Irina's phone numbers, she's already texting them and giving instructions for their parts. With Mom distracted, I start clearing the table.

"Are you done, Sir?" I whisper.

"Yes, baby girl. Thank you." I take his plate.

"You should be waiting on her while pregnant," Mom quips. "Not the other way around."

"Don't be silly. I'm pregnant, not incapacitated." I laugh and shake my head as I take the dishes to the sink.

Alex and Dad move to the couch and turn on the TV. Mom joins me.

"Is everything okay between you and Alex?" she asks.

"Why would you ask that?"

"Things seem different. You're waiting on him hand and foot." She looks over her shoulder to where they're sitting in the living room. "And I heard you call him sir?"

"Oh, that." I wave my hand. "That's just a silly nickname, and I enjoy waiting on him." I put the last plate in the dishwasher. "I seem to recall you caring for Dad the same way."

"I guess so," she says, but her words lack conviction.

I dry my hands and start the dishwasher. "Alex and I are perfect, Mom. I promise." I look into the living room and catch my husband's gaze. He gives me a panty-dropping smile, and I immediately wish we were still alone. "He's everything I've ever wanted and more. Come on, let's go watch the movie."

Chapter Ten

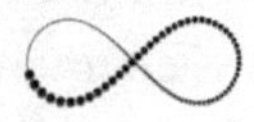

ALEX

It's been a long week with Natalie's parents here. I thought our apartment was big. However, I stand corrected. Nothing is big enough when Charlotte's around. Thankfully, everyone else has arrived, and her attention is now entirely centered on Natalie's baby shower, an event that's happening after Thanksgiving dinner tomorrow.

Today is the Clarke Family's famous Pie Day. Everyone's up extra early for the occasion. Charlotte brought her treasured apron, and Natalie is wearing her matching one. Charlotte was kind enough to make aprons for Luna, Irina, and Amelia—how, I'm not sure, with such short notice. She also brought one for Lana, but she didn't come today. Brandon said she wasn't feeling well but would be here tomorrow. Something's up with those two, but neither's talking about it. That's an issue for another day.

Right now, the women are gushing over Charlotte's talent as a seamstress. All their cell phones are out taking selfies in their new baking attire. I'm watching from the edge of the kitchen, imagining Natalie wearing her apron with nothing under it and what I'd like to do to her on the granite counter.

"Are you ready to go?" Dad asks.

"Sorry, I got distracted." I push off the door frame.

He laughs. "Come on, let's let the ladies do their thing."

Viktor, along with my dad, Stanley, Brandon, and Maxim, waits at the elevator. We ride down together to the parking garage and hop into the car. Maxim insists on taking the back seat while we navigate through the congested streets. Since preparations for tomorrow's parade are in full swing, we're forced to take a longer route to reach our destination.

"We could've gotten here faster if we walked," Viktor mumbles when we finally pull into the underground parking.

"Everything's almost finished," I say as we ride up to our floors. "We're waiting on some of the medical equipment. Our goal is to open right after the New Year."

"What is this place, Alex?" Stanley asks.

"This is why I stepped away from my company." The elevator doors open, and we step out into the newly completed reception area. "Welcome to Jelena's Hope, NYC. It's a shelter for abused women and children." That's a basic explanation and should be enough for him not to ask too many more questions.

"I had no idea you were doing this."

"I know how passionate Natalie is about helping youth. And since Maxim's already involved in something similar in Russia, we decided to expand on his efforts here in the city."

As I look around the space, I realize it's the first time I'm seeing it completed. I take a few minutes to appreciate the transformation. At the end of the room, there's an exquisite teak reception desk, and behind it, sparkling letters spell out *Jelena's Hope*.

Instead of the typical waiting room vibe, there are sofas and chairs arranged in a relaxed sitting room fashion with live flowering plants placed amongst the furniture. Rather than television, the room's highlight is the acrylic saltwater aquarium installed in the center, with a colorful live reef as its centerpiece. The reef has small inscriptions worked into it, displaying positive affirmations like *strength*, *hope*, and *love*.

I spend a few minutes observing the diverse range of fish in the tank. Natalie worked closely with the designers to select the ideal fish species to represent our mission. Among the sea creatures present are clownfish, which are recognizable from a popular animated movie and believed to be spirit guides for overcoming challenges. The tank is also home to a Flame Angel, a Yellow Watchman Goby, a Hawk fish, a Blue Hippo Tang, and a Yellow Tang, among others. It feels as though we've brought a piece of the ocean into our reception area.

"Alexander, this design truly speaks to the heart of Jelena's Hope," Maxim says, clearing his throat in an attempt to hide his emotions. "It is about restoring hope to those who have endured the worst of what humanity has to offer."

"It was all Natalie's idea." I smile proudly.

"Mr. Montgomery," Steve says, rushing up to me. He skids to a stop when he sees I'm not alone. "Mr. Solonik, I wasn't expecting you today."

"I find unannounced visits tend to be the most productive."

"Yes, sir."

"I was informed there was an issue with an employee. A fire?" Maxim begins to interrogate Steve.

"One of my welders didn't follow the safety guidelines, resulting in a small fire in a medical room. It was put out immediately, though." Steve stumbles over his words. "I covered the costs for the repair, and the employee was fired. I assure you, I take job safety seriously."

"Viktor. Please accompany Steve to ensure the quality of the operation. We would not want any more *accidents*, would we?" Maxim glares at Steve.

"Yes, sir. Let's go." Viktor starts walking down the hall while Steve scrambles to keep up.

I shake my head and chuckle. "Do you enjoy scaring people?"

"This project is of the utmost importance, and I expect nothing but the best from the people we have hired. Scaring people is just a bonus," Max says, cracking a smile. "Will you lead our tour, Alexander?"

Viktor is waiting for us in the reception area when we return from touring the facility.

"Everything looks good, boss," he reports. "I don't foresee any further issues."

"Excellent. Now we can concentrate on celebrating the American Thanksgiving and *moya vnuchka.*"

"This baby is one lucky little lady," Dad adds. "She has three sets of grandparents."

"Poor thing will never get a date," Viktor quips.

"Good," we answer in unison.

Viktor rolls his eyes and almost cracks a smile.

Chapter Eleven

NATALIE

Mom has a captive audience with Amelia. She went wild when she saw the apron my mom made for her. The fabric has Amelia's favorite boy band on it. I have no idea how Mom pulled that off, but it's perfect. Once she put it on, she even talked my mom into taking selfies with her.

Now, Amelia and Mom are rolling out the homemade pie crusts. Mom instructs Amelia on how to flour the surface so the dough doesn't stick. But when Amelia tries, she ends up with a face full of flour. She and Mom share a laugh. It's so nice to see Amelia smiling and carefree.

Irina, Luna, and I are sitting at the table watching the mayhem at the kitchen island. Irina's peeling apples, Luna's slicing them, and passing them to me. I'm eating them—well, that and mixing the apple slices into the seasoning.

"Amelia seems like she's doing well," I say quietly.

"She's come a long way in a short time." Irina sets her peeler down and gazes at the young teenager. "When Amelia first came, she'd wake every night screaming from nightmares. It broke my heart because she would be inconsolable. We couldn't touch her or hold her. All we could do was make sure she was safe until she calmed down and fell back to sleep." She shifts her gaze to me. "Thankfully, the nightmares seem to have subsided. She still has much healing to do, but she's a tenacious young lady. I think she will be successful."

"I'm grateful she's getting a second chance."

"It's all thanks to you." Luna places her hand on mine.

"I can't take credit for it. It was Michael and his team that rescued her."

"Are you three done with those apples yet?" Mom asks. "We're ready to fill the pies."

"We are." I get up and bring my bowl of sliced apple pieces over to the counter.

Amelia picks up the bowl. "Do I just dump them in?"

"No," Mom shrieks, making me laugh.

"Mom is super particular about how the apple pieces go in the crust."

"The inside needs to look as pretty as the outside," Mom says.

"But I think it tastes yummy either way." I smile and pass Amelia a cinnamon and sugar-covered apple slice.

Amelia takes a bite. Her eyes open wide with delight. "I've never tasted anything like this. It's delicious. Can you show me how to put them in neatly, Mrs. Clarke?"

"Of course, dear." Then, Mom and Amelia set to work layering the apples.

"I'm going to get started on the spiced pecans," Luna says, grabbing the bag of nuts and bringing them to the stove.

"Irina, would you like to help me make the pumpkin pie?"

"I would love that." She joins me at the other end of the island.

This year's Pie Day is turning out to be one of the most enjoyable days we've had yet.

I don't even realize how much time has passed until I hear masculine voices approaching the kitchen.

"It smells delicious in here, ladies." Alex comes from behind and plants a kiss on my cheek. "How are you and baby Rose doing?"

"We're good. How did the inspection go?"

"Everything looks good. Should be smooth sailing from here."

I look over Alex's shoulder and see my dad and Mr. Montgomery carrying several brown paper bags.

"Oh my God, is that Chinese takeout?"

"You didn't think we'd have Pie Day without it, did you?" Dad chuckles.

Luna and Irina begin clearing the table, and Amelia joins them to help. I excuse myself to take a trip to the bathroom. When I come out, mom's waiting in the hallway.

"I'm so glad you and Daddy came out here." I hug her. "And you're doing a great job with Amelia. She seems to be enjoying herself."

"She's a sweetheart," Mom says, looking over her shoulder. "I don't understand something, though." Oh no. I know exactly where this conversation is going. "How did a young girl from Australia end up in Russia?"

"I'm not entirely sure." I shrug.

"She seems to be very attached to you." Mom cocks her head to the side. "How did you meet her?"

"She was at Max and Irina's home when Alex and I visited a few months ago. We really hit it off."

"And they're adopting her?"

"They are."

"It's all very strange." Mom crosses her arms. "There seems to be something I'm not being told."

Mom's perceptive and quite a bit nosy. I know she won't drop this, so I have to tell her what I can. The last thing I want is for her to start asking Amelia questions she's not ready to answer.

"Come in here." I lead her into my bedroom and close the door. "Have a seat."

She perches on the edge of my bed. I sit beside her while I tell her about Jelena and how she was kidnapped. I leave out the details of the trafficking ring.

"I had no idea." Mom puts her hand over her heart. "I can't imagine the heartache that's caused for Max and Irina."

"It was a challenging time for them. But they took their tragedy and decided to help others. I'm pretty sure that's how they found Amelia, but I don't know the details. Those are things they like to keep private. I'm sure you understand."

I continue to explain a bit about Jelena's Hope, saying that it was born to help women and children who needed a safe place to start their lives over.

"Does this have something to do with the secret project Alex is working on?"

I nod. "It does. We've been so moved by what Maxim is doing that we decided to open Jelena's Hope- NYC. That's where they went today. Max wanted to see how it was coming along, and Alex couldn't wait to show it off."

"So, it's a place for abused women and children?"

"Pretty much, yes." She's more correct than she knows.

"You aren't planning on working there, are you?"

"I am."

"How will you do that when you have a new baby?"

I've been asking myself those same questions, but I really don't want to get into that discussion right now. "It won't be full-time, only what I'm comfortable with. We should get back. They're going to think we got lost."

Mom stands and looks at me, concern marring her face. "You know I disapprove of you working outside the home while you have an infant. As wonderful as this place sounds, I also sense that it could be dangerous—"

"There's security at the building." My stomach grumbles loudly. "I'm starving. Can we talk about this later?"

Mom nods, and together, we walk back to the kitchen.

"I was just about to send a search party out for you two," Dad jokes.

I grab a plate and fill it with Alex's favorite foods. Mom looks on as Luna and Irina do the same for their men. I can see the questions forming in her head, but luckily, she doesn't voice them.

While we eat, the timer on the oven goes off. Mom removes perfect-looking pies from the oven and sets them on cooling racks.

"Those smell delicious," Maxim says. "Do we get to taste them tonight?"

"Absolutely not." Mom places her hands on her hips. "They're for dessert after dinner tomorrow." Maxim's deep laugh fills the room. He gets a kick out of getting under Mom's skin. "Are we ready to watch the movie now?" Mom asks, her brow furrowed.

"We're going to deviate from tradition just a bit," I say cautiously.

"Oh?" Mom asks, surprised.

"They're inflating the balloons for the parade in Central Park. We want to take Amelia and anyone else who wants to come to see it," Alex says.

"Can we go, Sir?" Luna asks Sam.

"Of course. Get your jacket. It's going to be chilly." Luna hurries off to their room.

"Same goes for you, Amelia," Max instructs.

"Okay." She skips off to grab her jacket.

"Will you two come?" I ask my parents.

"As much as I'd love to," Dad says. "I'm feeling pretty worn out from our outing earlier. So, I think we'll stay back."

"Okay." I sigh. "I'll video call when we get there so you can see it. Then, when we get back, we'll watch the movie."

"Sounds great, sweetheart."

"Don't overdo it," Mom adds.

"I won't," I call over my shoulder.

The group of us heads out.

Despite his protests, Max and Sam talk Alex into taking the subway, something I'm grateful for. If he'd insisted on driving, we'd never get there before they closed off the park to visitors.

Chapter Twelve

ALEX

Central Park is buzzing with activity. Amelia grabs Natalie's hand, her eyes huge with delight as she takes videos and pictures of the iconic balloons being inflated.

"She's so patient." Dad comes up next to me. "She's going to be an amazing mother."

"That she is." I try to smile, but I've been distracted since we arrived. "Viktor?"

"Yes, boss."

"Keep a close eye on Natalie, please."

"What's wrong?"

"I don't know. Something feels off."

"I don't see anything out of the ordinary." Viktor looks around. "But I'll stick with her and the kid."

Logically, I know it's most likely a trauma response, but I can't shake the feeling that we're being watched—followed. Although I remain aware of the surrounding crowds, I keep my thoughts to myself. I don't want to say or do anything to ruin the fun.

I startle when Maxim puts his hand on my shoulder. "Are you okay?" he asks, concerned.

"I'm good. Just a lot of people."

"Thank you for giving us this wonderful experience. Amelia is having such a wonderful time," Maxims says while watching his daughter laughing at something Natalie said. "I love to see her smiling." "She's really enjoying herself." I smile, watching her.

"You are giving her experiences she'll never forget. I am certain she will ask to come back again." Maxim laughs.

I look at my pregnant wife, her hand on her round tummy as she points out the Olaf balloon. Amelia may be a teenager, but she missed out on so much of her childhood. Natalie's taking her role of surrogate big sister seriously. She's been introducing her to all the Disney movies. Right now, *Frozen* is her current favorite.

"And next year, you and Natalie will have your child with us," Maxim adds.

I didn't think about that. Next year, Natalie and Amelia will be showing these balloons to our little girl. Another shiver runs down my spine, and the hairs on my neck stand on end. I'm done ignoring this. "Hey, everyone, how about we head back? I'm sure Stanley and Charlotte are anxious to continue with their family traditions."

"That's a good idea," Natalie adds. "Anyway, my feet are killing me."

"Let's get you home then, baby girl." I take her hand as we all make our way to the subway station to return to the safety of our apartment.

Chapter Thirteen

XAVIER

IT TAKES ALL MY FREE TIME BEFORE AND AFTER WORK, but I'm able to keep tabs on the movements of the Montgomerys. Most people are creatures of habit and don't pay attention to their surroundings. I'm not complaining because it works in my favor.

Right now, they're among the crowds wandering Central Park, watching these ridiculous balloons being blown up. The number of people milling about makes for the perfect cover. I can follow them from a short distance without worrying about being spotted.

Montgomery must be feeling paranoid these days. Natalie never leaves the apartment alone. Even now, he has his lapdog sticking to her side like glue. He should be the one by Natalie, but instead, he's hanging back, talking to another man.

I'm not certain, but from what I've heard from the guys at work, he's a Russian named Maxim Solonik. I've done web searches on him and found out he's some hotshot in Russian oil. Why he hangs out with Montgomery is beyond me. I'm not sure who the other man is, but by how much they look alike, my guess is that he might be Montgomery's father.

Everyone in their little group seems to be enjoying themselves right now. Everyone but Montgomery. He looks tense.

Can you feel me watching you?

Don't worry. Your time's almost up.

We'll see each other soon.

Chapter Fourteen

NATALIE

THE TANTALIZING SCENTS OF TURKEY AND STUFFING drift into my bedroom from the kitchen, waking me. I'm sure Mom and Dad were up at the crack of dawn and are already hard at work preparing the meal. I stretch and turn to discover that Alex's spot in the bed is vacant. He must be helping cook, too.

Recognizing that this may be my only moment of tranquility for the day, I take advantage of it. I remain in bed, enjoying being alone with the baby, who's currently performing acrobatics. It's a peaceful start to what promises to be a busy day.

"You'll be out here with us next year, Rose." I rub my belly. "Thanksgiving's your mama's favorite holiday. Last year almost ruined that, but we aren't going to talk about that. This year's a new beginning. We're going to make new memories—happy memories."

"Hopefully, all our family will come here to celebrate with us every year. I want you to be surrounded by people who love you. Today's also our baby shower." I feel a strong kick in the center of my stomach as I sit up. "I guess you like that idea."

Before going out to the kitchen, I change out of my pajamas and into a casual dress that'll be comfortable to wear with my expanding waistline. Then, barefoot, I pad down the hall in search of something to eat. The sounds of happy chatter and laughter fill the room. I try to remain unnoticed and peek around the doorway, taking in the sight.

Everyone's here today, and they're all in my kitchen. Mom has clearly taken charge. She's paired off the couples and delegated many of the responsibilities. Everyone's hard at work and looks to be enjoying themselves, except for Brandon and Lana. I can feel the tension between them from here. Mom tasked them with making her sweet potato casserole. Although they're working side-by-side, they're certainly not working together. Their movements are stiff, and their conversation is nonexistent. I need to get Lana alone for a few minutes to find out what's going on.

"Are you going to join us or just keep watching?" Mom asks.

My cover's been blown. "I was just watching everyone together." I walk over to Mom and put my arm around her. "You have no idea how happy this makes me."

"I think I do, sweetheart." She points to the food tray on the counter. "Alex was kind enough to buy breakfast for everyone. Grab yourself a bagel and then get over there and help your husband set the table."

In the dining room, I spot Alex and Amelia, both of whom are engrossed in something on their cell phones. Amelia has a pile of cloth napkins and is trying to fold them into what looks to be turkeys. I'm impressed. She's doing a great job.

Alex has the table set with our Mikasa Love Story China dishes. He's standing in front of a pile of silverware, going back and forth between the different-sized utensils and whatever he's looking at on his phone. Mom's very particular when it comes to formal dinners, and Alex takes his task seriously, making sure each utensil is put in the right place.

I quickly toast a bagel and add cream cheese before taking my dish and joining them. "You two are doing a great job," I say and take a bite.

Alex looks up at me, confusion marring his gorgeous face. "Your mom issued her warning that the table must be set correctly. Thank God for YouTube, because I don't have a clue as to what goes where. And then there's this horn thing," he says, holding up Mom's cornucopia and pointing to the fresh foods on the table. "She told us we had to arrange this, too."

"What is that, Natalie?" Amelia asks with genuine curiosity in her voice. I tell Amelia the story of the cornucopia while I finish my bagel. Her eyes widen as she listens to me tell her how that used to be Michael and my favorite thing to do.

"You have a brother?" she asks.

I swallow over the lump in my throat. "Yes."

"Is he coming today?"

"He died when I was a teenager." And I'd give anything to have him back.

"I'm sorry," she says, looking down at her hands.

"It's okay." I reach out and touch her arm.

This year, more than any other, I wish Michael were here. He and Evan would've been over the moon about becoming uncles. And having everyone together, without arguing, was all either of us ever wanted.

"He's still with me here." I put my hand on my heart. "Let's get this table set before Mom comes over and scolds us." I quickly change the subject before I get too emotional.

With the three of us working together, we get the table set perfectly in no time. Then, Mom comes over and inspects it. "Did you make these yourself, Amelia?" she asks, pointing to the little turkeys in the center of everyone's plate.

"Yes, ma'am."

"I've never seen anything like it." She picks one up to inspect it. We all hold a collective breath. "But I love them."

Amelia beams with pride.

A few hours later, we're all gathered around the table that's loaded with the food everyone's worked so hard to prepare. I snap a few pictures on my cell phone to document the occasion.

"Before we eat, we always go around the table and say something we're thankful for," Dad says. "I'll start. I'm thankful to be here, in this crazy city, celebrating with my daughter and son-in-law."

"This is the first time I'm celebrating an American Thanksgiving," Amelia says. "I'm thankful for being safe, for having food to eat." She looks at Max and Irina. "And for having a new family."

"Our family has much to be thankful for," Maxim adds. "Amelia's adoption was finalized last week. She is now legally Amelia Solonik, our daughter," he says, a proud smile lighting up his face.

I think about the first time I saw Amelia. I didn't know how long she'd been there, but it was long enough that fear of disobeying was instilled in her. The emptiness I saw in her eyes—she'd already given up.

What Alex and I went through was horrible, and I wouldn't wish it on anyone, but so much good has come from it. I hate knowing Amelia was raped before Michael's team found her. But they did find her and got her to safety. That's the most important part. And her being adopted by the Solonik's is truly the cherry on top of it all.

Alex goes last. He grabs my hand before speaking. "This amazing woman sitting beside me has made me the happiest man in the world. She's given me so much more than I ever thought I'd have. Thankful doesn't come close to expressing my feelings today." He leans over, kisses my lips sweetly, and whispers, "Thank you, baby girl."

I look into his blue eyes, forgetting that anyone else is in the room—it's only us. "i love You, Sir."

"Let's hold hands and say grace," Dad interrupts our moment.

After the blessing, everyone fills their plates and enjoys the feast before us. The Thanksgiving meal is delicious, but what makes today truly special is being surrounded by my family.

This past year has been marked by so much heartache and near-tragedies. It's as if today's celebration has brought us full circle. All the bad is behind us now. Our family only has wonderful things to look forward to.

Chapter Fifteen

∞

NATALIE

After dinner, Mom shoos me from the apartment. "You and Viktor should go downstairs for a bit. I'll call you when we're ready." Her eyes dance with excitement.

I look to Alex for approval. He nods.

"Come on, Vik." I start walking to the elevator. "We're being kicked out."

Viktor follows me, laughing. "Your mom is—" He pauses. "A lot."

"Tell me about it."

"Natalie, wake up." Viktor shakes my shoulder gently. "It's time to go upstairs."

I stretch and yawn. "Sorry about that. I didn't realize I had fallen asleep."

He laughs. "We were only five minutes into the movie, and you were snoring."

"Snoring?"

"I had to turn up the volume because you were so noisy." He winks at me.

"You're terrible." I elbow him as I walk by. "Let's go. We have a baby shower to get to."

"This'll be a whole new experience."

To say I'm shocked at what I see when we get back upstairs is an understatement. Not only are several of our friends from Fire and Ice here, but in a matter of a few hours, Mom successfully transformed the entire dining room from a Thanksgiving celebration to a baby shower. The room is adorned with pink crepe paper that stretches from end to end. Shiny spiral streamers displaying baby bottles, booties, and pacifiers hang from the ceiling. A pink tablecloth covers the table, and several stuffed elephants sit atop a bed of baby-themed confetti. In the corner is a stack of exquisitely wrapped presents.

"How did you do all this?"

"Your mother's a very efficient party planner," Irina says.

"I've missed seeing you," Mistress Star says and squeezes me in a hug. "I was so happy when Lana called and invited me to your shower."

"Look at you, girl," Leo exclaims as his hands go straight to my tummy. "How's my little niece?"

"She's very active today."

"I feel that." He laughs.

"You look terrific, Natalie." Tony embraces me. "Pregnancy suits you."

His compliment makes me blush.

Alex comes over and takes my hand. "Let's have dessert, shall we?" He pulls out a chair for me to sit on.

Our guests take their seats while Mom and the other ladies bring over the pies and a two-tiered cake. It's covered in pale gray and pink fondant to match the colors of our nursery. On top is an elephant holding several pink balloons.

"Look at that cake," I exclaim. "It's adorable. How did you manage to get this on a holiday?"

"I told you Maxim is bossy," Mom chuckles. "He's responsible for that."

I look at Max, "Thank you so much, *Dedushka*."

"Nothing will stop me from giving you and *moya vnuchka* everything."

Plenty of pictures are taken before we cut into the desserts. The cake is decadent chocolate with a chocolate ganache between the layers. When dessert is served, our guests rave over the pies.

"Mrs. Clarke," Anthony says. "You must give me your recipe for this pecan pie. My customers will love it."

"You want to use my recipe for your restaurant?" Mom sounds shocked.

"Of course, I'll compensate you for it," he adds.

"There's no need for that, Anthony," Mom says, waving him off. "I'd be honored for you to have it."

We take our time enjoying the plethora of desserts on the table. By the time we finish, there's only half a slice of pumpkin pie and one tier of cake left. I'm so stuffed, I don't think I can move.

"Let's get to the presents," Lana chimes in.

"That sounds like a great idea. I can't wait to open them."

Alex moves an armchair from the living room, placing it next to the stack of presents. "Come sit over here."

"Gladly." My back's aching from sitting on the unforgiving dining chairs for so long. Alex pulls another chair from the living room so he can open gifts with me.

"Amelia," Mom calls. "Come help me with the ribbons."

Lana begins passing us presents, one at a time. Carefully, I take the ribbons off and hand them to Amelia. She and Mom are making the traditional ribbon *hat* for me to wear after opening the gifts. I have no idea how the tradition started, and although I'll look ridiculous, we'll have a laugh looking back at the pictures.

The first gift I open is from my parents. "Oh, Mom. It's stunning." I hold up a handmaid patchwork baby quilt. In the center are two elephants.

"The ladies from church worked on it with me. I was hoping you'd like it."

"I don't just like it. I love it."

"It's exquisite, Charlotte," Alex says as he runs his hands over the impeccable stitching. "This was truly a labor of love, and we'll cherish it."

Mom wipes at the corner of her eyes.

Lana and Brandon's gifts are next. The first is a designer baby pram.

"I read it's all the rage with high society in the city," Lana says, waving her hand.

I don't care about keeping up with trends, but the pram is stunning. The second present is a fancy bassinet that rocks.

"The lady at the store said this thing is magic," Brandon adds, uncertain.

"It's a smart bassinet," Alex says as he reads the box. "It'll sense if the baby is fussing and gently rock her."

"I figured if it works, I'll get the award for best uncle."

We all share a laugh.

"These gifts are from us," Maxim says. "As you know, we do not have these baby showers. Most Russians believe it is bad luck. However, I am not like most Russians and do not subscribe to such superstitions. We are here and wish to participate in your traditions."

He hands me a beautifully wrapped gift. The paper is so pretty, I don't want to tear it. But Maxim encourages me to open it. I lift the lid off the box, and Alex takes out a set of wooden nesting elephants.

"We had these made special for *moya vnuchka,*" Maxim says proudly.

Alex opens them one at a time and places them on the dining table for everyone to see. Each is painted with unique designs. The details on them are unlike anything I've ever seen.

"Max, I don't know what to say."

"There's more," Irina says, pointing to the gift in Lana's hand.

When I open it, I find a set of baby books in Russian.

"These are so Rose can learn our language from the beginning."

"Alex is going to have to read these to her. But maybe I'll finally be able to learn Russian as well." I giggle.

I've known Lana for years and have traveled to Russia several times, but other than a few simple words, I've not been able to master even basic communication.

We've been opening presents for what feels like hours. We're finally at the last of the gifts, and they're from Sam and Luna. Opening the box, we pull out a hand-painted trio of elephant pictures that read: *First, we had each other. Then we had you. Now we have everything.*

"This is perfect. We'll hang these over her crib." I look around at everyone. "Thank you all so very much. This is more than we could've asked for."

"You've made today extra special for my family." Alex places his hand on my belly. "Thank you all so much."

"We're not done yet," Mom says.

She and Amelia are heading in my direction with their ribbon hat. Alex looks at me with his eyebrows raised. Mom places the ribbon-covered paper plate on my head and ties it under my chin. Amelia giggles and grins as she snaps pictures with her cell phone. We don't have to wait for a day in the future. We're all getting a good laugh out of my new accessory right now.

After everyone's taken their fill of pictures, Alex and the other men move the gifts into the nursery. Unpacking and organizing them is a job for another day. Mom and the other ladies go to the kitchen to start the clean-up. But Lana quietly wanders off.

It's time I find out what's going on, so I follow her. She enters the guest room, where her parents are staying, and closes the door. I knock, but there's no answer. I open the door and ask, "Do you mind some company?"

"That's fine. Just close the door, please. I don't want anyone else to know I'm in here."

I sit on the bed next to Lana. "Are you going to tell me what's going on?"

She looks away and stays quiet for the longest time, and I'm starting to think she's not going to answer me.

"Things aren't okay between Brandon and me," she finally says.

"I know."

"Is it that obvious?"

"To me, yes. What's going on?" I ask.

She turns and sits cross-legged on the bed facing me. "He wants more."

"What's wrong with that?"

"I don't."

Sometimes Svetlana confuses me. She and Brandon have been together for a little over two years. When they moved in together, Lana was ecstatic. She always said she wanted the whole package —a husband, a few kids, and a dog.

"What do you mean you don't? I thought you loved him?" I ask, confused.

"He's a great Dominant, and I care about him."

"I sense a but coming." Nothing is making sense right now.

"He's ready to settle down. He wants what you and Alex have —the husband/wife thing," she sighs. "He wants to be a father."

"And what do you want?"

"I love the club and public scenes. I want to try adding other people," she says. "I'm not ready for marriage, and I don't want kids."

"Have you talked to him? Told him how you're feeling?"

"I told him what I want and what I don't want. He pulled out the contract and said we could renegotiate some things, but we haven't reached any agreements."

"What does that mean?" I ask, concerned.

"We're not on the same page anymore. So, we put our dynamic on hold," she replies, but her voice holds no emotion.

"Don't do anything you'll regret. Give it some more time," I encourage her. "Keep trying to work it out."

The door opens. "There you two are. Alex is looking for you, Nat," Brandon says.

"Please give what I said some thought," I say as I stand up.

Lana nods but says nothing.

As I walk by, I put my hand on Brandon's arm, and he gives it a reassuring squeeze. I hate this. My friends are hurting, and I don't know how to help them.

With a final look over my shoulder, I leave the room to find Alex.

Chapter Sixteen

ALEX

The majority of our guests left, but we were able to convince Natalie's parents to stay for an extra week. Charlotte's enjoying helping Natalie put Rose's nursery together. I think it's been a good activity for them to bond over. Stanley and Charlotte even went with us to a check-up the other day. The doctor did an ultrasound, which thrilled the grandparents-to-be. They were amazed at the images of their unborn grandchild and are going home with their own set of pictures. I can't believe how quickly Natalie's pregnancy has seemed to go. Rose will be here in just eight weeks.

Viktor and I have just finished our workout for the day, and I'm heading for a shower when my phone rings.

"I hope I got you at a good time," Steve says.

"What's up?"

"Good news. Construction's complete, and all the equipment's in place," he says. "I'm going to need you to come down and do a final walkthrough so you can sign off on everything."

I thought we still had a few weeks to go, but I won't complain about being ahead of schedule.

"Give me about two hours, and I'll be over."

I shower and am waiting for Natalie and Charlotte to return from their walk before I leave. I don't like letting her go out without Viktor, but she has her phone with the tracking app Dimitri's team installed, and she promised she wouldn't go far. She's fallen in love with a park down the street. There's a quiet little spot where she likes to sit and watch the water. I think it reminds her of her favorite place at Finn Lake.

Stanley stayed back to watch TV, but instead, he's fast asleep on the couch. Quietly, so I don't wake him, I make my way into the kitchen to get a bottle of water and a sandwich. While I'm eating, Natalie and Charlotte arrive back home.

"Did you enjoy your walk, ladies?"

"We did," Natalie says, her cheeks pink from the brisk November air.

"I'd much rather you use the treadmill in our gym."

"But then I wouldn't get to feel the sunshine and breathe the fresh air." She bats her beautiful green eyes at me.

"Fresh air? In the city?" I shake my head.

"You're being an overprotective father already." Mom waves him off. "Natalie needs to be outside. It's healthy for her and the baby."

Overprotective. If she only knew the things we've been through over the past six months. How I almost lost Natalie and the baby, she'd understand why I don't want to let her out of my sight. But those are things I can never tell her. Instead, I'll have to accept that she thinks I'm a nervous father-to-be.

"You have a good point, Charlotte," I concede. "It's a big city, though, and you can't blame a guy for wanting to keep his family safe."

"I guess you're right. Maybe you should think about relocating to Northmeadow permanently," she says nonchalantly. "I'm going to wake Stanley and see if he's hungry." She doesn't miss a beat as she walks away.

"Gee, that was subtle." Natalie looks over her shoulder. "Sorry about that. The good news is they'll only be here for a few more days."

"It's fine." I stand and kiss her forehead. "I'm thankful they agreed to stay.

"Me too. It's been nice having Mom here to help get the nursery ready." She looks up at me wide-eyed. "Not that you aren't helping—"

"I understand. Charlotte's your mom. She can help you prepare in ways I can't." I brush a stray curl behind her ear. "On another note, I have some good news for you."

"Oh? What is it?"

"Steve called. The construction on Jelena's Hope-NYC is done. I'm going to run over and do the final walkthrough."

"Can I come?"

"You just got back from a walk, and you still need to eat."

"Yes, Sir." She looks disappointed.

"I'll bring you down tomorrow." I put my empty water bottle in the recycling bin. "I'm leaving Viktor here."

I pull her into my arms and kiss her. "I have stuff laid out in our room for a scene tonight." She walks me to the elevator.

"Are you sure you have to go? Can't you wait and go tomorrow?"

"I won't be long, I promise." The doors open, and I step inside. "Have something to eat and get some rest while I'm gone."

"Yes, Sir." The doors start to close, but she sticks her hand in, stopping them. "i love You."

"I love you too, baby girl."

Chapter Seventeen

XAVIER

"Xavier," Steve calls from across the room. "Can I talk to you?"

"Yeah, boss. Be there in a minute."

I finally have everything in place and am ready to strike. Montgomery was here a few days ago, and I almost pulled the trigger. The only thing that saved him was that he wasn't alone.

The plan involves him and him alone.

My patience has finally paid off.

The project is done, and I overheard Steve tell his crew that Montgomery is set to arrive any minute.

I shoot a quick text to a friend who, after a bit of bargaining, has agreed to help me.

X: It's time. Bring the car with the package.

Jinx: Got it. I'll be there in ten.

Act normal, Xavier. You don't need any unwanted attention.

I put my tools away and stride across the room where Steve is talking to one of the other guys. When he finishes, he turns my way. "You've proved yourself as a loyal and talented worker, X-man. Have you decided if you'll stay on with us?"

"It's great working with you. I'd like to take you up on your offer."

"I'm glad to hear that." He slaps my shoulder. "I don't have time to go over the specifics right now. Mr. Montgomery is on his way so that we can finish up here. How about we meet at my office on Monday to iron out the details?"

"Sure thing." I look at my watch, knowing that if Montgomery's coming, I need to get out of here. "Break time. I'll see you Monday."

I make quick work of gathering my supplies and take the staff elevator to the basement. Once I'm sure I'm alone, I check my texts.

Jinx: I'm in place. Waiting on your cue.

X: Stay out of sight. He'll be here any minute.

I grab the product I promised Leon, slipping it into my pocket.
Then I watch and wait.

Chapter Eighteen

ALEX

While in the elevator, I have a silent debate over taking the subway instead of driving. If I take the subway, I can get there and back faster, but I'm still not over my issues with crowded, confined spaces, especially ones I have no control over. Control wins over speed, so I take the car.

I'm met with the usual city traffic, but I've lived here so long, it's something I'm used to. After hitting every red light possible, I finally pull into my designated spot in the underground parking garage. While I walk to the elevator, I make a mental checklist of things that still need to be done.

The majority of the staff have been hired and are in training. Maxim sent several of his most experienced employees to train my new staff, including a few recovered people who now work at Jelena's Hope. Having the shared experiences of the people who will eventually walk through our doors affords them a unique ability to connect with these individuals when they're at their lowest. And our new employees will only benefit from their experiences. I'm thankful they've been able to travel to New York City to help out.

As the elevator makes its way up to our floor, I find myself struggling with conflicting emotions. I'm thrilled that the construction is finally complete, and Jelena's Hope-NYC is almost ready to open its doors. But on the other hand, being excited feels out of place. After all, the existence of Jelena's Hope-NYC is a direct result of the unfathomable evil that exists in the world.

Centers like this and others around the world exist only because, every day, innocent individuals are ripped away from their lives and treated as nothing more than commodities to be exploited and abused.

I step into our facility and am reminded that there are ongoing efforts to rescue these victims, some of whom will soon be entering our doors to embark on their journey toward recovery and healing.

When Steve sees me, he jumps up. "Mr. Montgomery, glad you could make it on such short notice."

We shake hands. "I'm anxious to see the place."

"Then, let's not waste any time."

Steve hands me a binder that holds the specs for each room before we begin our walk-through. I review the checklists as we go and sign off on each section. When we finish the office area, we go up to the residences. The finished apartments look incredible. After the last signature, I pass the binder back to him. "I'm impressed with the quality of the workmanship."

"Thank you, Mr. Montgomery."

"I have some other properties that require remodeling, and I need them done quickly. Would you be interested?"

"I'd be happy to take a look at what you need done. I'm sure I can accommodate your schedule."

"I'd like to get the work started before the holidays. I'll email you the information."

"Sounds good. I'll be in touch."

I put my finger on the scanner to summon the elevator. While I wait, I text Natalie to let her know I'm on my way home.

The elevator stops a few floors down, and a well-dressed man wearing a business suit steps in. The doors shut, and a wave of anxiety washes over me. I try to regulate my breathing, reassuring myself that the individual sharing the confined space with me poses no harm. He's merely a fellow office worker from a lower floor. Maybe I do need to start seeing a therapist?

The elevator chimes, signaling our arrival at the parking garage. I reach into my pocket to retrieve my key fob.

Chapter Nineteen

NATALIE

Alex texted me that he was on his way home hours ago. Even with the insane holiday traffic, he should've been here already. I try to reach him on his cellphone, but it goes straight to voicemail. A sense of panic begins to bubble within me, but I recognize that it's likely residual anxiety from our ordeal in Mexico.

The most likely explanation is he's stuck in traffic, and his phone battery has died - he tends to forget his charger.

"Hey, guys." I pop my head into the living room, where my parents watch TV. "I'm going down to Viktor's to see if he wants to join us for dinner."

"Okay, sweetheart. We'll be here watching the end of this movie." Mom smiles.

My parents have turned into total couch potatoes while they've been here, watching as much TV as possible. They refuse to pay for cable at home, insisting they prefer to keep busy. They work very hard between keeping up with things at home and their store. So, it's nice to see them relaxing.

I'm just about to press the elevator call button when the

doors open. Viktor's standing there, his face devoid of all color. Two NYPD officers are with him. "Viktor? What's going on?"

"Let's go sit down." He takes my arm, but I shrug from his grasp.

"No. Tell me what's going on. Why are there police in my house?"

"Mrs. Montgomery?" The female officer speaks.

"Stop." Viktor puts up his hand. "I'll tell her."

My heart pounds. The last time I got a call from the police—

"What's going on?" Dad asks from behind me.

"Natalie," Viktor says softly. "There was an accident. An explosion."

"Where's Alex?"

"He was in the explosion." Viktor's voice is laced with pain. "He's gone."

"No," I scream and hit his chest. "You're lying."

"I wish I was." He grabs my hands. "His car exploded. He didn't make it, Natalie."

Everything goes fuzzy, and I feel myself falling.

When my eyes open, I'm lying in my bed. Mom is sitting beside me, wiping my forehead with a cool rag. Viktor's words slam back into my consciousness, and I shoot upright. "Tell me it's not true, Mama," I cry. "Please, tell me it's not true."

She wraps her arms around me, holding me tight. "I'm so sorry, honey." Her voice catches on a sob. "I'm so sorry."

"No." I push her away and get out of bed. "Viktor's lying. Alex is not dead. I would know it here." I put my hand over my heart. "I would feel it if he were gone." Storming out of the room, I set off, intending to find Viktor.

"Natalie," Mom calls after me, but I don't turn around.

I hear Viktor's voice coming from inside Alex's office. Pushing the door open, I storm into the room and stop in front of the desk, crossing my arms over my chest.

Viktor meets my penetrating glare. "I'll call you back." He disconnects the call and stands up.

"Don't come any closer," I warn.

"Natalie, please." He takes a step toward me.

"Why are you lying to me?" I shove his chest. "This isn't funny. Where's my husband?"

"You know I'd never lie to you." Viktor moves closer. "Alex is gone."

"No." I punch him over and over. He makes no move to block my strikes. "You're lying. He's not gone." Hot tears sear my face. My body shakes with sobs. Viktor wraps his strong arms around me, and I fall into his chest. "We're having a baby." I struggle to take a breath. "He can't be gone."

Slowly, Viktor slides us to the floor, never breaking his hold as he shifts me onto his lap. He rocks me back and forth while I continue to cry.

"I'm so sorry," he whispers. "Let it all out. I've got you."

I can't form thoughts. There are no words.

My world has just come crashing down around me.

Chapter Twenty

VIKTOR

"I don't know what the fuck happened," I growl into the phone. "Cars don't just explode. Is it possible one of Moreno's men made it out?"

"I will have Dimitri access the security system," Maxim says, trying to keep his tone even. "Natalia, how is she?"

"Not well. She fainted when I told her. Her mom's with her right now." I drop my head in my free hand. "Max, what do I do?"

"I do not have a full plan yet," Maxim replies. "But I will not rest until we find out who is behind this. They will pay."

The door to the office flies open and slams into the wall. Natalie marches into the room and stands in front of the desk. She stares at me, pure hatred in her eyes.

"I'll call you back." I hang up, needing to go to her.

"Don't come any closer," she warns.

"Natalie, please." I take a tentative step closer.

"Why are you lying to me?" She shoves my chest. "Where's my husband?"

"You know I'd never lie to you." I move a step closer, hoping to give her some comfort amid this nightmare. "Alex is gone."

"No," she yells and bunches her tiny hands into fists, punching me over and over. I don't move or try to stop her. Instead, I let her take all her anger out on my body. "You're lying. He's not gone." Her strikes slow and are replaced with a torrent of tears as she breaks down.

I wrap her in my arms, and she falls against my chest.

"We're having a baby." She struggles to take a breath. "He can't be gone."

Slowly, I lower our bodies to the floor, keeping her close. With my back against the large wood desk, I hold her on my lap and rock her gently. "I'm so sorry," I say softly. "Let it all out. I've got you."

She cries against my chest while I whisper softly to her, trying my best to console her but failing miserably. The woman in my arms is precious and doesn't deserve this. I struggle to hold back my tears, but they betray me and escape against my will. On the inside, I'm feeling red-hot rage. The bastards who took Alex from her will wish they'd never been born. I plan to hunt them down. I won't stop until every one of them is dead. But right now, my most important job is to make sure Natalie and the baby are okay.

Looking up, I see Charlotte standing in the doorway, her face tear-stained. "I'll take her." She walks toward where we sit on the floor.

"No." I don't release my grasp on her.

"I'm her mother," Charlotte argues. "I'll be the one who takes care of her."

"Please close the door on your way out." My tone is clipped.

With a huff, Charlotte spins on her heel and leaves us. She didn't deserve my temper. I realize that, but I won't let her take Natalie from me. I hold her tight until her tears subside, and her body relaxes—she's cried herself to sleep. I rest my head back and close my eyes. The task ahead will be difficult. I'm not sure where to start, but I'm confident in my skills. I'll find whoever's responsible and make them pay.

What scares me most right now is the promise I made to Alex. Why did I say yes to that? Because I didn't think any of this was a possibility. But here we are. Sure, I know how to protect her, and yes, I have feelings for her—feelings I never intended to act on. I don't know how to love. And I know even less about how to care for a child. I sit with my thoughts in silence, allowing Natalie to sleep for as long as possible. Right now, it's her only escape from the nightmare she's been forced to live. Unfortunately, I know reality will return all too soon.

The door opens slowly, and Stanley peers around the edge. The rage I felt earlier when her mom tried to take her from me has subsided, although I retighten my protective grip on her.

"Is she asleep?" he asks quietly.

I nod.

He disappears, and I'm relieved he's left us alone. A few minutes later, the door opens wider. Stanley walks into the office, a blanket in his hand. He bends down and spreads the blanket over Natalie's sleeping body. "I don't want her to catch a chill." Stanley meets my eyes, and I see his heartache. "Her mom's making soup for when she wakes."

"I called her doctor earlier. He's agreed to come by and look over her and the baby." I keep my voice quiet.

"This isn't going to be easy for her."

"She won't be alone. I'll be by her side."

Stanley nods and turns to walk away. "Bring her out when she wakes."

"Yes, sir. I will."

Chapter Twenty-One

NATALIE

"NATALIE." I HEAR VIKTOR'S VOICE, BUT IT'S NOT right. I'm with Alex, and he's holding our baby girl. We're happy. "I need you to wake up."

I try to resist and stay with Alex, but it's useless. My eyes blink open, and I lift my head. I'm in Viktor's arms on the floor of Alex's office. "Dr. Young's here."

"Why?"

"I called him after you passed out. I want to make sure you and the baby are okay."

"Come on, Natalie." Mom's walking across the room toward us. She reaches out to help me, but Viktor keeps his arms around me. They exchange a heated glare before he reluctantly shifts his position to help me up.

"The doctor's in your room." Mom leads me by the hand. "I'll take you to him."

I look over my shoulder. "Are you coming?"

Viktor begins to take a step.

"He can wait with your father in the kitchen," Mom quips.

We walk down the hall to my bedroom, where Dr. Young is waiting, a sullen look on his face.

"I'd like to see the doctor alone."

"Wouldn't you rather I stay with you?"

I understand and appreciate her concern, but I need to do this without her hovering.

"I'll meet you in the kitchen when we're done." I step into my room and close the door behind me.

"Natalie." Dr. Young embraces me. "I'm so sorry for your loss."

"It doesn't feel real."

"That's understandable. It was quite a shock." His voice is soothing.

My whole body begins shaking.

Dr. Young touches my arm, "How about you lie down?" He leads me to the bed and helps me recline against the pillows as tears trickle from the corners of my eyes. "I'd like to examine you and the baby if that's alright."

I nod.

The doctor takes my vitals. "Your blood pressure is a bit higher than I'm comfortable with, but that's to be expected right now. So, we'll keep a close eye on it." Next, he uses the Doppler to listen to the baby's heart.

Swoosh. Swoosh. Swoosh.

"The baby's heart rate is perfect." He smiles. "How about we take a peek at her? I brought the portable ultrasound."

My body's numb. Although I hear his words, it's as though they're floating around me, and I'm unable to form a response.

"Let's see your little girl," he says. "I'm going to pull your shirt up now."

The screen comes to life with the image of my unborn daughter moving about inside my body. She's unaware of the events that have taken place today, not knowing that she'll never get to meet her Daddy. It's too much for me, and I have to look away.

Dr. Young continues the exam, murmuring, "Baby Rose looks perfect, but I'd like her mommy to take it easy the next few days." He finishes the exam and cleans off the gel before replacing my shirt. "Would you like me to get your mom?"

"No, thank you. I could use a few minutes alone."

"Okay. Try to get some rest." He pats my hand before gathering his things and going to the door.

When he opens it, I see Viktor standing outside. Always my guardian.

"How is she, Doc?"

"Her pressure's a bit high, but that's expected after such a shock. I'd like to see her in the office in a few days to recheck it. If her pressure doesn't resolve, it can cause complications."

"I'll call in the morning and get an appointment," Viktor assures him. "What else do I need to do?"

"Make sure she's eating and drinking. It'll be hard, but it's important for the baby. I'd like her to rest as much as possible until I see her again."

"I'll see to it."

"Are you done with her exam?" I hear Mom ask.

"I am, Mrs. Clarke. I gave my instructions to Viktor," Dr. Young says patiently. "I'll see myself out."

"I'm going to get my daughter." Mom walks across the room and sits on the edge of the bed. "I made soup. How about you come to the kitchen and have a bite to eat?"

"I'm not hungry."

"You need to eat."

I really don't want to swallow anything.

"Doc said you need to eat, for the baby's sake," Viktor says as he walks into the room.

"Perhaps you should knock first," Mom says, clearly annoyed by Viktor's presence.

"Yes, ma'am. I apologize." He stands there for a minute, looking at me as if he wants to say something, but instead turns and leaves the room.

"Mom, you need to be kinder to him. He may be an employee, but he's also one of our closest friends. He's lost Alex, too."

"He's too familiar with you. I don't like it."

"We've been through a lot together. I trust him with my life." I stand up. "Can you please try? For me?"

She ignores my plea as she takes my arm. "Let's get you some warm soup."

Chapter Twenty-Two

NATALIE

The past few days have melded together into a hazy blur. I've been navigating through the routine motions of life without truly being present. Despite my mother's objections, Viktor has remained faithfully by my side. He tends to my every need, anticipating my wants and ensuring that I lack for nothing. Recognizing that I'm not up for socializing or conversation, he has taken it upon himself to screen my calls and visitors. He notes the names of those who've reached out to offer their love and support.

Most importantly, Viktor's there for me in moments of anguish, holding me tight as I sob through the nightmares that plague my sleep. Due to my high blood pressure, Dr. Young has instructed me to rest as much as possible. This hasn't been a challenge as I've found myself lost in a daze, lying on the couch and staring blankly at the television.

"You need to get dressed today," Viktor reminds me. "The detective will be here in about an hour." I shrug, not caring if I'm in my pajamas or not. "Let's go." He takes my hands, pulling me to my feet. "You're going to shower and put clean clothes on."

I roll my eyes but follow him down the hall. He opens the door to the primary bedroom. "I'm not going in there," I say as I freeze in place. The memories of Alex and me are too strong. I know they'll suffocate me if I step into that room again.

Viktor's features soften. "Okay, we'll go to the guest room then." He stops outside the bathroom door. "You go shower. I'll get some clothes and leave them here for you."

When he leaves, I strip and step under the hot spray, letting the water run over me, praying it will wash away the overwhelming grief. The emotion originates in the depths of my soul, intensifying with each passing moment until it erupts uncontrollably. I'm unaware of my screams until Viktor flings open the shower door and lifts me from the floor. He envelops me in a towel before carrying me to the bed.

"You scared the shit out of me." He sits next to me on the bed. "I thought something happened."

Silent tears mixed with water droplets run down my face.

"Stay here." He locks the door. "I don't want anyone coming in while you're not dressed. Viktor helps dry my body, never letting his gaze drop from my face. Then, I dress in the leggings and T-shirt he brought in. He's caring and gentle as he combs and blow-dries my hair.

There's a knock on the door. "Natalie, are you in there?"

"Wait here." Viktor goes to answer the door.

Mom's eyes are huge as she looks between the two of us.

"There's an officer here to see you."

"Please tell them we'll be right out," Viktor says.

She looks past Viktor to me before walking away.

"Are you ready?" he asks.

"Do I have a choice?"

"No. I'm sorry, but I'll be there with you."

Viktor and I make our way to the living room, where my parents are talking with an NYPD officer. When I enter the room, their conversation abruptly stops.

"Mrs. Montgomery, please accept my deepest condolences," the officer says.

"Thank you," I murmur as I take a seat on the end of the sofa.

Viktor perches on the arm next to me, and Mom gives yet another disapproving glare.

"I'm Detective Walters. I've been assigned to your husband's case." The older man introduces himself. "We've concluded our initial investigation and have ruled your husband's death a homicide."

Although I already knew Alex was murdered, hearing the words spoken out loud by law enforcement seems to make it even more real. I grab Viktor's hand for support.

"It's still an ongoing investigation. We have forensic experts sifting through the debris looking for anything that will give us a cause and hopefully a suspect," he explains. "Do you know if your husband had any enemies?"

"Of course he didn't," Mom interrupts. "Alexander was a model citizen. A business-owner. A husband and soon-to-be-father."

"Charlotte," Dad interrupts. "As difficult as this is for us, the office doesn't deserve our anger. He's only doing his job."

"I mean no disrespect, ma'am. These are the standard questions." He tries his best to appease her.

"I'm sorry. This is all very difficult. Please excuse me." Mom hurries out of the living room.

"Excuse me." Dad stands. "I need to go to my wife."

"Certainly," Detective Walters replies before returning to us. "I'm sure this is very difficult for you, but are you aware of anyone who may have been looking to hurt your husband?"

"As Mrs. Clarke said, Alex was a respected member of the community," Viktor answers. "I worked with him every day. He had no enemies."

The detective looks at me. "There's no one I can think of."

"Here's my contact information," Detective Walters says, handing me his business card. Viktor intercepts it. "Please call me if either of you thinks of anything that might help our investigation."

"We will," Viktor assures him.

"We weren't able to salvage much from the scene. But we were able to save a few of your husband's personal belongings." The detective holds out a small bag.

My hand trembles as I reach out and take the bag. "Thank you, Detective." Tears fall silently as I clutch the bag to my chest.

"If there's nothing further." Viktor stands. "Mrs. Montgomery needs to rest."

"Yes, of course. Thank you both for your willingness to meet with me. Again, if you think of anything, please call."

"I'll be right back," Viktor says before turning back to the officer. "I'll see you out." They exchange a few words that I'm unable to hear before the officer steps into the elevator and the doors close.

Chapter Twenty-Three

VIKTOR

After the officer leaves, I return to Natalie, who's clutching the bag of Alex's belongings and silently crying. I sit next to her.

"Do you want to open it?"

"Will you do it?" She hands me the opaque bag.

The first item I take out is Alex's wallet, charred around the edges. Did he drop it before he got into the car? Opening it, I find all his cards and ID are mangled but still in their places. I rule out an attempted robbery.

Natalie leans forward and opens the pocket where his cash is. She pulls out a piece of paper from behind the ruined money—an ultrasound picture. A fresh wave of tears pours down her cheeks. I set the wallet on my lap and wipe her face with my thumbs. "He was so excited about the baby."

"The day I found out I was pregnant, I was afraid to tell him. I didn't think he'd be happy."

"Why would you ever think that?"

"We'd talked about having a baby someday—" Her voice trails off.

I reach back into the bag and pull out two more objects: his wedding band and a small key on a chain. Natalie's hand immediately goes to the collar around her neck.

"I don't want to take it off. Not yet."

"I don't expect you to." I slide the key into my pocket. I know who this needs to go to.

"May I have his ring?"

"Of course." I give her the platinum band, which she slides onto her thumb.

There's another subject I don't want to bring up, but we can't avoid it any longer. "We need to plan a memorial service for Alex."

"I don't even know where to start."

"I know where there's a private chapel." I take her shaking hand in mine. "If you want, I'll call and set a date for the service."

"I'd appreciate that. Viktor?" Her voice is full of desperation.

"What is it?"

"I need you to find out who did this. Find who took Alex away from me."

I look into her determined, pleading stare. "I won't stop until I do."

Pulling out my phone, I make a call to the chapel. At Natalie's insistence, we schedule an evening candlelight memorial service.

Chapter Twenty-Four

NATALIE

My phone is propped on my makeup table, and I'm talking to Lana on video chat while I try to make myself look presentable for Alex's memorial service this evening.

"I hate that I'm not there with you today," she says.

"I wish you were here too."

After Thanksgiving, Lana returned to Russia with her family. She and Brandon are going through a very rough time and have decided to take some time apart while they consider the fate of their relationship.

I set the make-up brush down, frustrated. My attempt to hide the red, puffy spots on my face from crying failed. "I don't think I can do this, Lana."

"I know this is hard, honey." Lana gets close to the camera. "But you have to be strong. For Alex."

Two weeks.

That's how long Alex has been dead.

How long my world has been dark and lonely.

A part of me died with him in that explosion. Sometimes, it begs me to follow him.

Instead, each morning, I force myself to get out of bed. My body is going through the motions of living on autopilot. My mom places food in front of me at mealtimes, but I have no appetite. I gag it down to nourish my unborn baby—she didn't ask for any of this.

Yekaterina, my therapist from Jelena's Hope, offered to fly to New York City to help me through these first few months, but I declined her offer. Instead, we've been video-calling every day. She assures me it'll get easier with time, and although I nod in agreement, I don't believe her.

Life can never possibly be okay. If it weren't for this baby growing inside me, I'd have no reason to go on.

There's a knock on my bedroom door before it opens. Mom steps in.

"Sam and Luna just got here," she says. "He'd like to see you."

"You can send him back." I turn to the phone. "I have to go. We'll talk soon?"

"I don't care what time it is. If you need me, just call. I love you, Nat."

"Love you too, Lan."

I don't know how to face Sam. Losing his wife was hard enough, but no parent should have to lose a child.

It was a call I didn't want to make. I dreaded it with every fiber of my being. Viktor offered to do it for me, but I knew that wouldn't be right. Trembling with fear and sorrow, I mustered up the courage to speak, and my heart sank to the pit of my stomach.

The words were a crushing weight on my soul as they left my lips, informing Sam of the unfathomable loss of his beloved son. The deafening silence on the other end of the line was shattered by the sound of the phone dropping to the ground. The air was filled with the sounds of his anguished cries - sounds that were almost inhuman.

My heart broke at the sound of Sam's pain, causing the fragile semblance of composure that I had maintained to crumble. Luna had to step in to finish the phone call with Viktor as I was left wracked with grief and despair.

"May I come in?" Sam asks from the doorway.

I nod, already unable to speak.

Sam shuffles into the room, not as his usual confident self but as a weary man who looks like he hasn't slept in days. He holds his arms out, and I go to him, seeking refuge. Allowing him to envelope me in a fatherly embrace as we mourn the loss of the man we loved so much.

"I'm so sorry, Natalie." He rubs his hand in circles on my back. "I know how hard losing a spouse is. With you being pregnant, I can't even imagine how much harder it is."

This man just lost his only child, and he's apologizing to me —grieving for me. Sam leads me to the edge of the bed, and we sit. My body goes rigid.

"This is the first time I've been in here since—" I can't say the words. "I haven't been able to sleep in our bed." I look at the spot that was Alex's. "I can't bring myself to without him."

"I understand." He takes my hand. "It took me nearly a year to sleep in the room I shared with Rose. I wish I could tell you it gets easier, that the pain goes away, but it doesn't. Grief doesn't go away. We learn how to live with it." His gaze drifts off as though he's reliving the pain from losing his wife.

"It's been many years since I lost Rose. Although I eventually allowed myself to love again, sometimes, a sound or a smell pushes those memories to the surface. The pain hurts as much as it did in the beginning."

"I feel like I'm stuck in a nightmare. This can't be real." Sam puts his arm around me, and I rest my head on his shoulder. "I keep expecting Alex to walk through the door any second, but he never does. He's not coming back."

Tears stream down my face as the weight of the situation becomes even more overwhelming. "I don't know how to live without him," I confess, my voice choked with sobs. "Alex was my everything."

"You don't have to know right now. Take it one moment at a time, one breath at a time. And don't be afraid to lean on those who love you."

I cling to Sam, grateful for his presence in this moment of darkness. But the thought of facing the days ahead without Alex feels unbearable.

There's a quiet knock on the door. "I'm sorry to interrupt, but it's time to leave," Viktor says.

"I don't want to say goodbye."

"Tonight isn't going to be easy," Sam says as he steels his emotions. "But my son married a strong woman. I know you don't feel that strength right now. That's why you have all of us. We'll hold you up until you can stand on your own again." He rises from his place next to me. Gone is the weary man who entered the room, replaced by the strong and sure, dominant man I know him to be. He offers me his hand, and I reach out, placing mine in his.

The small stone chapel, lit only by the flickering glow of candles, is overflowing with Alex's business associates and friends. The air inside feels thick with sorrow, and the scent of burning candles only adds to the weight of it all. I sit there, numb and hollow, as person after person approaches me with kind words and memories of Alex. Their sentiments are like a knife, twisting in my heart and reopening the wound of his loss. Through it all, Viktor's steady presence is the only thing keeping me from collapsing in on myself.

As Brandon takes the stage to deliver Alex's eulogy, my heart feels like it's about to beat right out of my chest.

"Today, we gather to remember and honor a dear friend who left us too soon. We're all shocked and heartbroken by the suddenness of his passing. Alex was a wonderful person who impacted the lives of all those he encountered. He had a unique ability to bring joy and laughter to any situation." Somehow, Brandon found a way to tell everyone about me calling the police on him, making everyone laugh. Thankfully, he left out several key details.

"Alex's kindness knew no bounds, and although he's no longer with us, we can take comfort in knowing he's left a lasting impact on our lives." While Brandon speaks, it's like Alex is here with us, his spirit filling the room. Brandon's voice breaks with emotion as he talks about his friendship with Alex, and I can feel tears streaming down my face.

"I always admired you, Alex," Brandon murmurs as he looks upward, voice catching on a sob. "Until we meet again, brother."

He steps down from the small stage at the front of the chapel and stops where I'm seated. "You were his world, Natalie. Thank you for loving him." His words wrap around me like a warm blanket, and I break down. I can feel his arms around me, offering comfort and support, but it's like I'm a million miles away, lost in my grief. All I can think is that Alex should be here, with me, not in a coffin at the front of the room. And as the service comes to a close, I'm left with the crushing weight of the realization that I'll never see him again.

The repose is being held at Italiano Desiderio. When I called Anthony, he didn't even give me a chance to ask. He insisted on shutting down the restaurant for the night.

As our driver pulls up to the venue, Anthony and Leo are standing outside, waiting for us at the entrance. "Can we steal you away for a moment?" They guide Viktor and me through the restaurant, where our guests are starting to arrive. Upon reaching the back door, they hold it open. "Take all the time you need out here."

The walk down the path is hauntingly beautiful—peaceful despite the suffocating grief. Chinese lanterns sway gently in the breeze, casting a warm glow on the surroundings. But as we approach the gates, I feel a knot form in my stomach. This is the spot where Alex collared me, where our lives changed forever.

"Viktor." My hand covers my mouth. My heart aches as I take in the scene before me. The garden is aglow with lanterns and fairy lights, but what catches my eye are the framed photos of Alex and me lining the circular area.

Viktor takes a step back as I walk from picture to picture, vignettes frozen in time that tell our story. There are photos of us sitting in the restaurant from the night of our first date. Another of me sitting on the balcony of the bed and breakfast. Several selfies we took the day we got engaged. Seeing them all together is overwhelming. Memories flood my mind, and tears start to flow down my cheeks.

I continue my journey along the path and find a picture of Leo and me lying on the floor with the wax mural on us. There are pictures from our collaring and our wedding. The photo that hits me the hardest is Alex and me on the carriage ride in Central Park. Viktor must've taken it. I remember the feeling of Alex's arms around me and how it felt like we were the only two people in the world.

As the snow begins falling, Viktor's arm wraps around me, and I lean into him. We stand silently, surrounded by the memories of a love that will never fade.

Anthony prepared an extravagant meal with all of Alex's favorite foods. My plate sits on the table in front of me, my food untouched. People mill about, their voices hushed, but it's all become too much.

"Viktor, can you take me home?"

"You haven't even touched your food." He looks concerned.

"I'm not feeling well."

Without another second of hesitation, he stands and helps me from my seat.

"Where are you going, Natalie?" Mom asks.

"I'm not feeling well. I need to leave."

"You can't just leave when you still have guests."

"I'll speak to Tony on the way out. He'll handle everything," Viktor assures her. "Natalie isn't feeling well. So, I'm taking her home."

Mom clearly disagrees, but thankfully, she doesn't cause a scene. We say our goodbyes to a few people on the way out. Then, just as he said, Viktor speaks to Tony.

"If there is anything Leo and I can do for you," Anthony says, embracing me in a hug. "Just call."

"Thank you both so much. For everything."

Viktor must have called ahead because the valet is waiting with our car when we exit the restaurant. The ride back to the apartment is somber. The city that never sleeps is reverently silent as if it knows of my loss, and it allows us to have a smooth passage home.

We walk into a quiet apartment. I used to feel Alex's presence here, but now it feels empty.

"I'm going to go change. Will you wait here?"

"Sure." Viktor sits at the kitchen island while I return to the guest room where I've been staying.

I slip into pajama pants and a T-shirt and make my way back out to the kitchen.

"Your mom texted they're on their way. I should go to my place."

"Can you stay, please? I don't want to be alone."

We sit on the couch, and Viktor puts the TV on. But I don't think either of us watch it. It only serves to fill the silence.

Chapter Twenty-Five

∞

NATALIE

"I ASSUMED YOU'D BE COMING BACK TO NORTHMEADOW with us," Mom argues as I fold clothes, helping her pack her suitcase.

"This is my home. Why would I leave?"

Mom sets down the shirt she's folding. "There's nothing left for you here. You belong home with us, where we can help you."

I had a feeling she would try to convince me to go back with them. Fortunately, I'm not the timid girl I once was. I've grown and can stand my ground.

"Mom, I love you, and I know you think you're doing what's best for me. Alex is gone, but *this* is my home. This is Rose's home. We're not going anywhere."

"You won't have anyone to help you," she says, genuinely concerned.

"I have Viktor."

"What does a single man know about raising a baby? Besides, it doesn't look proper for you to be here alone with him."

Not wanting to be disrespectful or discount her concerns, I resist the urge to roll my eyes. "I don't only have Viktor. There's also Brandon and Lana and all my other friends. Rose and I will be okay."

"Well, I disagree, and I hope you'll eventually see reason. But I don't want to argue right before we leave."

"Good. Neither do I."

After we finish packing, Viktor takes their suitcases down to the car. We follow behind him and start the drive to the airport. Viktor drops us off at the door so I can walk my parents to the security checkpoint.

"We're going to miss you." Dad hugs me. "Let us know if you change your mind and decide to come home."

"I love you, Dad."

I say a tearful goodbye to my mom and watch as they make their way through security. They may be overbearing at times, but I know they love me.

When we get back to the house, I make sandwiches for Viktor and me. There's a task I've been avoiding, but I can't put it off any longer. Today's the day.

"I think it's time I go into Alex's office." I take a bite. "Alex told me a long time ago that if anything happened to him, there would be a file on his desk with important papers. I blew him off then, but it's time I take it out and go through them."

"Do you want me to stay with you?"

"I need to do this alone. I'll call if I need you."

Viktor looks uncertain, but he doesn't argue. I've successfully managed to make the rest of our lunch awkward, and we eat in silence. "I'll be in my apartment. I have some calls to make," he says when he's done eating.

I stand outside the closed door of Alex's office, debating whether or not I really want to go inside. Before I lose my courage, I turn the handle and open the door. As soon as I step in, I smell Alex's cologne. It's both comforting and painful. "Oh, Sir, I miss you so much." A warmth envelops me, and I know it's Alex.

Pulling out his well-worn leather desk chair, I lower myself into it. Everything is where he left it, as if his belongings are waiting for him to return. Although Alex was never secretive about his business or forbade me from being in his office, I never came here alone. Even now, it feels wrong to be in here without him. Unlike the other room, which he converted into an office for us to share, this was his space.

I sit back and take a few minutes before entering the code that will open the locked drawer. Once I input the numbers, the lock clicks, and the drawer opens. Just as Alex said, there's a large manila file with my name on it. Inside are several legal papers listing various assets I'm the beneficiary of. There are directions for bank accounts and investments, including all the business information for Jelena's Hope-NYC. It's a lot of information, and I'm overwhelmed with it all. I'll know Viktor will help me make sense of it.

Under the stack of papers is a white envelope with my name written on it. My hands shake as I open it. Inside is a note in Alex's handwriting.

My Dearest Natalie,

My heart is heavy with sorrow and regret as I write these words to you. Writing this letter is the hardest thing I've ever had to do because if you're reading this, I am no longer by your side. My beautiful baby girl, I am so sorry for leaving you.

Where do I start? That first phone call from Brandon. The one where he asked me to babysit the roommate who called the cops on him. After I got done laughing, my first thought was, there's no way I'm going to spend the night with a college girl who'll be freaking out—I came so close to not showing up.

But something pulled me toward Fire and Ice that night. Little did

I know that it would be the start of something that would change my life forever. The night I met you felt like the first day of my life—it was when I decided to start living again. I'd finally found the missing piece to my puzzle, and that piece was you.

Since that day, you've challenged me, made me laugh and cry, and shown me what it means to love unconditionally. You gave yourself to me, willingly submitting to me in every way possible. I never knew I wanted to be a father until the moment you told me you were pregnant. That first ultrasound, when our baby was no more than the size of a peanut, I fell head over heels in love. You and our daughter are everything to me. Please don't ever doubt how much I love you both.

As I write this, I realize that there are some practical things that you'll need to take care of moving forward. You are now the owner of everything I possess. You'll need help keeping Jelena's Hope-NYC running—don't be stubborn. Allow Maxim and Viktor to help you. Viktor is aware of all your assets and will arrange a meeting with my attorney to ensure everything's taken care of. You and Rose will always be safe and secure.

But now, I've come to the hardest part. I need you to listen to me very carefully, my love. This is my final request to you as your husband and Dominant.

There's another man in your life who has loved you for a long time. He's someone I trust wholeheartedly to love and protect you and Rose with his life. I cannot bear the thought of you being alone and vulnerable after I am gone. Imagining you in the arms of another man kills me, but I refuse to let you go through life alone.

I've already spoken to Viktor, and he's agreed to be that person for you. I want you to open your heart to him—accept the love he has to give you and our daughter.

Move on, be happy, and give Rose the family she deserves. My only request is that you tell Rose about me and make sure she knows how much her daddy loves her and that I'll always watch over her.

Please don't be sad, baby girl. I'm setting you free, but I will always be a part of you. I love you more than words can express, and

although I won't be there with you every day, I'll always be a part of you.
With all my heart
~Alex

The tear-stained paper falls from my hand, fluttering to the floor. Everything makes more sense now. Viktor hasn't left my side since the day of the accident. He's made doctor appointments, helped plan the memorial service, and run interference between my parents and me. He's stayed on the couch with me every night and held me when I woke from nightmares.

I drop my head in my hands and cry. Viktor's known about this, and he's said nothing. I should be furious with him for keeping it from me. And Alex. How dare he ask that I move on with another man?

"You promised you'd never leave me," I yell. "You lied." I stand and swipe my arm across the desk. Papers and pens fly in all directions. Alex's laptop crashes to the floor. "How could you do this to me? I hate you." As soon as the words leave my mouth, I want to take them back. "I'm sorry, Alex. I don't hate you. I could never hate you." I slide down the wall and sit on the floor. "But you left me. You left us."

A black box at the bottom of the drawer catches my eye. It's aged and worn, but I don't recall ever seeing it. I lean forward, lifting it out of the drawer. The top has etchings of a dagger piercing through a crown. The name *Moreno* is inscribed on it. What is this? I debate whether I should open the lid. My gut tells me that whatever's inside is going to change everything.

Chapter Twenty-Six

VIKTOR

"Did you get the security footage?" I ask Dimitri, one of several men on the video conference.

"I did. But so far, nothing. It looks just like every other day in a mundane office building," he says dryly. "I also have the data from the fingerprint logins and a complete list of all the building's employees. There are no red flags."

"Can you email that stuff to me? It won't hurt to have another set of eyes on it." I turn my attention to Maxim. "Anything on the Moreno front?"

"I have checked with all my sources. No one from Moreno's organization made it out alive. We have eyes and ears on the usual suspects, but everything has been quiet," he reports.

"That's not possible. We have to be missing something." I slam my fist on the desk.

"Calm down, Viktor." Maxim's voice is steady. "Getting angry is not going to solve anything. It will only cloud our vision."

"I just sent the files," Dimitri interrupts.

"Someone has to pay for killing him. For leaving Natalie alone."

"How is she doing?" Maxim asks.

"Not well. She's barely eating and has nightmares every night." I hesitate to say the next part, but I have to get it off my chest. "Alex has asked something impossible of me, and I don't know how to honor his request." I drop my head in my hands.

After hearing that, Maxim asks everyone to log off the video call, leaving only him and me. "What has he asked?"

I take a few minutes to tell him about the conversation Alex and I had in his kitchen shortly after they were rescued from Mexico. That I made a promise to love Natalie. "What do I do, Max?" I plead. "Tell me how to help her."

"She is grieving. She needs you to be strong and patient. Do what you have always done for her."

What I've always done? I put a Band-Aid on things until Alex came back. That's what I've always done. But that's not going to work this time. Alex isn't coming back. This time, I'm the one she's going to depend on. There's no one coming to take over. Max tells me not to push Natalie, to show her love and support until she's ready to move on. He's confident that, in time, everything will work out.

After we disconnect the video call, I lean back in my chair. Maybe I should've made her go back to Missouri with her parents? It's probably best if she's with her family instead of me. "Why the fuck did you put us in this situation, Alex? I only know how to keep her safe. You're the one who knew how to love her."

I stay in the silence of my office, trying to compose myself—to get my thoughts together. But when I look at the time, I realize it's been a few hours, and I still haven't heard from Natalie. I know she's going through the files Alex left, and I know the letter she'll find.

Although Alex didn't tell me everything he wrote, I know she'll learn what he's asked me to do—what he's asked her to do. I don't expect her to accept it or to love me right now, maybe ever, but I'll do everything I can to honor my friend's wishes. I head back up to her apartment and find it silent.

"Natalie," I call out, but get no response.

My senses go on high alert, and I hurry down the hall and find the door to the office cracked open. I see the mess and rush in. Papers are everywhere. A laptop lies smashed on the floor. Behind the desk, I find Natalie huddled on the floor, Moreno's box in her hands. Oh, God. I hope she hasn't opened the box yet—fear courses through me as I sit on the floor next to her and wait.

"You know what's in here, don't you?" she asks without looking at me.

"I do."

"I've been sitting here holding it, trying to imagine what's inside. But I'm not coming up with anything." She looks up at me. Her green eyes are seeking answers. "Why does Alex have this?"

"I'll be honest. What's in there has a story that won't be easy for you to hear. Hell, it's not going to be easy to tell. This was supposed to be Alex's story to tell you when he was ready."

"He's not here to tell me. So, you need to." She opens the box and comes face to face with the dagger that Alex used to cut Moreno's beating heart from his body.

Natalie listens quietly, her eyes never leaving the dagger, while I tell her everything I know about that night.

"Alex killed Moreno?" I see the fragmented pieces from that night coming together in her mind. "Why didn't he tell me?"

"He wasn't sure what you'd think of him if you knew he'd taken a life. He didn't want you to look at him any differently."

She sits quietly for several minutes, pondering what I just said. "This is the same dagger Alex used on my skin at Moreno's club. The one I wear the scar from?"

"It is."

"Why did he keep it?"

Michael told me how Alex held onto that dagger as though it were his lifeline. I suppose it was shock, but I don't know for sure. "I tried asking him, but he told me never to talk about it again. I didn't want to push him."

Natalie takes a long, last look at the dagger before she replaces the lid and hands the box to me. I put it back in the drawer and close it, not wanting to be reminded of that time either.

"I told him I hate him," she whispers.

"What do you mean?"

"After I read Alex's letter. I got angry." She motions to the mess on the floor. "And I yelled that I hate him." A lone tear slides down her cheek.

"It's okay. Alex knows you don't hate him." I move to put my arm around her, but pull back quickly. "You know what he asked me to do?" She nods. "I don't expect anything from you. I know you aren't ready to move on—you may never be ready. And if one day you are, you might not choose me." My words come out hurried. "I won't force anything—"

"Stop, please," she whispers. "Everything's too new, too raw. I'm not ready to make any decisions or promises." She takes my hand and holds it tightly. "Just please don't leave me. I can't get through this without you."

This time, I do reach out and put my arm around her. Natalie moves closer, allowing me to hold her. "I'll always be here for you."

My phone vibrates with a text alert. I pull it out to see who's texting me, hoping it's Dimitri with new information.

Steve: I hate to bother you during this difficult time, but I have some documents Natalie needs to sign.

Me: Documents for what?

Steve: The explosion damaged the building. The city insists that the repairs be made immediately. The new business license also needs to be signed by the end of the day tomorrow, or it could jeopardize the whole project.

Me: Is there a way to get an extension?

Steve: I already did. The city won't let it go past tomorrow without issuing fines and possibly shutting everything down.

. . .

I set the phone on my legs and rest my head against the wall.

"Who is it?"

"It's Steve. There are papers the city wants signed for Jelena's Hope. We have to go down there today."

Her body jerks up. "I don't want to go there."

"I know, but if we don't sign the papers today, Jelena's Hope could be shut down before we even get it open." I take her hand. "I'll be with you."

"Viktor—"

"We can't let whoever did this win. We have to show up and prove we're stronger. That we won't back down," I say with more confidence than I'm feeling.

"I don't think I *am* stronger," she admits quietly.

"Natalie," I cup her face in my hands. "You're the strongest woman I know."

"You'll stay with me?"

"I won't let you out of my sight," I promise.

"I need to take a quick shower and get dressed." She looks up at me, an odd expression on her face. "And, um, I need help getting up. I'm stuck."

"Is that why you were on the floor when I came in?"

"I sat down." She half cries and half laughs. "But then, when I wanted to get up, I couldn't."

I smile and do my best to hold back my laughter.

"Don't you even think of laughing at me, Viktor Dobrow," she warns.

"I wouldn't dare." I stand up and take her hands in mine, pulling her to her feet. "Problem solved."

Chapter Twenty-Seven

∞

NATALIE

I knew, eventually, I'd have to face going to Jelena's Hope-NYC. This project isn't going away, and I don't want it to. I didn't think it would be this soon. Alex has only been gone a few weeks, and the repairs haven't even been made where the explosion happened. How does anyone expect me to go where my husband's life was violently taken? And be okay with it?

The problem is, if I don't go, the whole project could end up being shut down. And we've worked too hard to let that happen. But that does little to quell my nerves. My entire body trembles on the ride across town. Viktor keeps the conversation light, discussing everything except what we're about to do. He's trying so hard, but nothing he can say or do will make this any easier.

Viktor turns from Central Park West to West 73rd Street, where our building sits on the corner. I think part of Alex's reason for choosing this building is the view of Central Park Lake from the upper floors. While we're stopped at the red light, Viktor puts the turn signal on.

"Can we do street parking?"

"The street's full. We could circle for hours and still not find a spot," Viktor replies, his voice steady.

"There's a parking garage a few blocks down."

"Natalie, the closest parking garage is nearly a mile away."

"I'll walk. Please, Viktor, park anywhere other than here," I beg.

My words seem to fall on deaf ears because he turns into the building's garage, anyway. My only solace is that he parks on the opposite side, in a guest spot. But I know that just a few feet away, around the corner, is the place my husband died.

Viktor shuts the car off and gets out. I don't move. I can't move.

He rounds the car and opens my door. "You can do this."

Panic rushes through my body. I'm cold—numb. Calmly, Viktor leans in and takes my hands, gently tugging me from my spot. When I get to my feet, I feel a gush of water.

"What's that?" Viktor asks.

"I think my water broke." I look at him. Fear of a different kind fills me. "My due date is still five weeks away. It's too soon."

"Fuck." He rubs his hand over his bald head. "This is my fault. I shouldn't have brought you here. I should've handled it myself."

My hands fly to my stomach as every muscle tightens until I'm in agonizing pain.

"What's going on?"

"I think I'm in labor."

During my shower, I wasn't feeling well. I assumed I was having more Braxton Hicks contractions. I've been having those for the past few weeks. Dr. Young told me they're perfectly normal, so I didn't think anything of it. The only thing different was the pain I was having in my back. But at this point in my pregnancy, I'm so uncomfortable that I blew them off. Now, I realize I should've paid more attention.

"I'll call Dr. Young." Viktor helps me back into the car and leans in, looking me in the eye. "Everything's going to be okay."

The hospital's on the other side of the city. With Christmas being a little over a week away, traffic's at an all-time high. My body doesn't seem to care that we're only inching through the city. It keeps contracting. I try to hide the frequency from Viktor, doing my best to regulate my breathing. He's already noticeably shaken. I don't want to make it any worse while he's trying to drive, but a stronger contraction assaults me, and I grab his arm for support.

"They aren't stopping?"

I finish breathing through the contraction before I can speak. "It feels like they're getting stronger."

He glances at me, his gray eyes swirling with fear. "Just keep breathing. I'll get us there as fast as I can." He turns down a side street, undoubtedly trying to find a less busy route.

Nearly an hour later, we're finally pulling up to the hospital's valet parking. Viktor barks orders at a poor, unsuspecting attendant before rushing to help me out of the car. I don't know whether to laugh or cry when I stand up and realize the wet stains going down my pants. It feels like all eyes are staring at me.

"It looks like I had an accident," I say, embarrassed.

"Nobody's looking. Even if they are, I dare them to say something." Viktor takes my arm. "Come on, let's get you inside."

Walking proves challenging between the wet denim chafing my skin and the pain from the contractions. Thankfully, the wheelchairs are just inside the doors. Viktor helps me into one and pushes me to the elevator. "What floor?"

"Seven."

He pushes the button, and we wait. The hospital elevators are notoriously slow. Finally, a car arrives, and he rolls me in. Viktor's hand nervously taps on the chair as we stop at several floors on the way.

I reach back to still his hand. "You aren't helping anything."

"This is taking forever," he complains.

I'm usually the impatient one, so this is an odd turn of events. Finally, the doors open onto the labor and delivery floor. Viktor wheels me to the nurses' station, where two ladies sit, their heads down, doing paperwork.

"Excuse me," Viktor says. "Where's Dr. Young? He's expecting us."

One of the women looks up. "Name?"

"Viktor."

She laughs and points to me. "The patient's name."

"Oh." Viktor blushes, another thing I've never seen before. "Natalie Montgomery."

She studies her computer screen before standing. "Right this way, Mr. and Mrs. Montgomery."

Viktor opens his mouth to correct her, but I grab his hand and shake my head. At my last appointment, I took the opportunity to ask Dr. Young for a rather unusual request.

"May I ask for a favor?"

"Depends on what you need." Dr. Young smiles.

"When it's time to have the baby, I don't want the nurses feeling sorry for the poor widow having her baby alone." I stop to get control of my emotions. I intend to get through this conversation without tears. "Viktor will be with me. Please let them assume Viktor's my husband and Rose's father."

"Natalie—"

"This is going to be hard enough without Alex. I don't want to see the look of pity on their faces. I want Rose's entry into the world to be a happy experience. Besides, Viktor will be raising her with me. He'll be the only father she knows."

Dr. Young doesn't answer right away. He studies my face for what feels like forever.

"Because of the publicity surrounding Alex's accident, I think it'll be better for me to designate one nurse to your care for the duration of your stay."

It was a huge relief, but I thought I had more time. I haven't told Viktor what I've done yet. I'll have to fill him in as soon as we're alone.

The nurse leads us to a beautiful delivery suite. "My name's

Esperanza, and I'll be your nurse while you're with us. I've let Dr. Young know you arrived." She opens a drawer and takes out a hospital gown. "As soon as we get you changed and hooked up, he'll be in."

"Hooked up?" Viktor asks.

Her smile is kind as she explains, "We'll attach a fetal monitor to Natalie's abdomen for a short time. It'll monitor the baby's heart rate and her contractions." She hands me the gown. "I'll give you a few minutes, and then I'll be back."

Once we're alone, I look at Viktor. "I'm scared."

"Everything's going to be okay. You're exactly where you need to be right now." He smiles, but the uncertain look in his eyes betrays him. "Do you want me to step out while you change?"

I double over from the pain of another contraction. Viktor hurries to my side and grabs my arms. "Look at me. Take slow, deep breaths. Like this." He emphasizes his breathing until I'm mimicking him. "Good girl. Just like that." He continues to talk me through the rest of the contraction.

When it finally passes, I ask, "Is there nothing you can't do?"

"What do you mean?" He looks confused.

"Where did you learn to coach a woman in labor?"

He shrugs. "I figure the pain is like a gunshot wound, and I'm familiar with that."

Viktor makes me laugh. That's not the answer I expected. "Can you help me change? With these contractions, I don't think I can do it myself." Viktor helps me out of my clothes and into the hospital gown. "There's something I need to tell you."

"Right now?"

"A few weeks ago, I asked Dr. Young not to tell the nurses about Alex. To let them refer to you as my husband and the baby's father." I pause, trying to gauge his reaction. "I didn't want to answer questions, and I didn't want pity."

"I see," he says stiffly.

"Are you mad?"

"I'll do whatever you need to help you get through this. It's my job."

I'm about to respond to his *it's my job* comment, but Dr. Young walks in.

"I wasn't expecting to see you kids so soon."

"Me either." I groan as another contraction grips my stomach.

Viktor sits on the edge of the bed and makes eye contact, again helping me breathe through the pain.

"I'm impressed," Dr. Young says. "How far apart are the contractions?"

"About every four or five minutes."

"I'm going to put the monitors on for a few minutes to see how your little one is handling the contractions, and then I'd like to see if you're dilated."

Dr. Young puts two stretchy bands around my stomach. The room fills with the sound of my baby's heartbeat. Viktor moves closer to the top of the bed while the doctor discreetly checks my cervix.

"Let's have a chat," he says and pulls up a chair. "You're almost seven centimeters dilated."

"I'm only thirty-five weeks. Isn't it too early?"

"You're a few weeks early, but Miss Rose is the boss here. And it seems she's ready to make her grand appearance. I have every confidence she'll be just fine." He looks at the readout from the machine. "Her heart rate is perfect at 155, and you're having some fairly significant contractions." He removes the straps. "Everything looks good here. There's no reason to keep you tethered to the bed."

"So, what do we do now?" Viktor asks.

"Now, we wait. Natalie's body knows what to do. She's opted for an all-natural delivery. Your job is to help her through her contractions. She can get up and walk around. There's a tub she can relax in if that makes her more comfortable. Whatever she needs to bring this baby into the world."

Chapter Twenty-Eight

∞

NATALIE

AFTER DR. YOUNG GIVES HIS INSTRUCTIONS, HE LEAVES
a wide-eyed and terrified-looking Viktor and me alone. Another
contraction hits. Viktor holds my hand and guides me through it
like a pro.

"Should we call your parents?"

"I'd rather wait until she's born. This is going to be hard
enough."

Viktor's phone rings. He pulls it from his pocket and looks at
the screen. "It's Max, but I can take it later."

"It might be important. You should answer it."

Viktor walks to the other side of the room. He's whispering,
so I only catch some of the conversation. They're saying something about documents that were sent to Viktor's email. I want to
know what's going on. So, I swing my legs over the side of the
bed, but as soon as I stand, a contraction hits hard, and I yell.

"Shit." Viktor races to my side, dropping the phone.

"That was a big one." I look at him.

"Why didn't you wait for me?"

"I can still walk, you know." I grin and point to the phone lying on the bed. "Is Max still on the line?"

Viktor puts the phone on speaker.

"What is going on?" Maxim's deep voice fills the room.

"Natalie's in labor."

"It is too soon for that."

"She's a few weeks early. But Dr. Young isn't worried."

"Why are you on the phone with me? Your attention must remain on Natalia," Max scolds Viktor. "Call us after the baby arrives."

"Will do, boss."

Viktor hangs up and sits on the bed next to me, a helpless expression on his face. Alex and I only took the first two birthing classes before the accident, so I'm feeling as ill-prepared as he is right now.

"How about we take a walk?" I suggest.

"A walk?" He looks at me, confused.

"Walking is supposed to help labor progress. Gravity and all."

Relying on Viktor's strength to hold me, we slowly make our way up and down the hall of the labor and delivery unit. We frequently stop to breathe through the contractions that seem to be getting stronger and closer together.

"I think we should head back to the room. I'm starting to feel a lot of pressure like I have to push."

Viktor takes my arm and starts leading me back when I nearly double over from the force of a contraction. "Nurse! Nurse!" Viktor yells as though the building's on fire.

"Stop yelling." I squeeze his arm, not wanting him to make a scene.

"But you need help. Here—" He reaches out to lift me. "I'll carry you back."

I slap his hand away. "You'll do no such thing." I stop to take a few breaths. "As soon as the contraction is over, I'll walk."

Esperanza comes over to us. "Everything okay here?"

"She's in pain."

She chuckles. "That's usually a guarantee during childbirth."

"You need to do something to stop it. Give her some medication—"

"I'm not taking any pain meds. I want to do this naturally," I say, turning to Esperanza. "I'm feeling a lot of pressure. Different than before."

"Let's get you back to your room and see what's happening."

With the increasing pain, it's an even slower walk back. Once we reach the room, I'm helped into bed, and the nurse checks my cervix. "I have good news. You're ten centimeters." She smiles.

"What does that mean?" Viktor asks.

"It means it's time to start pushing."

Viktor's face turns a nearly see-through shade of gray.

"Let's get you a chair, big guy." She drags a seat over for my trusty bodyguard and helps him sit. "It's always the big, tough ones that go down the hardest," she chuckles. "You stay here. We need to focus on the soon-to-be-mom, not the passed-out new dad on the floor. I'm going to get the doctor so we can have this baby."

Breathing through these contractions is getting more difficult. This is by far the worst pain I've ever felt. But Viktor quickly regains his composure and returns to my side, guiding me through my breathing.

As hard as I try, I lose the battle, and tears fall. "Alex should be here."

Viktor leans in close and whispers, "Close your eyes. Do you feel him?"

With my eyes closed, I see my husband's gorgeous face when I told him I was pregnant. The way his brown eyes lit up in a way I had never seen before. The awe on his face when he saw our baby on the ultrasound for the first time. A warmth envelops my body, and I know it's Alex wrapping himself around me. "I do."

The door opens, startling me, and Dr. Young walks in. "I hear it's time to have this baby. Are you ready to start pushing?"

"I think so."

Things start moving pretty quickly now. Dr. Young scrubs up and puts on gloves and a face shield. Esperanza plugs in some sort of contraption that looks like it has a French fry warmer on it before coming over to my bedside.

"I need you to help hold her leg," she says to Viktor. "Just like this." She demonstrates on my other leg. Viktor follows along. "With the next contraction, I want you to push."

It feels like only seconds until the next contraction hits. I bear down and push with all my might. I'm surprised that it actually makes the contraction more bearable. We repeat this process for what feels like forever. Sweat pours from my face—I'm exhausted.

"I don't think I can do this anymore."

"Don't you dare give up." Viktor turns my face so I'm looking at him. "You can do this."

Another contraction.

Another push.

"I can see her head. Give me your hand." Dr. Young guides it between my legs to feel the top of my baby's head.

The magnitude of the moment overwhelms me.

Esperanza points to a mirror set up behind the doctor. "It's so you can watch your baby come into the world," she explains.

The next few contractions are difficult. The pressure becomes increasingly more painful.

"Her head's out. I don't want you to push quite as hard this time," Dr. Young instructs.

Viktor leans close to me. "You're doing so good, Natalie. She's almost here." He kisses my forehead gently.

While I push, I watch in the mirror as the doctor maneuvers the baby's shoulders out one at a time, followed by the rest of her body. A moment later, my newborn's cries fill the room. Dr. Young places her on my bare chest, and I wrap my arms around my precious daughter.

"Viktor, would you like to cut the cord?"

He looks to me for approval. "Alex would want you to."

With shaky hands, he takes the offered scissors and cuts where the doctor instructs. Esperanza brings over a blanket and, much to the dislike of Rose, helps me dry her off.

"I need to steal her for a few minutes."

She brings Rose to the warming bed, where she finishes drying her off. Then she gets a weight and measurement.

Dr. Young comes to my side, taking my hand in his. "I know how difficult today is for you. Celebrating the beginning of a new life while you're still grieving the loss of another." He squeezes my hand. "You did good. She's beautiful. Alex would be very proud."

I manage to smile through the tears pouring down my face.

Esperanza returns to us with a tiny bundle swaddled in a blanket, a pastel pink hat on her head. "She's 6lbs 3oz and 17 inches long." She places the baby in my arms. "We'll give you some time alone."

I look down and see familiar blue eyes looking back at me. "Hi, Rose," I say softly. "I'm your mama." She's tiny and absolutely perfect. I lift her hat and gently run my hands over her head, which is full of curly blonde hair.

Viktor sits on the bed beside me, his gaze fixed on the baby in my arms. "She's beautiful."

"Would you like to hold her?"

"I don't know." He freezes. "She's so tiny."

"She won't break." I adjust my position and pass my daughter to Viktor. Somehow, she looks even smaller in his large-muscled arms.

"*Printessa,*" he says softly. A lone tear slides down his face.

I reach over to the table beside the bed and grab my cell. I want to capture this tender moment. Then I send a text and the picture to Max and Irina.

Me: She's here, and she's perfect. As you can see, Viktor's already quite taken with her.

Rose begins to fuss. "What's wrong?" Viktor panics and passes the baby back to me.

"She might want to eat." I lower the hospital gown and help Rose latch onto my breast for the first time.

"I'll leave and let you two have some time alone."

"Please don't go."

"But you're feeding her." He motions to my partially exposed breast. "I shouldn't be here."

"It's not like you haven't seen me naked before." I shake my head and laugh. "We live in the same house, and I'll have to feed her. Quite often. Do you plan on leaving the room every time?" I pause and look down at the infant suckling from my breast. "I know this isn't how it was supposed to be, but it's how it is. We both need to bond with her." I move over, making room. "Come, sit."

Chapter Twenty-Nine

∞

VIKTOR

Watching Natalie endure such pain and knowing I can't do a damn thing about it makes me feel more helpless than I've ever felt. She's in agony, and I can't fix it. What was Alex thinking when he agreed to let her do this without medication? If it were up to me, I would've insisted she take something to alleviate this pain. It's torture watching her and only being able to hold her hand and guide her breathing.

When the doctor returns to the room, things move quickly. Natalie's legs are pulled back, and I'm instructed on how to hold one while I coach her through breathing and pushing.

I've never witnessed a woman giving birth and never wanted to. Despite the pain, Natalie looks more beautiful than ever. Although she's exhausted, she doesn't quit. She's incredibly strong as she pushes with all her might, bringing her baby one step closer to being born.

Leaning close, I whisper, "You're doing so good, Natalie. She's almost here." I kiss her forehead gently.

Esperanza sets up a mirror so Natalie can watch her daughter enter the world. I don't know if I should watch, but I can't tear my eyes away from the miracle I'm witnessing. Somehow, Natalie's tiny body opens, allowing the most perfect little human to come out. The doctor quickly lays her on Natalie's chest.

"Viktor, would you like to cut the cord?" Dr. Young asks.

I look to Natalie. "Alex would want you to."

This is for you, brother. I take the scissors and cut where the doctor shows me, officially severing the cord connecting mother and child.

Esperanza takes the baby from Natalie to clean her thoroughly. I watch, already guarding this precious new life, as she's weighed and measured. Then, the nurse wraps her tightly in a blanket and returns her to her mama.

We're left alone.

Just a few hours ago, being alone meant there were only two of us, but now, by some miracle, we're three.

I can't take my eyes off Natalie. She's radiant as she holds her daughter and whispers to her. Rose gazes at Natalie adoringly, as if she already knows who she is, and I guess she does. Their bodies have been connected for nearly nine months.

"She's beautiful."

"Would you like to hold her?"

"I don't know." Every muscle in my body tenses in fear. "She's so tiny."

"She won't break." Natalie adjusts her position and passes the tiny bundle to me.

I look down, admiring this perfect little girl in my arms, already knowing I'd give my life for her. *Printessa,* I say softly. My chest aches when I see she has her daddy's brown eyes. He should be here, not me. A tear slips down my face. The baby begins to squirm and whimper.

"What's wrong?" I quickly hand her back to Natalie.

"She might want to eat." Natalie lowers her hospital gown and brings the baby to her breast. She quiets as she latches on quickly.

Rose cried in my arms because she knew I wasn't her father. I understand what Alex asked, but I don't see how this will work—I don't have a place in this little family.

"I should leave. Let you two have time alone."

"Please don't go," she implores.

I can't be here right now, not with the emotions warring inside me, but I can't tell Natalie that. I don't want to ruin this time for her. "You're feeding her. I shouldn't be here."

"It's not like you haven't seen me naked before." Natalie gives me an incredulous look. "We live in the same house, and I'll have to feed her quite often. Do you plan on going out every time?" she asks gently. "I know this isn't how it was supposed to be, but it's how it is. We both need to bond with her." She moves over, giving me room. "Come, sit."

Although I'm filled with uncertainty, I know she's right. Natalie and I have been through more together than most people. We've seen each other at our most vulnerable, but things are different now. In the past, I was nothing more than her bodyguard and friend, but now, I've been thrust into a role I never expected to find myself in.

Finding a woman and starting a family with her was never in my plans. I was happy on my own. I don't know how to be the man Alex asked me to be—the one who is to protect and love his family. I'll never measure up to the man he was. Natalie will never look at me with the same love and adoration she did him. And I certainly have no idea how to raise a child.

The promise I made to Alex is easily the most important promise I've ever made to anyone. I fear I'll never live up to the expectations he had for me.

Chapter Thirty

∞

VIKTOR

AFTER NATALIE FINISHES FEEDING THE BABY, SHE CALLS her parents to tell them their granddaughter has been born. It turns into an emotional phone call as Charlotte begs Natalie to return home. To let them help her raise her child. Natalie insists she's okay and wants to do this on her own. It's well over an hour before their phone call winds down. Charlotte is disappointed but, in the end, agrees to respect Natalie's decision.

Right now, Natalie and Rose are sleeping. She made me promise not to leave the room, but I need to call Maxim. So, I find myself standing in the far corner, trying to be as quiet as possible so I don't wake either of them.

"I did not expect to hear from you so soon," Max says.

"I guess her labor went fast. At least that's what the nurse said." I look over my shoulder to check that the girls are still sleeping. "Any updates?"

"Nothing of significance. Dimitri is rewatching the video footage from the security cameras, but nothing seems out of place." Max pauses. "How is Natalia doing?"

"She's doing as well as to be expected. I think Rose coming

early was the best thing that could've happened. It's given her something to smile about."

"That is all good, but what is it you are not telling me?" Maxim asks, perceptive as always.

"You know what Alex asked of me?"

"*Da.*"

"I don't think I can do it. I'm not the man Alex believed me to be." I put my forehead against the wall and close my eyes. "I know how to protect, and I know how to kill. But I don't know how to be gentle and love."

There's a long pause.

"Are you still there?"

"I am," Max responds. "Your concerns are understandable. You have been tasked with the most important job a man could have."

"It's a job I can't do. I've never been in a relationship, and I have no clue how to raise a child."

"You already know how to love her."

"Boss—"

"Do not interrupt me, Viktor," he reprimands. "Anyone who has seen you with Natalia knows you care about her. Alex was not blind to that. However, he knew you would never betray him. That is why he asked you to do this. Alex knew he would never have to worry because you already love her."

"Even if that's true, she doesn't love me."

"Not a romantic love, you may be right. But given your experiences together, you and she share a very special bond. She knows Alex's request, and eventually, she will be able to act on it," he pauses. "As for being a parent. You are the only father Rose will ever know. Your responsibility is to make sure she knows who Alex is, how much he loved her, and how much you love her. After that, the rest will fall into place." He says it like it's so easy. "When will she and the baby go home?"

"Tomorrow morning." Behind me, the baby begins to fuss. "I have to go. Rose is up, and I don't want her to wake Natalie."

I don't wait before ending the call and hurrying over to the baby trolley where Rose lies. "Shh, *Printessa*." I gently place my hand on her. "Go back to sleep." She pushes out her bottom lip, and I laugh softly. "Your mama does the same thing when I tell her what to do."

Rose's whimper begins to grow louder. Natalie's been going non-stop since she gave birth. This tiny human is a non-stop eating machine. "Okay, I guess we're going to do this." I put my hands under her little body and lift her, holding her close to my chest. "This isn't so bad, is it, *Printessa?*"

I walk her to the windows and turn my body so the baby can look out. It's night, and the city lights twinkle in the distance. "See, it's nighttime. This is when we sleep." She seems to settle and eventually falls back to sleep. I'm afraid to lay her down, so I sit in the recliner with the baby in my arms. Carefully, I press the button that makes the footrest pop up, and I recline with the baby lying on my chest. "You and I will hang out here so your Mama can get some sleep.

Chapter Thirty-One

∞

NATALIE

Esperanza wakes me when she turns the bedside light on. Even though I'd rather be sleeping, it's time for another routine post-birth check.

"Look at those two over there." She points to Viktor, who's asleep, his arms holding Rose, who's sleeping on his chest. "Looks like she's going to be a daddy's girl."

"I think so." I smile and fight to hold back the tears, but they fall anyway. I quickly swipe at them.

Esperanza passes me a tissue from the table. "It's postpartum hormones," she says as I dry my eyes. "Is there anything you need?"

"I was told I could ask for a pump. I'm going to have to go back to work, and I'd like to get Rose used to a bottle, so Viktor," I hesitate. "So, her dad can feed her, too."

Esperanza leaves but quickly returns with the machine. She explains how to use it, and it seems pretty straightforward. I keep the lights dim so I don't wake Viktor or Rose. While I pump, the words I spoke to the nurse repeat in my head. *So her dad can feed her, too.*

Suddenly, things I hadn't considered or didn't want to consider hit me hard. Rose will never know Alex. She'll never hear his voice. Besides what she's told, she'll never experience how much he loved her. All the dreams and plans Alex and I once shared were stolen. I've been left to pick up the pieces of my life and move on. I'm left with the knowledge that Alex's wish is for me to make new dreams and a new life with Viktor.

I look over at the man who's sleeping peacefully with my newborn daughter snuggled on his broad chest. He's a good man. A kind man. A man I trust with my life and now my daughter's life. He doesn't lack in the looks department either, but I'm still in love with my husband. There's no room in my heart for another man. I don't know how to put my love for Alex aside and make room in my heart for Viktor. I don't know how I'm supposed to honor Alex's request.

It's a chilly December afternoon. The weather turned wintry overnight, leaving a few inches of snow on the ground. I'm dressing Rose in a soft pink one-piece with little rosebuds. Alex chose it months ago for her coming home outfit.

Meanwhile, Viktor is pacing, an instruction booklet in his hand, looking between it and the alien invention, otherwise known as a car seat.

Esperanza walks into the room. "I have your discharge papers. You need to sign here." She hands me the papers and a pen. "I also have a cooler with your milk." She sets it on the bed and spots my cell phone. "How about I take a family picture before sending you off?"

Viktor stops pacing and looks at me. He knows the arrangement I made with the doctor, and he's gone along with it, but every mention of *family* makes us flinch. The wounds are too fresh.

I muster a smile and pass her my phone. "That would be great."

Viktor sets the instructions down and joins me on the bed, where I cradle Rose in my arms.

"Get closer, you two." She peeks around the phone. "Put your arm around your wife."

Although his body remains tense, Viktor slides his arm around me. Esperanza snaps a few pictures until she gets one she's pleased with. "You are a beautiful family, and you've been a pleasure to serve," she says kindly.

"Thank you, ma'am," Viktor says.

"Let's get the baby in her car seat, and you three will be free to go."

While Esperanza and I get Rose situated, Viktor calls the valet to have our car ready. Despite my protests, I'm put in a wheelchair—standard practice, I'm told, and my lap is piled high with everything we have to bring home. Who knew one little person could accumulate so much stuff so quickly? Viktor carries the car seat, and we walk out of the hospital to our waiting car.

Viktor opens the back door, where the car seat's base is secured. Then, lifting the car seat, he leans in and tries to attach it to the base. "Dammit," he mutters as he fiddles with the contraption, still not finding success.

"May I help you with that?" Esperanza asks.

Viktor glares at her over his shoulder. "I'm fine."

"They're always fine," she says and laughs.

"I guess you've seen this before?" I ask while watching Viktor and trying to suppress my laughter.

"Every day." She smiles. "First-time fathers are the most stubborn creatures."

I lose the battle, and we share a laugh.

"What's so funny?" Viktor asks, looking deflated by his continued failed attempts.

Esperanza walks up to Viktor. "Move over and let me show you how it's done."

With practiced ease, she snaps the car seat into place.

"I almost had it, you know," Viktor mutters as he takes the pile of stuff from my lap and puts it into the trunk.

"You'll get it next time," I say as he helps me into the backseat with the baby.

Today, bringing Rose home from the hospital is one of those defining moments in life. Something that should be met with happiness and celebration. Instead, it's a quiet ride, both of our hearts heavy and missing Alex.

Chapter Thirty-Two

∞

VIKTOR

OUR FIRST FEW DAYS HOME ARE CHAOTIC, TO SAY THE least. While we were in the hospital, I read a bunch of articles on Google about taking care of a newborn. I thought I had it all under control, but damn, was I wrong. Rose is a pleasant baby, but I've learned that even pleasant babies are surprisingly high-maintenance.

While we were in the hospital, she seemed to understand the difference between daytime and nighttime. But once we got home, something happened. Now, she sleeps all day and stays up all night. When Rose is awake, she's either eating, which she seems to do all the time, or needs her diaper changed.

Natalie's running on fumes, so I try to make sure she naps when Rose does. While the girls sleep, I try to clean up the house and have learned how to work the washer and dryer. It's a juggling routine unlike anything imaginable. This crazy new schedule also means I've had no time to even think about opening the email from Dimitri.

Natalie's asleep in the guest room because I still can't get her to sleep in the primary bedroom, and Rose is asleep in the bassinet beside me. We agreed to keep all business related to Maxim down-stairs, but I can't wait any longer to open my laptop to review the documents Dimitri sent. I only make it halfway down the first page before Rose fusses.

Leaning over the bassinet, I peer down at her perfect little face. "*Printessa,* I believe you came pre-programmed to know when I'm trying to work." I can't help but smile as I lift her into my arms. "Your mama said you'd be hungry soon. Fortunately for both of us, she left a bottle."

This is my first time feeding her without Natalie's supervision, and I hope I don't screw it up. Holding Rose with one arm, I warm up the milk in a cup of hot water and test it on my wrist like Natalie showed me. Then, I get comfortable on the couch and offer Rose the bottle. At first, she turns her head and refuses. "I know, it's not the real thing, but Mama's exhausted." I rub the nipple gently on her mouth, and eventually, my efforts pay off. She wraps her tiny pink lips around the nipple and sucks the milk greedily, finishing the bottle in record time. Then I readjust her position on my chest as I burp her.

"You two look like pros," Natalie says as she sits beside me and gently caresses Rose's head.

"We managed to figure it out." I smile proudly. "How was your nap?"

"It was well-needed. Thank you for watching her."

"So, while I was sitting here, I started thinking about some-thing." I adjust my hold on Rose.

"What's up?"

"Christmas is only a few days away, and we don't have a tree."

"I'm not in the mood for celebrating."

"I understand, but it's Rose's first Christmas." I pass the baby to Natalie. "We have to do it for her."

"She won't know the difference."

"But we will. And Alex would expect us to give Rose the best first Christmas possible." I turn to face her. "We need a tree, deco-rations, and presents."

"Whatever you want."

"Let's bundle Rose up and take a walk to the tree lot down the street."

A part of me longs for her sassy mouth to argue with me, but there's nothing. She just shrugs and goes along with my plan. None of this is ideal, but something has to give. Rose shouldn't be living in a home shrouded by grief. We have to start moving forward, if not for us, for the baby.

With the three of us bundled up, I buckle Rose into her pram and tuck an extra blanket around her to keep her warm.

Outside, flurries dance in the breeze, adding to the spirit of the holidays. With Christmas less than a week away, the lot is pretty well picked over, but luckily, we still manage to find a decent tree. The lot attendant wraps the tree tightly in netting, making it easier to transport. Natalie laughs when I hoist the bundled evergreen onto my shoulder. It's the first time I've heard her laugh in weeks, and it warms my heart. When we're back at the house, I set up the tree while Natalie goes to the closet to find the Christmas decorations.

"I told you this was a good idea," I say to the infant lying in her swing.

Natalie comes back into the room carrying two boxes. I hurry over and take one from her.

"This one has the lights in it." She says as she sets her box down.

Natalie nurses Rose while I string the colorful lights across the tree branches. Then, she gets Rose situated in her baby sling to have both hands free to help decorate the tree.

"I have something for you. Wait here." I rush down the hall to Alex's office to grab the gift I've been hiding and hurry back to Natalie. "It's nothing big." I shrug and hand her the little pink box.

She lifts the lid and looks inside. "Viktor, it's beautiful."

She holds up a silver tiara ornament with crystals inlaid across it. Engraved on it is *Baby's First Christmas*.

"I hoped you'd like it."

"I love it." She reaches out to hug me. Usually, I'd withdraw. Knowing I had feelings for her made any physical contact feel wrong. Things are different now, and I embrace her tightly. Holding Natalie feels incredible until Rose wriggles between us, prompting me to let go.

Natalie hangs Rose's ornament front and center on the tree. Together, we pull out the ornaments until Natalie comes upon a delicate porcelain snowflake. "It's Alex and mine's First Christmas ornament." She looks up at me. "I don't know what to do with it."

"Whatever you decide is okay."

Natalie holds it up, her gaze fixed on the object, seemingly unsure what to do next. After a moment's contemplation, she returns it to the box, but at the last second, she changes her mind and brings it to the tree. With great care, she hangs it on a branch, positioning it next to Rose's ornament. I'm not sure how it happens. Maybe the branch was damaged. But like a slow-motion movie, the snowflake slips from the tree. It crashes onto the floor, shattering into countless irreparable fragments.

Natalie is devastated when she sees the ruined ornament and collapses to her knees. She remains quiet, but tears silently stream down her cheeks.

"I'm so sorry. This is my fault. If I didn't insist on getting a damn tree—"

"It's not your fault," she says quietly. "It was an accident. The universe seems to be trying to erase Alex from my life." She walks away and sits on the couch, cradling the baby against her.

"We aren't going to let that happen." I place my hands on her legs. "He'll always be a part of you—a part of us."

"I know, but I'll never be able to move forward if I keep pretending he's coming back." She lifts her left hand and looks at her wedding rings. "It's time I accept that he's gone," she says as she slides the rings off her finger.

I don't know how to respond, so I say nothing and watch as she walks out of the room.

I debate whether I should go after her or allow her some space before settling on giving her a few minutes alone. While she's gone, I put Rose to bed and clean up the broken ornament pieces. Then, I sit on the couch and wait for her to return.

Natalie walks back into the room. No words are needed. I open my arms to her, and she crawls on my lap, burying her head against my chest as she cries.

There are no words I can say to make this better for her. All I can do is give her a safe place to express her grief.

Chapter Thirty-Three

NATALIE

Seeing the shattered fragments of our precious ornament scattered across the floor, a crushing wave of emotions washes over me. It feels like every piece of my life connected to Alex is being cruelly ripped away from me, and I am helpless to stop it. I'm exhausted from feeling like a mere bystander, waiting for the next disaster to strike. This time, I'm taking control and making the first move.

Without a word, I leave Viktor behind with the half-finished tree. There's something I need to do, a cathartic act that will bring some sense of closure. With a trembling hand, I slide my wedding rings off my finger, acknowledging the brutal reality that this is not a nightmare but my tragic new life. Alex is gone forever, and I can't bring him back.

I clutch my wedding rings tightly as I enter the bedroom that once belonged to Alex and me. My jewelry box beckons, and I pull out the little drawer where Alex's wedding band rests on the soft black velvet. It's time for my rings to join his, a symbolic gesture that brings both comfort and pain.

One day, I'll tell my daughter the beautiful story behind my ring. How it first belonged to her grandmother, Rose, and how her daddy redesigned it into something meaningful for us. Then, I'll pass the ring on to her, so she'll always have a special treasure from her dad.

I heard Viktor putting Rose to bed. So, before I return to the living room, I check in on her and find her sleeping soundly.

When I return to Viktor, he's sitting on the sofa. The mess from the ornament has been cleaned up. Our eyes meet, and he opens his arms, inviting me to go to him. I crawl onto his lap and let him hold me. Tears come in vicious waves as I allow myself to grieve for what I decide is the last time. After this, it's time to start fresh. To move forward.

It takes a while to compose myself, but eventually, the tears stop, and we finish decorating. The rest of the ornaments are hung on the tree, and then, with Viktor's help, we hang the wreath above the fireplace. I watch as Viktor strings some extra lights around the room. "I hate to admit it, but decorating was a good idea."

"Can you say that again?" Viktor teases.

"You were right." Then, in a childish move, I stick my tongue out.

Viktor laughs, and I join him, knowing it's these small moments that are going to be what heal my soul.

"Let's go to bed. I'm exhausted." I try to hold back a yawn.

"That sounds like a good plan."

We go to the bedroom we've been sharing since we brought Rose home. After I change into my pajamas, I crawl into bed. Viktor grabs his pillow and blankets and starts making his bed. "Viktor," I sit up. "It's time to stop sleeping on the floor."

"I'm fine down here."

"Come sleep in the bed." There's no way he's comfortable sleeping on the hard floor, and I see no reason he shouldn't sleep in bed. "We don't have to share a blanket if that makes you feel better."

"I don't know—"

"Please."

I hear him shuffle around, and then the bed dips next to me as he gets in and lies down.

He slowly slides my satin nightgown up my body, trailing kisses along my skin in his path. Stopping at my breasts, he sucks on each one, ensuring my nipples are hard, and I moan in response. It feels so good. I'm close to an orgasm, and he hasn't even touched me yet. Once he frees me from my nightgown, he tosses it to the side.

"You're beautiful, baby girl," he says from where he's standing next to the bed. "I want to fuck your mouth."

I adjust my position so my head is at the edge of the bed and bite my bottom lip, knowing this is his favorite position. I can take him deep in my throat this way. He moves closer, and I take his cock in my hand. I drag my tongue around the head before teasing his slit. Then, I lick the beads of pre-cum that have already formed there.

I open my mouth and take him deep. He lets out a growl of appreciation before he grabs my hair and starts moving. Tears drip from my eyes from how hard he's fucking my face. I love it when he loses control like this. It's a powerful feeling. He's close, I can tell, but instead of continuing, he pulls out. "Turn over," he demands.

I get on my hands and knees and look back at him, taking in every inch of his muscular body. My husband is amazing. He wastes no time thrusting himself inside from behind me. He's not gentle as he continues to fuck me with abandon. My hands clutch the blankets. He reaches around and squeezes my clit, sending me over the edge. I call out his name right as I'm about to—

"Natalie, wake up." Viktor shakes me.

My eyes fly open.

"You were having another nightmare. You were grabbing me, and then you called out for Alex."

How can I tell him I wasn't having a nightmare, that I was dreaming about sex with my husband while I was reaching out for him? "I'm sorry I woke you."

"That's what I'm here for."

I lay back down and roll over, questioning my decision to invite Viktor into my bed.

Chapter Thirty-Four

NATALIE

My heart aches each morning when I think about facing another day without Alex. The erotic dreams I have every night aren't helping. When I wake, I long to hear the sound of his voice, to feel his touch. It's a constant battle where I remind myself they're only dreams—he's gone.

Yekaterina and I have been discussing the grief process in my sessions. Where she can help me overcome the trauma from Mexico and the explosion, there's no prescribed treatment for grief. No timeline can be given for when the pain will ease. It's not easy, but each day, I'm learning a new *normal*. Learning how to exist in a world without Alex.

It started when Viktor insisted we celebrate Christmas—for Rose. I tried to convince him that she'd have no memory of it, but he's stubborn and said we were celebrating the holiday properly. He's gone over and above to make the day special.

I wake to breakfast in bed. Viktor made my favorite—French toast, bacon, and a cup of coffee. He got Rose up, changed her diaper, and dressed while I ate. Then, with a goofy grin, he videos me carrying Rose down the hall and into the living room. I'm not sure how or when he managed to pull this off, but there are stacks of presents under the tree.

"What in the world? How did you do all this?"

"Don't ask questions," he says, smiling. "Just enjoy it."

Viktor takes pictures and videos while I open the presents for Rose and me. Despite my initial resistance, I find myself smiling and enjoying the moment.

When I finish opening the gifts, I pass Rose to him. "Wait here. I'll be right back."

I hurry to my office and open the desk drawer to get my gift for Viktor. "I feel awful. I only have one present for you," I say, handing him the wrapped box.

"Seeing you smile is the only gift I need."

"Oh, so I can take this back then?" I pull the wrapped box away.

"Since you took the time to get it, I wouldn't want to be rude and not open it." He grins.

I laugh and hand him the present.

With a sleeping Rose in his lap, he tears the wrapping paper off and opens the box. Minutes tick by while he stares at it, saying nothing.

When he finally speaks, I swear I hear his voice crack. "I love it," he says without taking his eyes off the framed picture Esperanza took of us before we left the hospital. "It's perfect."

The following week, we get calls from Tony and Leo begging us to come to their New Year's party. However, neither of us is in the mood to celebrate the occasion, so we politely decline. Instead, we spend the evening curled up on the couch, intending to watch the ball drop in Times Square, but we fall asleep before midnight.

"Come here, Natalie," he orders. Naked, I climb onto his lap.

His erection rests between my legs, setting all my nerve endings on fire.

"Please, I need you." I rub myself against him.

"Natalie. It's me, Viktor. You need to wake up."

When I open my eyes, I'm straddling Viktor's lap, rubbing myself against his very prominent erection. Completely humiliated, I jump off. In a swift move, he grabs my waist, stopping me from having a collision with the floor.

"I'm so sorry. I didn't realize. I was dreaming about—"

"You don't need to apologize for having a dream." He tries to hide his arousal by pulling the blanket over his lap.

"Maybe I should go sleep in the other room?"

"Don't be silly." He puts his arm out for me to lie back down. "Come back to sleep."

Tentatively, I get back on the couch and lie against him.

What's going on? Why do I keep having these vivid dreams, and how do I make them stop before I do something I can't take back?

Chapter Thirty-Five

VIKTOR

I startle awake. Natalie's straddling my lap, rubbing herself against me, my body responding to her movements.

"Please, I need you," she begs.

Her eyes are open, and for a brief second, I allow myself to believe it's me she's talking to. But I know I can't do that. It's not fair to her to allow her to believe I'm Alex.

"Natalie, it's me, Viktor." I shake her gently. "I need you to wake up."

It takes her a minute before recognition creeps into her awareness, and she jumps off me as though I'm a flame threatening to burn her. This isn't the first time she's reached out to me while asleep. At first, I thought she was having nightmares. But now I know they're not nightmares. She's dreaming about Alex.

Natalie offers to sleep in the other room alone. But I've quickly become accustomed to being next to her, and selfishly, I don't want to give that up.

My wish is that one night, when she has that dream, it's me

she sees—me she's reaching out for. Until then, I have to find a way to be content with only holding her and making sure she's okay.

she sees—me she's reaching out for. Until then, I have to find a way to be content with only holding her and making sure she's okay.

Chapter Thirty-Six

NATALIE

"I keep having these vivid dreams about Alex."

"What kind of dreams?" Yekaterina asks.

"That we're together intimately."

"That's normal. It's part of the way you're grieving. It'll eventually pass."

She encourages me not to hyper-focus on them, which is exactly what I can't stop doing. Between the dreams and Rose's feeding schedule, I'm exhausted and not thinking clearly. I'm running on empty.

My parents have called every day for the past two weeks. They want to come for a visit to meet their granddaughter. But that would get complicated very quickly. First, they're going to ask why Viktor's living with me and what's going on between us. Both questions I'm not ready to answer. Then, they'll pressure me to go back to Northmeadow. I'm so tired and confused right now. I know I can't deal with it, and I'll end up exploding. I don't want that, so I keep making excuses and telling them they can come *soon*.

Lana and I video chat almost every day, but she immediately

changes the subject when I bring up Brandon. Now I understand how they felt when Alex and I broke up, but at least they had each other. I don't have Alex to go to for advice on how to get them back together, and when I ask Viktor, he tells me they have to work it out for themselves. All I can do is sit by and watch my friends hurting.

Mistress Star and Leo also keep calling. Star keeps inviting me to the club, and Leo wants to get together for coffee. As much as I love and miss them, they're a part of my life that no longer exists. I send their calls to voicemail and don't return any of their countless messages. I keep hitting delete, hoping they'll give up soon.

Aside from Viktor, Brandon's the only person I let close to me. He comes over at least once a week. Maybe I feel safe with him because we're both hurting. Brandon lost not only his best friend but also his submissive, who's still in Russia, unsure if she'll ever return.

Brandon's spending the afternoon with me while Viktor goes downstairs to work. He doesn't like leaving me alone, but he's also desperate to find out who's behind the explosion that killed my husband. It helps him to work without worrying when Brandon's here.

Rose's soft coos come through the speaker on my phone. She's just waking up from her nap.

"I'll get her," Brandon offers.

"She's going to need a diaper change," I call after him.

"I can handle that." Then, I hear the door to the guest room open. "Wassup? Wassup, my precious little Rose?"

I laugh at the usual greeting of his niece, but part of me fears *wassup* will end up being her first word. He continues talking to her, and I turn the baby monitor app off, not wanting to eavesdrop on their time together.

"Can I give her a bottle?" Brandon asks when he comes back to the kitchen carrying Rose.

I know how much he enjoys feeding her, and I'm already a step ahead with a bottle ready to go.

"Thank you, Mommy." He kisses my cheek and sits on the couch to feed the baby while I catch up on dishes. "Can I ask you a question?"

"Sure. What's up?" I dry my hands on a dishtowel and turn around, leaning against the counter.

"What's going on between you and your Russian?"

"He's only half Russian and nothing. Why?" My words come out hurried.

"Nothing?" he asks, clearly not believing me. "He moved in with you, and I see how he looks at you. The man's in love with you." Brandon adjusts Rose to his shoulder to burp her while he walks into the kitchen. "It's okay to move on, you know."

"Why don't you put Rose in her swing? We need to talk."

He buckles his niece into her swing and turns it on low before joining me at the kitchen island. As hard as this will be, I owe Brandon the truth. "You have to promise you'll try to keep an open mind," I say before explaining the letter Alex left me and his conversation with Viktor. When I finish, Brandon stays quiet for a few minutes. It's clear he's trying to digest everything I've just said.

"I had no idea," he says quietly. "So, you and Viktor are a couple?"

"Yes. No. I don't know." I'm unable to give him a straight answer. "I care about him, and I know how he feels about me, but it's too soon. I'm not ready to move on yet."

Brandon takes my hand. "You have my support with whatever you choose." Then he not so smoothly tries to change the subject. "Everyone at Fire and Ice has been asking about you. Any chance I can get you to visit? Maybe bring your *half-Russian* with you?"

"Bring me where?" Viktor asks, walking into the kitchen.

"I didn't hear you come in."

"I was just asking Natalie if there's any chance she'd come down to the club. Of course, you can tag along, too." Brandon smirks.

"Is that something you want?" Viktor asks.

"Thanks again for the invite. But I don't think so."

"Suit yourself." Brandon shrugs. "How are things coming with Jelena's Hope-NYC?"

"Everything's a mess." I sigh. "We've had a hard time getting a contractor who's willing to fix the damage caused by the explosion. That's put everything behind with permits and licensing. I don't know all the details. Viktor's been handling it all."

"Sounds like a headache."

"It is," Viktor agrees. "Needless to say, the grand opening's been postponed indefinitely."

"I'm sorry. I know how much this project means to you." He looks at his watch. "Shit. I'm going to be late. I have a meeting in an hour." He jumps up and plants a noisy kiss on my cheek. "Hang in there. I'll see you soon."

"I'll walk you out." Viktor follows Brandon to the elevator.

When he returns, he takes the seat next to me. "That's a subject we haven't discussed."

"The club?"

"The lifestyle in general."

"I didn't know you're into that sort of thing?"

"I went to the club with Alex a few times. Long before he met you."

"And?"

"There were some interesting things."

"Makes sense. You are the bossy dominant type," I say jokingly.

"True." He smiles, and his gray eyes light up. "I do like to take charge—in the bedroom. But a Dominant I am not." The smile falls from his face. "Is that something you want again?"

"No," I say without hesitation. "What Alex and I had was special. A once-in-a-lifetime experience. Submitting to him was natural—most of the time." I grin. "But I don't want that with another man."

Viktor lets out a relieved breath. "I'm glad to hear that."

"Did you find anything new?" I ask as I return to loading the dishwasher.

"No," he growls. "And it's starting to get frustrating."

"You'll find it. Don't give up."

"There's no chance of that. I won't rest until the person who did this breathes their last breath."

Chapter Thirty-Seven

VIKTOR

Since Natalie took her wedding rings off, things feel like they're starting to shift. Almost like she's beginning to give us a chance. At least I hope I'm not reading more into things than is really there.

Valentine's Day is next week. I want to do something, but I don't know what. Unfortunately, relationships aren't exactly my area of expertise. Sure, I know how to please a woman in the bedroom, but I never cared about the whole romance thing until now.

I need advice, but men in my line of work don't have a long list of friends. Dimitri isn't even a consideration. He's a fuck 'em and leave 'em before the sun comes up kinda guy. Maxim always gives good advice. He and his wife have been together forever, but I feel uncomfortable calling my boss to ask for relationship advice.

"Shit." I pace back and forth in my office. Then it occurs to me—Brandon. "He spends a lot of time with Natalie. Maybe he can help."

I pull up his contact and tap the green button on the screen.

The line rings several times, and I think he isn't going to pick up. I'm just about to disconnect.

"Hello?"

"Brandon. It's Viktor." I feel like a nervous schoolboy.

"Are Natalie and Rose okay?"

"They're fine."

"I got worried when I saw you come up on the caller ID." He lets out a deep breath.

"I didn't think you were going to answer."

"I was in a meeting. I had to excuse myself from the room."

I didn't stop to think about the time. It's the middle of the afternoon on a Thursday. He's at work, and I'm calling him with my dating issues.

"I'm sorry. I'll let you go."

"No. I'm good now."

There's a long and very awkward pause.

"Are you going to tell me why you called?"

"Well, Valentine's Day is next week."

"Did you forget my address to send me flowers?" Brandon asks.

He's being a smart ass, and I'm ready to hang up on him. But Natalie already told me Brandon supports us being together. I need to get over myself and just ask.

"I want to do something for Natalie—a date. But I don't know what to do."

Brandon laughs. "That's what all this is about?"

"Forget it. I'll figure it out myself."

"No. Don't hang up," Brandon says. "What are you thinking?"

I sink into the leather chair across from my desk. "I want to do something special for her—for us."

"Take her out to dinner."

"She won't leave the baby with a sitter," I explain. "I think she's scared to let Rose out of her sight."

"That's understandable. Why don't you wait until Rose is in bed for the evening and cook dinner for her? You know, flowers, romantic music, and candlelight. All the romantic stuff that girls love."

"Do you think she'd like that? Is it enough?"

"Natalie doesn't expect expensive gifts. She's not high maintenance like that."

Brandon's right. Natalie's the least high-maintenance woman I've ever met. The smallest thing, as long as it comes from the heart, makes her smile. Regardless, I still want to give her the world. She deserves nothing less.

"I think that's what I'll do. Thanks for the help."

He's still talking when I disconnect the call.

Wednesday was Valentine's Day. I didn't want Natalie to feel pressured, so I decided to wait until the weekend for our *date*. It's a lazy Saturday morning. We're still lying in bed while Natalie nurses Rose.

"I have to run a few errands today. Will you be okay here?"

This is the first time I'll be leaving her here alone. I'm apprehensive, to say the least.

"I'll get dressed quickly. Rose and I can come too."

"There are a few things I need to do on my own."

"Oh, Okay." Disappointment flashes across her face, but she quickly masks it. "I have a few loads of laundry to do, so it's probably better I stay home."

"Great." Knowing I don't have time to waste, I hop out of bed, grab some clothes, and go into the bathroom for a quick shower. There's a lot I need to get done for tonight.

When I come back out, Natalie's just getting out of bed. A

content Rose in her arms. I kiss Rose's forehead and then Natalie's. "I'll see you girls later."

"Don't you want breakfast before you go?"

"I'll grab something while I'm out."

Chapter Thirty-Eight

NATALIE

Viktor's acting weird today. It's not like him to go without breakfast or leave me home alone. I wish I knew what was going on. "Well, Miss Rose. It looks like it's just you and me today." She rewards me with a smile, something new she started doing this week. Then, I buckle her into her baby seat in the kitchen so I can keep an eye on her while I make breakfast.

I'm in the middle of cooking when my phone starts ringing. Mistress Star's picture comes up on my screen. She's called every day this week. I slide my finger across the screen, sending her call to voicemail again. Hopefully, she'll get the hint and stop calling. The friends I had from Fire and Ice are reminders of what Alex and I shared. That's over now. I've moved on.

I manage to eat and shower before Rose demands to be fed again. While I'm sitting on the couch nursing her, I get a text.

Viktor: I made plans for us tonight—8 p.m.

Me: Plans?

Viktor: Yes. It's a formal event.

Me: A formal event? You know I'm not ready to leave the baby.

Viktor: We aren't leaving the house. Rose should be in bed by then. Be dressed and ready. I'll meet you in the dining room.

Me: What's going on?

Viktor: I'll see you tonight. Oh, and don't cook. I've got it covered.

He'll meet me in the dining room? And he's handling dinner? Other than him using the microwave, I don't think I've ever seen him cook.

"Looks like Viktor's planning a surprise tonight," I say to Rose, who's currently fighting to keep her eyes open. "He's a good man, and he loves us both. I need to learn how to love him back."

When Rose finishes nursing, I put her in the portable playpen for her nap. Viktor keeps telling me she'll have to sleep in her crib at some point. But that's in her nursery, and I've been unable to go there. I've been silently questioning if I should look for a new apartment—one with no memories.

My phone, which I left on the couch, starts ringing. "This better not be Star again." When I look at the screen, I see it's Yeka-terina. I go to connect the call, but she's already hung up. Quickly, I call her back.

"Hello, Natalie," she says as the video call pops up on my screen.

"I'm sorry I missed your call. I just put Rose for a nap, and honestly, I forgot about our session today."

She asks how Rose is doing, and we chat briefly about the ups and downs of having a newborn. Yekaterina has a few children of her own and always has excellent advice.

"Is she sleeping through the night yet?"

"Not really, but it doesn't matter. I'm not sleeping through the night either."

"Are you still having those dreams?"

"Almost every night." I sigh. "Why is this happening?"

"Why do you think it's happening?" She always asks my opinion before offering her own. It can be frustrating, but I know that's how therapy works.

"Because I'm not ready to let go of Alex," I say honestly. "I know he's gone—"

"I hear a but there."

I hesitate before answering, "But something deep in my heart refuses to let him go. I can't explain what it is. Does that make sense?"

"It does. But I have a different take on your dreams. An angle you might not have considered."

"What is it?"

"You tell me that you're reaching out to Viktor during these dreams, correct?"

"Yes. And it's making things awkward. On my end, at least. I'm sure on his too, but Viktor and I don't talk about them once morning comes."

"Have you stopped to consider that maybe your heart is telling you it's time to move on? That it might be time to accept what Viktor's offering you?"

I'm stunned by her words. How can dreams about my husband mean I'm ready to move on? "My dreams are about Alex, not Viktor," I remind her.

"I understand it's Alex you see in your dreams, but I think there's more to it than what meets the eye." She stops, allowing me time to think about her words. "Are you ready to explore what's trying to blossom between you and Viktor?"

Am I ready? "I don't know if I'll ever be ready." Do I tell her about tonight? I decide I should. "He's planning some sort of date for us tonight."

Yekaterina smiles. "Consider this the push you need to take that leap of faith. Give him a chance."

"I don't know." There's something I can't explain that's holding me back.

"Natalie, Alex has already given you permission to move on. If you can't do it for yourself, at least do it to honor his last wish. You never know what might happen."

The rest of the afternoon goes by slowly. Viktor hasn't come back yet, so it's just Rose and me. The laundry and dishes are all caught up, and now I find myself sitting in the way-too-silent house. My mind is replaying my session with Yekaterina. *Are you ready to explore what's blossoming between you and Viktor? You need to take that leap of faith. Give him a chance.*

In my head, I know she's right. I think even my heart knows it. Somehow, I have to ignore that quiet little voice in my head that's trying to hold me back. Our date tonight might be the perfect time to do just that.

I bathe Rose and get her into her soft, warm jammies before nursing her for the last time. She should sleep for a good five or six hours.

Viktor: Don't come out until exactly 8-ok?

Me: Whatever you say, boss.

Viktor: Holy shit, she does know how to follow orders. LOL.

His comment makes me laugh. I set my phone down and go into the closet, searching for something appropriate for an official first date.

I've decided on a short red dress and black heels. My blonde curls hang softly down my back, and I even put some makeup on. It's the first time I feel like a put-together adult in months.

My phone says it's time. I leave the primary bedroom and am hit with incredible smells coming from the kitchen. My stomach grumbles in response, and I realize I haven't eaten since breakfast. I stop to peek in our bedroom to check on Rose, who's sleeping soundly.

Then, I take a deep breath and meet Viktor for our first date.

Chapter Thirty-Nine

VIKTOR

"*Babusya*, can you please tell me how you make your *Shashlik*?" I beg the woman as I walk through the market to get tonight's dinner ingredients.

"I do not give that recipe to anyone."

Somehow, I have to get it from her. It's the Ukrainian part of my surf and turf plan.

"What do you need it for, *onuk*? You do not cook." Little does she know I'm quite a good cook, but I don't put any effort into it when it's just for me. "I'm cooking dinner for someone tonight." I hesitate. "Like a date."

"A woman?" my grandma asks. "I do not hear from you for months, and then you call for my secret recipe. And there is a woman now. How did you meet?"

"It's a long and complicated story, *Babusya*."

"When will I meet this woman?"

"I don't know." Natalie and I haven't talked about my family. She knows nothing about my past. "Can I please have the recipe?"

"If you promise to come to visit and bring your woman."

"As soon as we can, I promise."

She tells me all the ingredients and directions for how to cook a dish she's famous for in her village. After I've gotten everything for dinner, I stop by another small shop to get candles. My last stop is the florist on the corner for a bouquet of flowers. I decide on a mix of soft pink and ivory roses and peonies. Hopefully, she'll like it.

As much as I hate leaving her alone all day, there's no way I can cook dinner at home and still surprise her, so instead, I stay downstairs in my old apartment to do all the prep work and cooking. Once everything's done, I turn the oven on warm and take a quick shower. I told her it was a formal occasion, so I pull out a pair of black dress pants and a dark blue button-down shirt. I still have to get everything upstairs and set the table—only a half-hour to go. I send Natalie a text, making sure she doesn't come out early. I don't want to ruin the surprise.

By the clicks of her footsteps, I'm almost certain she's wearing heels. Damn. I wasn't sure she'd take me seriously, but she did. I slide my hands into my pockets so she doesn't see how much they're shaking. When she comes around the corner and sees the dining room, she lets out a small gasp. The lights are dim, and candles are placed around the room and on the table.

"These are for you." I hand her the fragrant bouquet.

"They're beautiful, thank you."

"You look stunning." She's in a red dress that shows off her incredible body.

Natalie blushes. "Thank you. I should get these in water."

"I'll take care of it. Go sit down. Dinner's ready."

I take her to the dining room and pull out her chair. "Would you like some wine?" I made sure to get her favorite, a sweet rosé.

"Yes, please."

After pouring our glasses, I go to the kitchen and get our food. Returning to the dining room, I set our plates down and sit across from her.

"I didn't know you could cook."

"I've never had a reason to until now."

She takes a bite of the Ukrainian meat dish. Her eyes close, and a quiet moan escapes. My usual self-control is not functioning tonight, and my body reacts to the sensual sound.

"This is delicious, Viktor."

We eat our meals without our usual conversation. I think we're both nervous. Trying to break the ice, I ask about her day. She tells me how boring it was by herself.

When we've finished, I clear the plates. "There's Baklava for dessert."

"You made dessert too?" She raises her eyebrow in disbelief.

"Actually, no. That I got from the bakery." I smile.

"I would love some, but maybe in a little bit. I'm full right now."

I leave the dishes in the sink—I'll get to them later. Then, pulling out my cell phone, I find my playlist and put on Eric Clapton's *Wonderful Tonight*.

"May I have this dance?"

She places her hand in mine. "You may."

We sway to the music. At first, our movements are stiff, but soon Natalie relaxes and allows me to hold her close while she rests her head on my chest. I close my eyes, savoring the feel of her body against mine. It feels like heaven.

When she lifts her head, her green eyes are full of tenderness. No longer able to resist, my lips meet hers. The elevator dings, interrupting our kiss. I grab the gun from my waistband, the doors open, and I push Natalie behind me.

"Natalie, are you here?" A female voice calls.

"Star? What are you doing here?" Natalie asks.

Star looks around the room. "I'm sorry. It looks like I've interrupted something."

"You think?" I replace my gun and shut the music off, aggravated by her intrusion. "How did you get in?"

"Alex gave me the code a long time ago," she explains. "I tried calling, but my calls keep going to voicemail. So, I got desperate and came over. But I see you're busy. I can come back."

Mental note—change the elevator code.

"It's fine." Natalie adjusts her dress. "We were just having dinner."

"It looks like you were doing more than having dinner," Star says with a smile.

"*Were* being the keyword," I grumble. Everything was perfect until Star crashed our date. "I have some work to do downstairs. I'll let you two talk."

"You don't have to leave." Natalie grabs my arm.

"I'll be back later." I smile, but only give it a half-hearted effort.

I know I must look like a spoiled little boy stomping off in a tantrum. But I don't care because that's precisely what I'm doing.

Chapter Forty

∞

NATALIE

Viktor's clearly upset by our unexpected company. We were having a good time, but maybe Star's interruption is for the best. I turn the lights back up.

"You've been ignoring my calls," Star says.

"I'm sorry. I've been busy with the baby." I make up an excuse.

"Mhm." I know she sees—right through me and my excuses. "Can we talk?"

We sit on opposite ends of the couch. My nerves are on edge, and I bite my nails.

"Natalie." She motions to my hand.

"Sorry. Old habit."

Her expression softens. "I'm sorry I interrupted your evening. Brandon told me Viktor was planning a Valentine's date, but I assumed it was on Valentine's Day, not three days after."

"Brandon knew about this?"

"Viktor called him for advice on what to do."

I'm surprised to hear that Viktor called Brandon. "It's not what it looks like," I try to explain. "We were just—"

Star holds up her hand, stopping me mid-sentence. "There's no need to explain. You and Viktor are adults."

I look down at my hands in my lap. "Viktor kissed me, and I let him." Guilt is eating away at me. "I feel like I'm betraying Alex. Like I'm cheating on him."

"Oh, honey. You're doing no such thing. You know, I was once where you are now."

I don't know much about Star's past, but she begins to tell me that she had a longtime submissive named Jeremy.

"He and I met when we were way too young to be doing the things we were doing," she chuckles. "We were barely seventeen, but we both knew what we wanted." She explains they were together for fifteen years as Domme/sub. "Jeremy was my everything, and I was his."

"What happened?"

"We were returning from vacation and were hit by a drunk driver." Her eyes fill with tears. "I walked away with only some bumps and bruises, but Jeremy didn't make it."

My tears fall as I listen to the ache still present in her voice. "I had no idea. I'm so sorry."

"That was nearly twenty years ago now, but sometimes the pain hurts like it was yesterday." She dabs at the tears in the corner of her eyes. "I've wanted to talk to you because I know what it feels like to lose the love of your life."

Now I feel terrible for ignoring her. I thought she was trying to get me to go to the club, but all this time, she only wanted to share her story with me. She wanted to help me.

"I'm sorry for ignoring you. It was selfish of me."

"Trying to deal with grief does not make a person selfish."

"How did you move on? When did you know it was okay?"

"My situation was a bit different than yours." She tells me Brandon filled her in on Alex's wishes for Viktor and me. "Jeremy and I never married. He was collared, but we weren't interested in marriage and children. But it still took several years before I was ready to move on."

"I knew it. This between Viktor and me is going too fast."

"No, it isn't. Not if it's what you both want."

Star tells me that she never considered life without Jeremy. Much like Alex and me, they were young. Discussing their mortality didn't seem important at the time.

"Alex was always overprepared. He thought about and planned for things the rest of us would never have considered. But in this case, it was a good thing. Natalie, you know what Alex's wishes were for you if something happened to him. That's supposed to bring you peace."

"I wish it brought me peace." I kick off my heels and slump down on the couch. "I know what Alex asked, but I don't know how to do it. I don't know what it's supposed to look like." I turn my head to look at her. "How did you know when it was time?"

Her story explains her strength today. She joined a group for people who had lost their partners and found healing there. "I also had the whole BDSM community at Fire and Ice to lean on," she says. "At first, I felt like I'd be betraying Jeremy if I played with another sub. I had to give myself permission to move on. In my case, I decided I didn't want to look for a long-term collared relationship." She looks off into the distance before returning her focus to me. "What Jeremy and I shared can never be replaced. I'm comfortable having fun playing with different subs. It's filled the void Jeremy left behind, and I'm at peace with it."

I think about what she said.

"How you choose to move forward is up to you. There's no right or wrong," she adds.

"I can't see myself playing the field," I giggle.

"And you don't have to."

"I also don't see myself in the lifestyle anymore. That was something I could only share with Alex."

"And that's okay too—no right or wrong, remember?"

"Viktor's a good man. He cares about me, and he adores Rose. I know we could be happy together."

"Yes, I agree with all that," she says. "So, where are you getting stuck?"

It's that quiet feeling I have. But how do I explain that to Star when I can't figure out how to put it into words myself? "Fear of making the wrong choice. Fear of judgment."

"Natalie." She leans forward once again. "What I'm about to say will sound harsh, but I need you to look at me and hear me out."

I raise my eyes to meet hers.

"Alex is dead. He isn't coming back." She's right—her words sting. "There's a man downstairs who loves you and your daughter. A man, your husband, gave his blessing for you to love. Forget about anyone else's opinions. The only people who matter are Viktor and you. I know you care about him. Accept the love he wants to give you and allow it to grow."

Rose's crying interrupts our conversation.

"I have to go get her. I'll be right back."

I return with the baby in my arms. It's the first time Star's seeing her.

"She looks like her daddy." Star reaches out and touches Rose's hand. "She's so tiny."

"Would you like to hold her?"

"No, thank you. Babies are nice from a distance, but that's where I draw the line." She stands. "It's late, and I've already taken enough of your time."

I walk Star to the elevator. "Please apologize to Viktor again for me and think about what I said. It's okay for you to love again."

Chapter Forty-One

NATALIE

With spring in full bloom, the three of us are spending more time outdoors. We enjoy our daily walks to a pretty little park with a playground and a green grassy area. My favorite spot is a secluded area with a bench overlooking the water. We've just returned from our walk, and Viktor's on a call with Max. He's bouncing Rose gently on his knee while she babbles away. I think she's mimicking him talking on the phone.

"Thank you, Max. We couldn't have done it without your help."

The Jelena's Hope-NYC project has been on hold since the explosion. The city wouldn't let us move forward with anything until the damage was repaired. Our problem—no contractor wanted to touch the project, and who could blame them? Someone murdered my husband and still hasn't been arrested. I wouldn't be jumping at the chance to take a job with us either.

Viktor finally hangs up. "Maxim and Nicholai called in some favors. There'll be someone there tomorrow to do the repairs. They should be complete in about three weeks."

"That's such a relief. I didn't think we'd ever get it done." I hesitate, afraid to ask. "Have they found anything yet?"

"No, nothing. But we're not giving up. With time comes complacency. Someone will mess up, and then we'll make a move."

It's not the answer I want to hear, but it's the one I have to accept. With each passing day, I fear that instead of getting closer to finding Alex's killer, we're moving further away, and we'll never find the responsible person.

"Did you hear from the trainers?" Viktor asks.

"Yes," I turn my laptop so Viktor can see it.

He pulls his chair closer, putting the keyboard within grabbing distance of the baby. Her tiny fingers go straight for the keys.

"Here," Viktor hands her his cell phone. "You can play with this instead."

I shake my head, knowing that the phone is going to end up thrown on the floor within the next thirty seconds.

"The last set of house parents is in their final few weeks of training. Imani has been in touch with them and is redesigning their suite."

"What about the other staff positions?"

"It looks like they've finally been filled. But we still have a few months before the staff will be fully trained."

"That's okay. We can't move forward until the repairs are made." He holds Rose in the air in front of him while he finishes talking. "The city is being difficult in giving us the permits and licenses." Rose giggles and reaches for his face. "They want a reinspection before they'll allow us to open."

"I understand why they're being extra cautious, but it doesn't make waiting any easier."

The next few weeks keep us busy. Viktor spends most of his time running back and forth between the apartment and Jelena's Hope-NYC. With whoever did this still on the loose, extra security has been hired for our floors. Viktor's doing everything in his power to ensure we don't have any further issues.

Rose and I are playing on the floor when Viktor texts that he's coming home. She's so strong. She's holding onto my hands and standing.

"Did you hear that, princess? Viktor's on his way home."

"Fi," she babbles.

Viktor swears she's saying his name and brags that he is her first word.

"Mama," I say, smiling. "You need to say, mama." Rose giggles in response.

She's closing in on six months now and is full of personality. As much as I'm upset the opening of Jelena's Hope-NYC has been postponed, I'm also thankful that I've had all this time with her.

"When Viktor gets home, you get to try your first taste of baby cereal," I say in a sing-song voice.

"Did someone mention food?"

Startled, I pull Rose close to me. The abrupt action makes her cry. "I didn't hear you come in."

"I'm sorry. I didn't mean to scare you." He puts his arms out to take Rose, and she reaches up to him.

"Fi. Fi."

"*Ochen' khoroshiy, printessa,*" he says, smiling proudly.

I stand up and roll my eyes. "She's just making random noises. She's not saying your name." I walk into the kitchen to prepare her cereal.

"I think Mama's jealous. But that's okay." Viktor buckles her into her highchair. "You'll say mama soon." He kisses her forehead.

I bring the food bowl over to him. "Do you want to feed her?"

"I don't know how," he says. "Don't you want to be the first to feed her?"

"I'll take pictures while you do it." I love doing things with her, but I also love watching her and Viktor together. They share a very special bond. Besides, I have something I need to discuss with him.

Chapter Forty-Two

∞

VIKTOR

LAST NIGHT, I WOKE UP WITH NATALIE KISSING ME AND trying to free my hard dick from my boxers. Everything in me wanted to let her continue, but I knew she wasn't aware. Didn't realize it was me she was touching. When I took her hand and removed it, she began to cry. She didn't understand why I wouldn't let her touch me.

"Don't you want me anymore?" she asked through tears.

"You have no idea how much I want you."

"Then take me, please take me."

Her eyes may have been open, but she was clearly talking in her sleep, and I didn't have the heart to wake her.

"Let's sleep for a little bit while the baby sleeps." I placed a gentle kiss on her lips. "We'll be together later."

And just like that, she curled against me and fell asleep. I lay awake, my self-control fraying. I want this woman, but I need her to be fully aware of who she's with when we're together. *I hope that day comes soon,* is my last thought before I allow myself to fall back to sleep.

Alex's birthday would've been today, June eleventh. A few weeks ago, Natalie suggested we make a sizable donation to the Susan G. Komen Foundation in Alex's name to pay homage to him and his mom, who passed away from breast cancer.

Today, I have my own tribute to Alex that Natalie doesn't know about. She's in the living room on the floor with Rose. Lana's on video chat.

"Hey," I peek my head around the corner. "Can I steal you and Rose for a little bit?"

"Lana, I have to go. I'll call you tomorrow."

Svetlana says goodbye to Natalie but oddly ignores Rose before disconnecting the call.

"What's up?" Natalie asks.

"It's beautiful outside. Let's go for a walk."

"Do we have to?"

She's been quiet today. I know she's struggling.

"Yes, we do." I pick up Rose. "Tell Mama you want to go for a walk

Rose kicks her legs and makes a bunch of happy sounds as though she's trying to talk.

"See, Rose wants to go for a walk."

With Rose buckled into her pram, we head out toward the park. The closer we get, the slower Natalie moves. "Viktor, I'm really not up for this today."

"Do you trust me?"

"Yes."

"Then come on." I continue walking past the playground full of laughing children and follow the path around the back of the building to where Natalie and I often come to sit.

"Viktor," she whispers.

I got permission from the city to have a Japanese Maple Tree planted near the bench we visit. Natalie walks closer and reads the plaque installed in front of the tree. *In loving memory of Alexander Montgomery- beloved husband and father.*

"Did you do this?"

"I did. I hope it's okay."

She rests her head on my chest as tears stream down her face. "It's perfect, Viktor. Alex would've loved it."

I take Rose from the stroller and bring her to the tree, letting her touch it while I tell her stories about her daddy. Natalie sits quietly on the bench as she stares out over the water. Rose and I join Natalie. I put my arm around her, and she moves closer, resting her head on my shoulder. Rose reaches out, playing with her mama's face and giving her a baby's version of a kiss.

Together, we pay silent respect to Alex.

Chapter Forty-Three

NATALIE

Jelena's Hope-NYC's grand opening was supposed to be right after New Year's. But between Alex's death, Rose's early arrival, and all the complications with the construction, it was postponed. Actually, I doubted it would ever happen. It may be seven months late, but the grand opening is set for this weekend.

"Max and Irina will be here tomorrow," Viktor informs me

"Is Lana coming too?" I haven't talked to her in a few weeks. She's been avoiding everyone.

"Unfortunately, no. She's staying back with Amelia."

"Oh." My shoulders sag in disappointment.

"I'd like to take you to dinner before the ceremony?"

Lately, there's been a noticeable shift in our relationship. We're beginning to act like a couple. Despite my reservations about the right time to move on, I'm starting to let myself care about Viktor as more than a friend. Looking at it from the outside, our relationship probably seems unusual. We live together, sleep together, and are raising a baby together. But, except for the sexual advances I make while I'm dreaming about Alex, we haven't taken our relationship to the next level.

He's a man, and he can only take so much. I'm sure it's wearing on him. It's a topic Yekaterina and I discuss at every session. I'm working on building up the courage to take that next step.

"I think I'd like that."

"Really?" He looks surprised.

"Really. As long as you don't mind a baby tagging along?"

"If you're okay with it, Max and Irina offered to keep Rose while we go out. They'll bring her to the center and meet us there."

I've not been away from her at all since she was born. My belief, although erroneous, is that as long as I'm with her, nothing bad can happen—another thing Yekaterina and I are working on.

Viktor waits for my answer, his face full of hope. Outside of Viktor and me, if anyone will keep Rose safe, it's Max and Irina.

"Okay."

"Okay? You're saying yes?"

"I'm saying yes."

He lifts me off my feet and spins me around. "Thank you." He stops and slides me down until my feet touch the floor. His erection presses my body as he leans down to kiss me. The kiss starts tenderly. Viktor's hands move up my body and tangle in my hair as the kiss turns more demanding. Rose's cry interrupts us.

I step back, breathless from the kiss. Viktor's eyes don't leave mine. It's like we're frozen in time. Until Rose grabs onto his leg. He bends down to pick her up while I stay frozen, stunned by the moment we've just shared.

Chapter Forty-Four

VIKTOR

Max and Irina arrived yesterday. They've been nothing but doting grandparents since the second they walked in, even insisting on moving her playpen into their guest room so they could get up with her during the night.

Rose was sleeping through the night, but she's getting a couple of new teeth, which is wreaking havoc on her sleep schedule. When they offered, I gladly took them up on it. It's the first full night's sleep we've had the past month—something Natalie and I desperately needed.

Max and I are downstairs in the office reviewing the video footage Dimitri sent. We finally got a small break. Dimitri got his hands on some brand-new technology to find an almost imperceptible anomaly in the video. Minutes before the explosion, the video goes off the live feed to a recording of Alex walking to his car and then back to a live feed just as the car explodes. I'm furious we've missed it for so long, but it explains why we've found nothing on the video. But other than that, we're still coming up empty-handed.

"Why do we keep hitting dead ends?" I slam my fists on the desk.

"Sometimes, we have to wait these things out," Max says calmly. "This is proof that, given time, mistakes will be discovered, and we will find who is responsible. Alex's murder will not go unpunished."

"It's taking too long."

"Patience, Viktor." Max checks his watch. "Do you not have dinner plans?"

I look at the time. "Shit." I'm going to be late.

Maxim laughs. "Go, get changed. Tonight is a big night."

Natalie has to feed Rose one last time before we leave, so she's running more behind than I am. I showered and dressed in my black suit. Now, I'm pacing back and forth in front of the windows in the living room, waiting for Natalie to come out.

I finally hear the click of heels from the hallway. When I turn around, it feels like I've been punched in the gut and can't take my next breath. Natalie stops across the room from me. She's wearing a knee-length black dress that sits off the shoulder.

I take a few steps toward her. "You look breathtaking."

"Thank you." She blushes.

"Are you ready to go?"

"I want to say goodbye to Rose first. Irina's in the nursery, changing her. She'll be right out." Her eyes roam my body. "You look amazing."

Irina interrupts us, and I quickly step away toward the windows to allow my arousal to subside while Natalie says goodbye to Rose.

"Mama's going to miss you, sweet baby."

"Tell Mama you'll see her in a few hours," Irina says, half to Rose and half to Natalie.

"You know where the breast milk and bottles are, right?"

"Yes."

"I already packed the diaper bag. You know how to use the car seat?"

"Yes," Irina answers patiently.

"The list of emergency numbers is hanging on the fridge."

"Natalie, breathe. Maxim and I have everything under control. Don't worry about us. Go with Viktor and have fun."

"Sorry." Natalie shrugs. "This is all new."

With my body back under control, I return to Natalie's side and kiss Rose. "Be a good girl for *Babushka, printessa.*"

Rose kicks her legs and blows bubbles.

"We have our phones if you need us," I add. "We'll see you at the grand opening."

I found a little Asian fusion restaurant for dinner. We're seated in a quiet corner, which allows us privacy to talk.

"I'm nervous about tonight," she says.

"That's to be expected. There's been a lot mixed up in this, and tonight's a huge step. One I know Alex would be proud of."

"Yes, I know he would. This project meant so much to him."

Our food is served, and it looks delicious. While we eat, we continue our conversation.

"Are you sure we have enough security?"

"Dimitri and his team have set up surveillance inside and outside the building. Misha will be accompanying Max, Irina, and the baby. The rest of the security team is already in place." I take her hand from across the table. "We'll be safe."

"Okay." She doesn't seem convinced. "But we still have no

idea who's behind Alex's death. Do you think it's connected to what happened with Moreno?"

"I wish I had that answer." I wish that with everything in me, but the truth is, other than finding the security footage tampered with, we're no closer today than we were several months ago. "I promise, I won't give up until I find who's responsible and make sure they pay."

Chapter Forty-Five

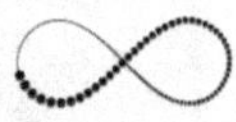

NATALIE

Dinner was delicious. I don't know how Viktor found this place, but it was perfect. It was, however, the quiet before the storm.

Outside the Jelena's Hope-NYC building is a rather large press gathering. People make their way down the sidewalk while cameras flash and reporters thrust microphones at them, trying to get someone to answer their questions. It looks like a circus.

"Good thing we're not going in that way," Viktor mutters.

"They aren't all going to be upstairs, are they?" I ask, panicked.

"Several journalists have been vetted and given admittance. The rest will remain outside," he reassures me. "I'm not taking any chances. One of my men has the approved guest list and is stationed at the door. The only people getting in tonight are the ones on his list."

I know Viktor and Maxim are more than capable of keeping the event safe tonight. I'm trying to take calming breaths, reminding myself to trust Viktor's plan.

When we pull into the underground parking, the anxious feelings return. Over the past few months, I've been here several times. Although the damage from the explosion has been repaired, it does little to erase the memories. I know where Alex's car was parked. I know the exact spot where my husband took his final breath. I don't know if I'll ever be able to come in here without feeling the suffocating sadness.

It takes all my willpower to push those feelings aside because tonight is an important night. I need to be strong—for Alex.

"Public speaking was Alex's thing, not mine," I say to Viktor while we ride up in the elevator.

"I'll be by your side every second."

He takes my hand and laces his fingers with mine. Together, we step out of the elevator into the lobby, already teeming with people. My heart begins to beat faster, and my anxiety level quickly rises. I squeeze Viktor's hand tighter as I look around, trying to find Max and Irina. I need to see my little girl.

"Do you see them?"

Viktor looks around, easily able to see over the people's heads. "Irina's behind the reception desk with the baby."

When Rose sees me coming, she reaches her arms out. I take her and snuggle her close. "Mama missed you so much," I say between kisses.

"She was a perfect angel," Irina beams. "How was dinner?

"It was very nice."

"*Printessa.*" Viktor leans in to kiss Rose.

Rose's eyes meet Viktor's. "Fik," she says and rewards him with her beautiful smile.

"May I?" He reaches out to take her, holding her close to his chest. "I missed you very much. I love you, *printessa.*" Viktor whispers.

Rose grabs his face.

"She loves you, too."

It's time for the grand opening ceremony to begin. Viktor, Maxim, and I are standing in front of the reception desk, the Jelena's Hope-NYC logo on the wall behind us. Irina is behind the desk, holding Rose. Misha's stationed next to them. In front of us is a room full of journalists, Jelena's Hope-NYC staff members, Steve and his crew, and public figures—some I recognize, others I don't. I know mixed in with the crowd are some undercover men as well.

Maxim calls the room to order and then turns it over to me.

"First, I'd like to thank all of you for joining us tonight to celebrate the grand opening of Jelena's Hope-NYC. This mission was born out of tragedy when Maxim and Irina's daughter, Jelena, was stolen and sold by human traffickers. Sadly, they weren't able to find her in time. Since then, they've taken their tragedy and have done something incredible for those who have suffered from being trafficked. Their efforts ensure recovered persons have access to everything they'll need to recover and rejoin society."

I look over my shoulder to Viktor, who takes a step closer to me before returning my attention to the room. "As many of you know, a few months ago, I lost my husband." I pause, swallowing over the lump in my throat. Viktor places his hand on my arm for support, and I cover it with my own.

There's movement in the back of the room that catches my attention. A man with almost shoulder-length dark blond hair sidles up next to Steve. They shake hands, and then the man turns in my direction. When his eyes meet mine, he smiles. Goosebumps cover my body, and I quickly break eye contact. It takes a moment to shake off the uneasy feeling and continue speaking.

"Jelena's Hope-NYC was a project that was near to his heart. My husband wanted his part in the fight against human trafficking to be more than only words. He wanted to transform those words into action." A tear slips down my face, and I look up. "I wish he were here in person to share this moment, but I know he's watching over us."

Maxim steps forward and hugs me. "Thank you, Natalia."

I nod and take a step back. Viktor puts his arm around me for support while Maxim speaks to the crowd.

"What's wrong?" Viktor whispers.

"A man came in. He's standing by Steve. They look like they know each other. But there was something unsettling with how he looked right at me and smiled."

"What does he look like?"

"He has long blond hair. He's right—" I look in the back corner. "That's odd. He's not there anymore."

When all the speeches are through, Viktor disappears. I stay with Maxim and speak to a few government officials pledging their support to Jelena's Hope-NYC.

After what seems like forever, the evening finally begins to wind down. The last of our guests has just left. So now, only us and our intake staff are sitting in the lobby. Maxim is briefing them on a small trafficking ring that was raided two days ago in Southern California. Our first clients are currently en route and are expected to arrive tomorrow.

I'm sitting on the couch nursing Rose when the elevator opens, and Viktor steps out. His tie hangs loose, the first few buttons of his dress shirt undone. My mouth hangs open at the sight of him before I catch myself.

"Where did you disappear to?" I ask.

"I was checking the identity of that guest. He's one of Steve's guys."

"I thought we met all of his employees. He must be new."

"Are you ready to head home?"

"Do you think we should wait for Max?"

"He'll be a while with the staff." Viktor reaches out to take Rose, who's fallen asleep. "I'd like to get you girls home. It's been a long night. And there's something we need to talk about."

"What's wrong?"

"Nothing's wrong. I don't want to discuss it here."

I can't imagine what's going on and why Viktor's being so secretive about it.

He carries Rose while we take the elevator to our car, where he buckles the sleeping baby into her car seat. I slide into the passenger seat and wait for Viktor to get in. He's tense as he pulls the car onto the still-congested Manhattan streets.

Chapter Forty-Six

VIKTOR

THE TENSION IN THE CAR IS NEARLY SUFFOCATING. THE drive home takes forever between the traffic and these damn red lights. I've been keeping something from Natalie that I was hoping to wait and discuss at home. But the longer I wait, the worse it's going to be. It's time to come clean.

"We're taking a trip. We leave in the morning." I spit the words out quickly.

Natalie's head whips around to look at me. "We're what?"

I take a deep breath and let out a long sigh. "Your mom called me last week."

"Oh?"

"She's worried about you. They both are." I glance at her before returning my eyes to the road. "Rose is almost eight months old. It's time she meets her grandparents."

"We've video chatted." Natalie's voice is clipped.

When Charlotte called last week, she was beside herself. She explained that every time she asks Natalie about coming to visit, she tells them *soon* or *no*. The past few weeks, Natalie hasn't even answered their calls. She and Stanley are worried about her, and they want to meet their granddaughter in person. After speaking with Charlotte, I felt I had no choice but to take the actions I did.

"We have a flight tomorrow afternoon. We're going to Missouri to visit your family."

Natalie crosses her arms over her chest. "Don't you think I should've been a part of this decision?"

There's the feisty girl I've grown to love. I smile, and a laugh slips past my lips.

"What's so funny?" She pouts.

"I haven't seen this side of you in a while. I missed it."

She lowers her arms. "I don't want to go. I'm not ready to see them. And how do you suggest I explain us?"

"I don't know what to tell them either," I say, resting my hand gently on her arm. "But we'll figure it out together. They need to meet Rose. She deserves to know her grandparents."

"I guess you're right. I wish you had talked to me first, though."

"And you would've agreed to go?"

"Well, no." She laughs softly.

I pull the car into our spot and turn off the ignition, but make no move to get out. I turn in my seat to face her. "Natalie, I love you."

"Viktor—"

"Let me finish, please. I don't expect you to say those words back, and I realize Alex put us in an uncomfortable situation. Maybe he had no right to ask me to take his place, but he did, and I accepted." I reach out and take her petite hand in mine. "Someday, I hope you might be able to return my love, but even if you never do, that's okay. I'll always be here for you and Rose. You'll always come first in my life." A lone tear drips down her face, and I wipe it with my thumb. "Don't cry, please."

"You've been my rock since Alex died. I don't know how I would've survived this without you." She looks in the back at the baby asleep in her car seat. "Alex is Rose's father, but you're the dad Rose will know and love." Natalie threads her fingers through mine. "I've been struggling to move forward. I haven't even tried to honor Alex's request, but I've been giving this," She motions between us, "a lot of thought. It's time for me to start moving forward. I want to give us an honest try."

My heart beats faster hearing her words. Did she agree to try? I reach up and cup her face in my hand. She leans into my touch and closes her eyes. "I don't know what our path forward looks like. We can take it as slowly as you need. I'll wait for you forever if I have to."

When she opens her eyes, I feel her emerald-green gaze deep in my soul. "I do care about you, Viktor. We've been through so much together already. Hopefully, the worst is behind us," she says with a sad smile. "When my parents ask, what do I say? It feels weird to call you my boyfriend." She scrunches her nose.

"Let's not overthink it. We don't have to put a label on it. When they ask, because we both know they will, I trust we'll find the right words."

Rose interrupts our conversation with a loud wail from the backseat.

"I think that's our cue. Someone's hungry."

"I'll get her."

We get out of the car. While Natalie grabs the diaper bag, I unbuckle, lift our precious baby girl, and hold her close to my chest.

With my line of work, being a father was never even a blip on my radar, but now that I've been thrust into this role, I couldn't imagine my life any other way. I know I have big shoes to fill. Even though she hadn't been born yet, Alex loved this little baby I'm holding. The knowledge that he would've been a better father than I ever could be is hard to swallow, but I strive to be a little better each day—for Rose because my *printessa* deserves no less.

Chapter Forty-Seven

NATALIE

Summer in Northmeadow is beautiful. I've always loved looking at the rolling mountains covered in their vibrant greenery, the forests teeming with life, and the fields flowing with wildflowers. The picture is so clear in my mind, I can almost smell their fragrance. The memories of last summer and how we celebrated our engagement resurface. Alex and I were so happy. We thought the worst was behind us. We had no idea what terrible things lay ahead for us. That before the year was over, there would be no us.

Viktor and I are in a rental car, driving from the airport to the lake house to drop our stuff off. We told my parents we'd meet them at their home this evening for dinner. I'm glad for the short reprieve because I'm exhausted. I didn't sleep last night. Instead, I tossed and turned, trying to come up with answers to questions not yet asked. Viktor turns onto our gravel driveway, and I shoot straight up in my seat. My parents' car is parked in front of the house.

"What are they doing here?"

"I'm not sure. But it's okay," Viktor says calmly.

"It's not okay." I raise my voice.

Viktor grabs my hand, just the way Alex used to. "Natalie, breathe. I'm sure they couldn't wait to meet Rose. It's okay. We've got this."

The front door swings open just as Viktor turns off the ignition, and my mom runs down the pathway to our car. She opens my door before I even have a chance.

"I've missed you so much," she says as she pulls me from the car and into a hug. "I hope you don't mind. Dad and I opened the cottages and freshened them up for you." She releases me. "And we couldn't wait until tonight to meet our granddaughter."

Viktor walks around the car, the baby held protectively in his arms. My heart melts a little each time I see them together. He sees Rose as his daughter, and he's head over heels in love with her. She had him wrapped around her little finger from the moment she was born.

Mom walks over and tries to take Rose from his arms, but she wriggles away and starts crying. "Fik." She clings to Viktor.

"What did she just say?" Mom asks, appalled.

"She's too little to be able to say Viktor, so she calls him Fik."

"Well, that's not what it sounds like to me." She crosses her arms.

I don't understand the hostility already pulsing from her. It's as though we're back to square one. Where we were when Alex and I first met.

"There's my little girl," Dad says, walking down the path with his cane.

"Daddy." I rush over and wrap my arms around him. Both happy to see him and equally happy for the distraction. "I've missed you so much."

"Me too, sweetheart." He kisses my cheek. "Did I hear my granddaughter crying?"

"You did. She gets a little nervous around strangers. Give her a few minutes, and she'll be fine."

"Let's get you inside. You look exhausted." Dad offers his free arm, and I slide mine through it.

Viktor, who's still carrying Rose, and my mom follow us. Once we get inside, Viktor passes the baby to me.

"I'll go out and get our bags," Viktor says and walks out of the house, leaving me alone with my parents.

"Why don't we sit down?" I ask and make my way to the couch. When I'm seated, I place Rose on my lap and turn her to face my parents. "Rose, this is your grandma and grandpa. They couldn't wait to meet you."

Mom, who's sitting next to me, reaches out and takes Rose's hand in hers as she talks sweetly to her. "I couldn't wait to meet you in person, gorgeous girl." Rose rewards her with a grin that shows off her brand-new tooth. "Do you remember me? We talk on that camera. But now I finally get to see you and hold you." Mom looks at me. The earlier hostility seems to have faded, and I nod.

Again, she reaches out, and this time, Rose willingly goes to her. Mom holds her close as tears slide down her cheeks. "I can't believe I'm finally holding my granddaughter." She peppers her with kisses while Rose babbles and blows bubbles, eating up all the love being showered on her.

Viktor's taking forever outside. I'm sure he's trying to give my parents and me some time alone. But I know the questions will start soon, and I'd rather he be here with me when that happens. Thankfully, the door opens, and Viktor walks in, rolling our suitcases behind him. I look up and smile, relieved he's back. He returns my affection with his own, and I see the love reflected in his eyes. I'm sure my parents can see it too.

"I locked up the other cabin. I'm going to put these in our room." The words come out so naturally as he heads down the hall toward the primary bedroom.

Mom's eyes nearly bulge out as she lowers Rose to her lap. "Our room?"

I knew it was a matter of time, and now the time's up. Somehow, I have to explain our relationship, which is hard because we haven't even labeled it. We're not dating exactly, at least not in the traditional sense, but we're more than just friends. He loves me, and I'm learning to love him. We live together and sleep together, but aren't sexually involved. We're in some weird, unclassified relationship that my husband pre-arranged before he died. How in the world do I explain that?

I haven't answered her question yet. I haven't been able to find the right words. Thankfully, the sound of Viktor's footsteps cuts through the uncomfortable silence. He sits next to me, unaware of the confrontation about to happen. I lean against him for support.

"Do you two care to explain what's going on? Why are *both* of your bags in Natalie's bedroom?" Mom snaps.

Viktor slides his arm around me. It's possessive and comforting. "Natalie and I are together."

"Together?" Dad asks. "What exactly does that mean?"

I look into Viktor's comforting gray eyes before steeling myself and turning back to my parents.

"Viktor and I are in a relationship. We're living together."

"Living together?" Mom quips. "Don't you understand what people will say about you?"

Once again, I feel like that young girl fighting to live on her terms. The insecurity that used to plague me comes back with a vengeance as I once again find myself sitting under my parents' scrutiny. The ingrained response of caving to their demands calls to me, but I fight against it.

Each breath gets harder to take, and I shrink back further against Viktor's body. Tension and anger hang heavy in the air. Since she was born, Rose has always seemed to be able to sense my emotions. She begins to fuss and reaches out for me. Taking her from my mom, I walk to the windows, whispering in her ear.

"Stanley, we're leaving."

"Wait," Dad interrupts. "Maybe we should give them a chance to try to explain this."

"I'm not interested in hearing any explanations."

"Please, Mom, don't leave." I walk back toward them. "Let me try to explain it better."

"I always got the feeling that something was off with the two of you." She waves her hand between Viktor and me. "And I was correct. The minute your husband is out of the picture, you jump right into a relationship with *him*."

"There was nothing off about our relationship, Mrs. Clarke. I was an employee—Natalie's bodyguard. We spent a lot of time together and became friends. It was never more."

"Nothing more than a friend. Is that what you call sharing a bed these days?" Mom hastily walks to the door.

"Dad, please." He's always been the one I could make more headway with—the one who could talk Mom down.

He shakes his head. "I'd like to understand, sweetheart, but I'm struggling with this myself."

Viktor follows them out on their heels while I clutch Rose close to me. It feels like the past is repeating itself, and I'm about to lose my family all over again.

Chapter Forty-Eight

$$\infty$$

VIKTOR

Charlotte and Stanley hurry down the stone path from the cottage to their parked car. I didn't think when I said where I was putting our bags. If I'd just kept my mouth shut. I feel responsible for this situation and follow them out.

"Mr. and Mrs. Clarke, may I please have a moment before you leave?" I have to try to fix this.

Stanley gets in the passenger seat. He still tires easily, but leaves the door open. Charlotte turns to face me, arms crossed.

"Natalie and I understand that our relationship comes as quite a shock. We realize it's unconventional. It's not something we would've ever done on our own. Alex should be the one here with his wife and baby, but the fact is, he's gone. It's not been easy for Natalie these past few months." I pause, allowing myself a minute to find the right words for the next part.

"We probably should have explained all this sooner. Before the accident, Alex approached me. He wanted to ensure that Natalie and Rose would be cared for if anything ever happened to him. He asked me to step in, to be there in his place. He gave his blessing for whatever develops between Natalie and me."

"That's ridiculous. Why would Alex do such a thing?" Charlotte asks.

I can't tell her about Alex's true association with Maxim. About what they went through in Mexico, and how that scared him. Forced him to face his mortality.

"Because he lost his mom at a young age. He remembered the toll it took on his father and how long it took his father to be able to move on. He didn't want that for Natalie. He wanted her to love and be loved. To know that if she chose to move on, she'd have his blessing."

Charlotte drops her arms and stands taller. "That may be true, but *you* are not the person Natalie should be moving on with. She belongs with her family. We'll help her raise Rose, and maybe one day, she'll meet a nice man here in Northmeadow." She takes a step closer to me. "And you need to convince her of that. Then, you are to leave and never come back."

This woman is incorrigible. Dealing with her face-to-face, I see why Natalie loses her cool so quickly.

"Tomorrow's Natalie's birthday. We're only here for a few days, then we're going home—together. Hopefully, after you go home and take some time to think this through, you'll change your opinion."

Charlotte closes Stanley's door and walks around the car to the driver's side.

"We'd like to spend more time with you before we leave. We both want Rose to know her grandparents."

Whether she hears me or not, she doesn't respond. She gets in the car and slams the door. I watch them pull away, wondering if I've done the wrong thing by bringing Natalie here. I take a few minutes to collect my thoughts before going back into the house. When I do, I find Natalie sitting on the couch nursing Rose. She looks up, her eyes filled with tears. I sit next to her and put my arm around her. Natalie settles in next to me, resting her head on my shoulder.

"I'm sorry. Maybe it was wrong to bring you here."

"There's nothing to be sorry for. This was going to happen sooner or later. I wasn't going to come on my own, and you knew that." She runs her fingers gently through Rose's curls. "You just wanted Rose to get to know her grandparents."

We sit, both lost in our thoughts, while Rose fills her tummy and falls asleep in Natalie's arms.

"Are you hungry?" I ask quietly.

"Very."

"We don't have any groceries, and it's still pretty early. Do you want to go into town to eat?"

"Honestly, no. I don't want to deal with any more people today." She wiggles a bit and pulls her cell from her pocket. "How about we order pizza instead?"

Chapter Forty-Nine

∞

NATALIE

"Touch yourself for me, baby girl." His hand guides mine between my legs. "You're so wet for me already. Do you know what that does to me?"

"Mmm." His erection against my back tells me everything I need to know.

My eyes fly open, and reality sets back in. The man who's asleep, his arm draped over me, and whose erection presses against me is Viktor, not Alex. Is today the day I give him access to my body? I get my answer when Rose begins rustling around in her portable playpen. Quietly, I slide out of bed and walk over to her.

"Good morning, princess." I reach down and lift my little girl, who rewards me with her babbles. "You have a lot to say this morning. How about we go to the other room so we don't wake up Viktor?"

"Fik. Fik," Rose says.

"Yes, Viktor. Shh," I whisper. "He's sleepy."

With Rose in my arms, I bring her outside onto the patio. It's a beautiful summer morning. The birds are chirping, and the little bluebird family from last year is back in their nest, raising a new generation of babies. While Rose nurses, I tell her about the birdie family that her daddy and I loved watching every morning. She smiles, and a trail of milk drips down her chin. "I know your daddy isn't here, but he loves you very much." Those words hang in the air as I swallow over the lump in my throat—I refuse to cry. I don't know how long she and I sit alone, talking about the animals and the boats on the lake while Rose kicks her legs in glee.

"There you two are. You should've woken me," Viktor says as he comes out onto the patio, a mug of coffee in each hand. "Happy Birthday." He leans down and places a soft kiss on my lips. "*Dobroye utro, printessa.*" Viktor kisses Rose on the head and then passes me one of the cups.

Viktor speaks Russian to Rose as much as possible. We're hoping she'll be bilingual since we'll most definitely spend time here and in Russia.

"Thank you." I take a sip and set the cup down on the table, out of reach of Rose's tiny hands.

"You should've been the one sleeping in today." Viktor sits in the chair next to me. Rose reaches out her arms to him, and he scoops her up, kissing her belly and making her squeal in laughter. "Okay, birthday girl. What do you want to do today?"

"Absolutely nothing. I would love to stay here and enjoy the quiet."

"Whatever you wish, it's your day." He smiles. "I hope you don't mind pizza for breakfast?"

"Sounds good to me."

"When we're done, I'll run to the market and pick up some groceries for a few days, and then maybe we can take the baby down to the lake. It's a beautiful day, and I bet she'll love the water."

After we finish eating, Viktor runs out to the store. While he's gone, I try calling my parents, but the calls go straight to voicemail. I don't leave a message. As much as it hurts, I won't beg them to be a part of our lives.

After putting the groceries away, we walk down to the lake. It's Rose's first encounter with a large body of water. Viktor was right. She loves it. I'm videoing on my phone while Viktor stands at the water's edge, his pants rolled up almost to his knees. He's holding Rose and letting her kick her chubby little feet in the water. Each time she makes a splash, she lets out a full belly laugh, followed by Viktor's deep laugh. He may look like a big, scary man, but Rose and I know the truth. Viktor has the kindest and most gentle heart. He has so much love to give. I realize how lucky I am to have had the love of one incredible man and to have the love of another now.

Since being with Rose and me, I've witnessed a transformation in him. He used to be serious and by the book. Few things could make him crack a smile. But something's changed. It's like a switch flipped, and he's come alive. Yes, he still has an air of danger. I know what he's capable of, but there's more to this complicated man.

When he's with Rose, he's protective. I know he'd give his life for her. But he's also gentle and nurturing. My baby girl has stolen his heart. I also see the tenderness in his eyes when he looks at me. I don't doubt he loves me with everything he has. He's solid and strong, my fierce protector who longs to be my lover.

It doesn't take long before Rose tires herself out. Her little legs stop kicking, and she begins yawning.

"I think that's our cue." Viktor carries Rose over, and I help him wrap a towel around her. "Naptime for Miss Rose."

As we walk back to the house, I struggle with an internal war of emotions. Days like today feel normal. We appear to be a happy family to anyone who doesn't know us. And at this moment, I am happy. It's my birthday, and I'm spending it with the two most important people I have in my life. Two people I love. While we were playing at the lake with the baby, I didn't have a care in the world. I didn't think about Alex. That's when the guilt settles heavily on my chest. How could I share a special moment with Rose and not think about Alex? Why does it still feel like I'm betraying him?

By the time we get back inside, Rose is asleep on Viktor's shoulder.

"I'm going to go lay her down. I'll be right back." When he returns to the room, I'm sitting on the couch, looking through the stack of papers. "We don't need to worry about that today. It's your birthday."

"There's no reason not to." I pass the papers to him as he sits beside me on the couch.

"Are you sure?"

I nod and pull out my cell to send Brandon the video of the baby at the lake. While we text back and forth, Viktor mumbles as he reads the names off the list. "Steve Martinez. Bill Johnson. Scott Maren." He flips to the next page. "Jonathan Orz. Brad Carlton. Xavier Moore. Paul Johnson."

"What was that last name?" I interrupt him.

"Paul Johnson?" he asks, a puzzled expression on his face.

"No, the one before that." I reach for the paper. "Can I see that?" I look at the name on the list. It can't be? Can it? How many people could have that name?

"What is it, Nat?"

"Xavier is Tommy's middle name." I pass the paper back to Viktor. "Could Xavier Moore be Tommy Moore?"

"Fuck." Viktor pulls his phone from his pocket and hits a button. "Dimitri, we might have a break." He explains everything before disconnecting. "He's going to look into it and call us back."

Chapter Fifty

VIKTOR

I can't sit still as I clutch my phone, waiting for Dimitri to call me back. Nine months. Nine fucking months, and it was right in front of me the whole time. How the hell did I miss this?

"Viktor, please sit down. You're driving me crazy," Natalie pleads from the couch, where she's biting her nails.

The screen flashes to life just before the phone begins to ring. "What did you find?" Dimitri fills me in on how Tommy was released early last September. Some shit about good behavior. "So, you're telling me he's been out for nearly a year, and we had no idea?"

Natalie jumps off the couch and comes to my side. "You'll break the phone if you don't loosen your grip," she whispers.

"Where is he?" I demand.

"We don't know."

I see red. "What do you mean you don't know?" How does one low-life punk not only get out of prison early but also manage to disappear without a trace?

"He's been off the radar since his release," Dimitri says. "Maxim's been briefed and is calling his contacts to start a search."

"Let me know the moment you hear anything." I disconnect the call and stare out the window.

Natalie wraps her arms around my waist and looks up at me. Her green eyes plead with me to give her answers. "Was it him? Where is he?"

"I don't know." I hold her tight and place a kiss on her head. "But I'm going to pay Delia Laurel a visit to find out."

"I'm coming too."

"No. You're staying right here." I know I'm in for a fight when Natalie pulls away from me and crosses her arms over her chest.

"I'm not waiting here. Rose and I are going with you."

This woman standing in front of me is a force to be reckoned with. How do I make her understand I'm trying to keep her safe? What if Tommy's there? I don't want her or the baby anywhere near Delia. But from the look on her face, I know there's no way she'll take no for an answer.

"We're safer with you rather than here by ourselves, aren't we?" She tilts her head and gives me a look that says she knows she's won.

I throw my hands up in defeat. "Fine."

Driving through Northmeadow, my nerves are on edge. It's not that I doubt my abilities. I know I'm damn good at my job. But today, the two most important people in my life are with me, and we're about to confront the aunt of a possible murderer. My mind is racing, trying to anticipate every scenario I might encounter.

How do I extract information from Delia while keeping my girls safe? What if Tommy shows up? He's already proven to be unstable. What if he goes after Natalie or, God forbid, the baby while I have my back turned?

I'm also berating myself for missing such a crucial detail.

Tommy Moore has no business being anywhere near Natalie or Rose. I don't know his exact role in Alex's death, but I know he's involved somehow. And this time, when I find him, he won't be walking away.

We arrive at a pale-yellow house, and I spot Delia Laurel on the porch swing, engrossed in a book. I hate what I'm about to do. Interrogating a sweet old lady isn't my usual approach. But in this case, it can't be helped. Delia is Tommy's only family, and she might know his whereabouts. "Stay in the car," I tell Natalie.

"No."

I'm not a Dominant, and we don't have rules, but right now, I'm ready to take her over my knee and spank her ass until she can follow a simple command. "Natalie, I'm not asking. You will wait here. Doors locked." We have a stare-off for several long minutes. I'm not giving in to her this time. Finally, she breaks our eye contact.

"Whatever."

"Thank you." I lean over and kiss her cheek.

Delia looks up when I shut the car door and puts down her book before heading towards her front door. I waste no time and march straight up her sidewalk and onto her porch, warning her to stay put.

"Who are you? What do you want?" she asks, feigning ignorance. But I know she's well aware of who I am. What she doesn't realize is that I won't resort to violence. I need answers, and if instilling fear is the only way to get them, then so be it.

"Where's Tommy?" I demand.

"What do you mean?"

"Where is he?"

"He's in prison," she answers.

"Don't play games with me," I insist, my tone firm. "I know he was released last year. Where's your nephew?" Delia's gaze drifts past me towards the car where Natalie and Rose are waiting. A surge of apprehension prickles the back of my neck. I don't want anyone connected to Tommy laying eyes on either one of them. "This is the last time I'm asking. Where is Moore?"

"I don't know. I haven't heard from him in months."

"Did he come here?"

"No. He only called me," she answers.

"Where was he when he called?"

"Last I knew, he was in New York."

"New York? What the hell? Why was he in New York?" I yell.

"When he went to jail, he was addicted to so many drugs. They claimed that the correctional system here lacked adequate resources to assist with his detoxification. They told me he had to be transferred to Rikers Island."

"How did he get early parole?"

"Tommy said it was because of good behavior."

"Why didn't he come back here?"

"Why are you asking all these questions?" This woman may look frail, but she's either putting on a brave face or she's as crazy as her nephew.

"Just answer them," I demand. "Why didn't he come back here?"

She lets out an exasperated sigh. "Tommy had just gotten clean. His probation officer thought it would be best for him to remain there until his sobriety was more established. He arranged for Tommy to go to a halfway house and join a support group. Tommy told me they'd allow him to complete his parole here once he proved he'd stay sober."

"When's the last time you heard from him?"

"Why do you want to know?"

"When was the last time you heard from him?" I'm beginning to lose what little patience I came with.

"A few weeks after he got out. Since then, he hasn't called, and I don't know how to contact him." Her eyes dart back and forth, avoiding eye contact. She knows more than she's telling me.

"What else do you know?"

"That's it."

I take a step forward, hoping to intimidate her.

"I got a phone call from someone who said he was his probation officer a few weeks ago, wondering if I'd heard from him. That's all I know, honest."

"Did the person leave their contact information?"

"No."

I find Delia's reaction interesting. If Tommy had shown up, his probation officer would've wanted her to contact him. Delia nervously fidgets with the book in her hands. I glance back at Natalie, who's focused on Rose. I'm still uncertain if Delia is covering for Tommy or just repeating what he told her.

"Is my nephew in trouble?" she asks. Stress and old age show on her face. Her hazel eyes, wrinkled at the corners, are filled with tears.

My anger subsides a bit as I realize that this woman did her best to raise Tommy, and despite his issues, she still loves him. Tommy's actions as an adult are not a reflection of her, and she's not responsible for his current behavior.

"Yes, ma'am. He is."

"Did he—?

"Thank you for the information." I turn and start walking down the steps.

"Please tell Natalie I'm sorry for whatever Tommy's done this time. Whatever happens, will you make sure Tommy stays safe?"

As much as I feel for her, that's a guarantee I won't make.

I stop mid-step. "I can't make that promise," I reply firmly, without turning back to face Delia Laurel. Those are the last words I say to her before I head back to the car and give Natalie a brief rundown of our conversation. Despite whatever emotions she may be experiencing, Natalie maintains her composure. I start the car and merge onto the road. "Take my phone and send the information to Dimitri. My code is—"

"I know what it is." She smiles. The fact that she knows my

passcode fills me with pride. I watch out of the corner of my eye as she types out the information and sends the text.

"We need to go back to the cottage and grab our things. We're taking the next available flight back home."

"So much for a calm, quiet day."

I feel awful that all this is happening on her birthday.

"I'll make it up to you. I promise."

Chapter Fifty-One

XAVIER/TOMMY

As soon as I was released from parole, I ditched the halfway house and found myself an apartment. I sit on the tattered chair in this dump of a place I'm renting in Hell's Kitchen. But the rent is cheap, and the neighboring units are filled with plenty of others who are also trying to hide in plain sight. It's been the perfect place to go about my daily life and stay undetected.

How did I end up in New York City, you ask? When I was sentenced for shooting Stanley Clarke, I figured I'd get a few months in the local prison. My plan was to keep my head down, do my time, and go right back to my life. What I didn't plan on was being shipped to Rikers. Apparently, I was addicted to so many things that no prison in Missouri was *medically appropriate*. As soon as I got there, I was forced to spend several weeks in detox.

Muscle cramps.

Nausea.

Shivering so hard, I swore my bones would shatter.

And the hallucinations—they were a special kind of hell.

Those first few days, I was sure I was going to die. Wished I would die.

After they deemed me cured, I was transferred to the general population. I quickly learned there was a pecking order among the inmates. Those on the bottom aren't likely to make it out, and I sure as shit wasn't going to be among that group—I had a life after prison to look forward to.

During those first few weeks, I stayed on the outskirts, watching and learning who was in charge. Slowly, I weaseled my way into the group that held power. Seems corruption knows no bounds, and I had no problem selling my soul to secure an early release.

I played by the rules, wore my ankle monitor, and showed up clean for all my parole appointments. That lasted only long enough to prove to the powers that be they could trust me. Money transferred hands, and my ankle monitor was removed.

What did I have to do in return? It was simple, really. All I had to do was agree to run drugs for one of the most powerful crime families in New York City. I'd make good money while I repaid my debts. Once we were even, I'd have a clear path to achieving my goal—getting my girl back.

What I didn't realize was how quickly things would work out for me. While I was visiting a neighbor, I noticed an article in the newspaper on his kitchen table. New York City's golden boy, Alexander Montgomery, was on the front page. Seems he was out playing the hero once again. The article said he was opening up some kind of shelter for abused women or some shit like that. As luck would have it, my neighbor happens to work in maintenance in the same building. He couldn't stop going on and on about what a great guy Montgomery is and what a hot wife he has— how he wished he could get a piece of ass like hers.

My first instinct was to kill him for talking about Natalie like that, but then I had a brilliant idea.

"Do you know if your boss is looking for any more help?" I asked. "I could really use a job."

"I'm pretty sure he is. I'll tell him about you tomorrow."

And that's all it took. By the end of that week, I was on the payroll.

In preparation for this phase of the plan, I'd already grown out my hair and changed the color. I also got contact lenses to change my eyes. And that's how Xavier Moore was born. I laugh at how easy this has been.

By night, I sell drugs on street corners and in dark alleys. By day, I play the strait-laced, hard-working guy who's looking to work his way up.

First, I got in good with Steve, the foreman on the shelter project, and have been working right under Montgomery's nose. After some snooping around in the paperwork, I hit pay dirt—I found their home address. It felt like old times, hiding out and watching Natalie from a distance, all while I planned my next move—getting rid of Montgomery for good, and I planned to do it right where he felt safest.

I've learned to spot weaknesses and exploit them. Leon, the head of security, has a sick wife. Cancer, he says. The doctors keep throwing treatments at her, but nothing's working. Bottom line —she's going to die. But Leon can't stand seeing his old lady suffer. So, I dangled a carrot in front of him, some free product guaranteed to make her forget her pain, in exchange for a favor when I was ready. He didn't even bother asking. He jumped on it.

Since Alex's accident, Natalie's bodyguard hasn't left her side. That's not surprising since they spent so much time alone together in Missouri. It's obvious the guy couldn't wait to fuck her. That is, if they weren't already screwing each other when Montgomery wasn't around. I probably did him a favor by taking Montgomery out of the picture.

He'd better have his fun with her now because soon she'll be mine.

There's only one complication I didn't expect. Montgomery

knocked Natalie up, and now she has his spawn. There's no way in hell I'm going to raise his kid. I have to get her alone. Then I'll offer her a deal she won't be able to refuse.

It won't be too much longer before she's back in my bed where she belongs.

Chapter Fifty-Two

NATALIE

WE'VE BEEN BACK HOME FOR A FEW WEEKS NOW. I'M sure Delia Laurel called my parents to complain about Viktor. However, my phone has been silent, and I can't help but worry that my relationship with Viktor may have caused irreparable damage with my parents. Despite my fear, I stand by my decision to honor Alex's wishes.

In the meantime, Rose has been making strides in her development and has recently mastered crawling. Today, I created an obstacle course for her in the living room with various toys. I love watching her determination as she moves from one toy to another.

I'm about ready to set one up for Viktor, too. He's been restless and agitated, pacing back and forth in front of the windows, constantly checking his phone for updates. Dimitri promised to call us this evening with the information. But each passing hour without an update is causing Viktor to become increasingly irritable.

"You know you can't make the phone ring." I try to make him laugh, but fail.

"It's been hours, and he hasn't called yet."

"He'll call as soon as he knows something. Come here and watch the baby."

Viktor obliges and slides his large frame onto the floor next to me. Rose gets excited when she sees him.

"Fik," she says and tries to move to get to him faster than she can coordinate her arms and legs. She tumbles forward—her bottom lip quivers.

Viktor scoops her up before she cries, kisses her nose, and then sets her back down. Then, he picks up her favorite stuffed elephant, making it dance on the floor a short distance in front of her. *"ty mozhesh' eto sdelat."*

"What did you tell her?"

"You can do it." He continues encouraging her to try again. Finally, she gets back on her hands and knees and successfully crawls to him, getting her prize and then rolling onto her back. He praises her in Russian as she brings the toy right to her mouth.

"I think she's getting another tooth."

Before Viktor can respond, his phone rings. "It's him." He connects the call. "You're on speaker. Natalie's with me. What did you find out?"

"I hacked into the old lady's phone records. The call wasn't from any parole officer. It came from a burner phone. After some searching, I found the real parole officer. He was hesitant to talk at first, but after some *persuasion,* we got answers." According to him, Tommy got in front of a sympathetic judge who felt Tommy earned an early release. What makes the story even more questionable is that he had his ankle monitor removed and his parole requirements canceled sooner than his original release specified.

"Seems corruption runs deep even in America," Dimitri adds. Then, he continues the tale. While Maxim was reaching out to some business associates, the Scartelli family name came up. It appears Tommy made some interesting friends during his time at Rikers. "We don't have all the details yet, but we know Luciano

Scartelli had something to do with his release in exchange for Tommy running drugs for them."

"Why the hell would Scartelli give a fuck about Tommy?"

"Because he agreed to do his dirty work."

"So, what happened? Where is he?" Viktor asks.

"That's where this story gets even more interesting. Once he was out of the criminal justice system, all records of a *Thomas Moore* went cold."

"How's that possible?"

"Because that's when he started going by Xavier Moore. That was a great catch, Natalie." Dimitri gives a rare compliment. "With that information, I was able to get pictures of Moore from the building's employee files. He changed his physical appearance, but Xavier and Tommy are one and the same."

"X-man," I whisper.

"What are you talking about?" Dimitri asks.

"Steve kept telling us about this new guy, X-man. He wanted Alex to meet him, but every time we were there, *X-man* was gone." The ground falls out from under me. I can't take my next breath and grab Viktor's arm.

"Look at me, Natalie." Viktor turns my head to face him. "You need to breathe."

"All that time, he was right there. Tommy killed my husband." The words leave my mouth in a strangled cry, and I break down.

Viktor pulls me against him and holds me tight. My crying startles Rose, and she begins to cry, too. Viktor scoops her up with his free arm and holds her close. "It's okay, *printessa*. Don't cry. I'll take care of you and Mommy," he murmurs and kisses my head. "Moore will pay for this."

"There's more," Dimitri says.

"What the hell else could there be?"

"A few months ago, one of the other lowlifes Scartelli employs put a call into the boss. He suspected Tommy was skimming from the product he was supposed to be selling. Said Tommy's high all the time." Dimitri hesitates. "He was concerned because Tommy was bragging about crazy shit like killing—"

"Enough." Viktor stops Dimitri mid-sentence.

"Please let him finish."

"Tread cautiously," Viktor warns.

"Tommy must've gotten a heads up and disappeared because Scartelli's been looking for a Tommy Moore. At least until Maxim spoke to him and told him to start looking for an Xavier Moore instead. Now that his cover's blown, he won't be able to hide for long." Before Dimitri continues, there's a long pause. "I found one more thing."

"I don't know if I can hear anymore."

"I'm sorry, Natalie, but you need to hear this. Knowing Tommy's past and his affinity for stalking you, I pulled footage from the security cameras outside your building."

"And?" Viktor says with an edge to his tone.

"Tommy's been watching your building."

"No, not again." My body trembles.

Viktor takes the phone off speaker and balances it between his cheek and shoulder. "I need to take care of things here. Send me everything. I'll call you back later."

He disconnects the call and turns all his attention to me.

"Viktor," I look into his gray eyes, which are usually calm, and see nothing but rage. "He killed Alex. He's been watching me— watching Rose." I try to stand, but Viktor doesn't let me go. "We have to get out of here." My instincts urge me to pack up and run. To take my baby somewhere far away. Somewhere Tommy will never find us.

"We aren't going anywhere," Viktor says sternly. "Moore will answer for what he's done, and this time, it'll be with his life."

I know I should cringe in disgust. My morals should be screaming that taking a life is wrong, but they aren't. Tommy stole my husband from me. He took Rose's dad away—she'll never know him. I don't want to hate, but I can't stop myself.

Rose continues to fuss on Viktor's lap. "This was a lot for our little girl, too."

Rose reaches out for me, and I hold her close. "I'm sorry I scared you, princess. Everything's okay," I say and look at Viktor.

"Everything's going to be okay," he echoes my words, giving me the reassurance I so desperately need. "It's getting late. How about we get Rose some dinner and then a nice warm bath?" Viktor suggests. "Once we get her tucked in, I'll call Dimitri back.

I get Rose settled in her highchair while Viktor makes her cereal. She's starting to eat a little more solid food, and I'm not sure who loves it more, Rose or Viktor, who's feeding her, playing airplane, and making all sorts of silly noises. With each bite, she giggles, spitting food everywhere. Watching them play is exactly what I need. Their pure enjoyment makes it impossible to continue worrying, at least for now.

After Viktor bathes her, I get her into jammies and relax on the bed to nurse her. It only takes a few minutes before her little eyes close, and she's sound asleep. She's still sleeping in the portable playpen in the guest room that Viktor and I share. I feel bad that she hasn't used the beautiful nursery Alex made for her, but I can't bear to go in there. It holds too many memories. Viktor asked if I wanted to change it, but I couldn't do that either, so he moved most of Rose's day-to-day things into our bedroom to make it easier.

Chapter Fifty-Three

∞

VIKTOR

WITH ROSE IN BED, NATALIE AND I RETURN TO THE living room and sit on the couch. Although it's the early morning hours in Russia, I know Dimitri's awake. He hasn't slept since we started putting the pieces together. I hit the green button to connect the call.

"What's the plan?" I ask as soon as I hear it connect.

"Maxim's getting his plane ready. Misha, Timur, and I will be leaving in the next few hours. We've also been in contact with Michael. He and a few of his men are on a plane en route to you as we speak. The plan is to find Moore and take him out."

"How do you plan on finding him?" Natalie asks.

"According to our surveillance, we know Moore's using the coffee shop across from your building to hide and watch Natalie. Unfortunately, he has a sporadic pattern. Once he's out of range of the security camera, we lose track of him. The plan is to put someone inside the coffee shop who'll follow him once he leaves. The hope is to catch him in a less populated area, preferably before Scartelli. Either way, he's a dead man, but I want us to have the satisfaction of carrying out his sentence," Dimitri explains.

Natalie quietly listens as we discuss the finer details of the plan. Dimitri has the technical aspects covered, and Michael will provide snipers if needed, but a shoot-out on the streets is not preferable. Timur and I will be on the ground to capture Moore, and Misha will remain at the apartment to cover Natalie and Rose.

"Do you need a ride from the airport?"

"No. Maxim has arranged transportation for everyone."

"Sounds good. Have a safe flight, and we'll see you tomorrow."

I disconnect the call and turn to face Natalie. She's staring out the window, lost in her thoughts. Gently, I place my hand on her shoulder. "Are you okay?"

"Yes. No. I don't know." She looks at me. "What am I supposed to be feeling right now?"

"There's no right or wrong answer." She leans into me. I love the way her body feels curled against mine. "A lot of information has come out in the past twenty-four hours. I know how I'm feeling knowing Moore's behind this. I can't imagine what you're feeling." I stroke her hair.

"I never would've imagined Tommy was capable of murder." Her voice catches on a sob. "He shot my father, but I thought that was because of the drugs. Why did they let him out? He should've been in jail. Then Alex would still be alive."

I don't know how to answer her. We live in a corrupt world. What something looks like on the surface is rarely how it is. Greed and corruption are all around us, and whether we like it or not, money talks. It's that corruption and money that got Moore released from prison. I hate that Natalie's life has once again been tainted by evil, except this time, it's not something I can fix. We're forced to live with the consequences. Left to pick up the shattered pieces while trying to move forward.

"There are a lot of bad people out there who only look out for themselves. They don't care who gets hurt in the process."

"I hate it. I hate every part of it."

"I know." I take her face in my hands. "I'm sorry I can't bring Alex back, but I'm going to do everything in my power to fix this as best I can." I lean in and kiss her. "I'll take care of Thomas Moore."

She places her hand over mine. "I know you will."

"Come on. We need to get some sleep. We have a long day ahead of us."

"Oh. I promised the clinicians we'd stop at Jelena's Hope in the morning. The Mothers-To-Be program asked if I could bring Rose by."

"Are you sure you're up for that?"

"Yes. The last time I brought Rose in, it brightened up a lot of faces. It was the first time I've seen some of those women smile since they came to us," she says. "These women, whether they've decided to keep their babies or not, are facing a difficult road. Spending time with Rose seems to help."

"As long as you're certain, we'll be there, but that's even more reason to get to bed."

Chapter Fifty-Four

NATALIE

Viktor is sound asleep with his arms protectively wrapped around me, but I'm wide awake. It's been several weeks since I last dreamed about Alex. Yekaterina's words are starting to ring true. Because as soon as I decided to let myself care for Viktor and accept the love he's giving me, the dreams stopped. However, in the hushed darkness of the night, the pain in my heart is screaming.

I yearn for Alex's embrace, how our limbs would entangle together. The fear of forgetting him looms over me. It's been ten months, and I'm struggling to recall the sound of his voice. Sometimes, when I'm alone, I listen to his last voicemail repeatedly, willing myself not to forget him.

Turning onto my side, I reach out and drape my arm across the man lying next to me. I hope that whatever this connection is between us will be enough. Alex knew what he was doing when he orchestrated our relationship. He realized that, given our shared history, it would be impossible for us not to be drawn to one another. He didn't want us to feel guilty for finding love after his death.

Since the day Alex died, Viktor's been by my side. He was my pillar of support during Rose's birth, cutting the cord and becoming the only father figure she'll ever know. On days when I couldn't muster the strength to face the world without Alex, Viktor held me up. He's kind, caring, strong, and capable. When we enter a room together, I can feel the jealousy from other women as they whisper about us. But the only woman Viktor sees is me.

I run my fingers over the chiseled muscles of his abdomen. I love Viktor, but am I truly in love with him? His body is a source of comfort and security, but my heart still longs for Alex's touch. Will that ache dissipate if I allow myself to be intimate with Viktor? I let my fingers wander lower, teasing the waistband of his pants. Even in his sleep, his body responds to my touch. He stirs, and I freeze. Viktor is waiting for me to give the green light to take our relationship to the next level. To show me with his body how much he loves me. But I'm hesitant, fearful of hurting him if I can't reciprocate his feelings. When we do take that step, I want my heart to beat only for him instead of wishing he were another.

As I contemplate this, my phone vibrates on the nightstand. I carefully slide out from under Viktor's arm to check the text. It's Lana. I haven't heard from her in weeks.

Lana: What's going on that the guys all left in such a hurry?

Me: Didn't your dad fill you in?

Lana: He and I aren't exactly on speaking terms right now.

Me: Why? What's going on?

Lana: He doesn't approve of the way I left things with Brandon. But stop changing the subject.

Me: Tommy's the one who killed Alex. They're coming to help Viktor find him.

Lana: Holy shit!! Tommy? I thought he was in prison.

Me: Yeah, me too. It's a long story. One that I'm not even sure I understand. Now, back to you and Brandon. When are you coming back?

Lana: I don't think I am. We both want very different things.

"Who are you talking to?" Viktor rolls over and pushes up on his elbow.

"I'm sorry I woke you," I whisper. "Lana texted."

Viktor takes the phone from my hand.

"What are you doing?"

"I'm telling her to let you sleep."

Me: It's Viktor. It's late, and we're in bed—sleeping, or at least we were until you texted. Natalie will call you tomorrow. Goodnight, Svetlana.

He hits send and passes the phone back to me before lying down.

"Bossy much?" I grin.

"When I need to be." He gives me a peck on the cheek.

Lana: What's Viktor doing in your bed?

Besides knowing Viktor is staying in my apartment, I haven't told her anything about our relationship. She has enough on her plate right now with whatever she's dealing with. I didn't want to add my problems to the mix. But after that text, I have some explaining to do.

Me: That's another long story, but not for tonight. I do need to get some sleep. Love ya.

Lana: You'd better call me in the morning! Love you too.

I power off my phone and set it back on the nightstand.

"Better?"

"Alex said you'd be a handful." Viktor pulls me close to him once again. "Now, close your eyes and sleep."

I slap his shoulder. "Maybe you should go back to sleeping on the floor."

"Too late for that. You can't get rid of me now," he says, a goofy grin on his face. "Good night."

And somehow, he falls right back to sleep while I continue to toss and turn.

Tonight, I dream of Alex once again. He's just out of reach. Each time I step toward him, he gets further away. When I finally get within reaching distance and stretch my hand out, he disappears. I'm left standing in a dark room, calling his name, but he doesn't answer. He's gone.

When morning comes, I'm still tired from the restless sleep and unsettling dreams. But I don't have time to analyze what they mean. I have to be at Jelena's Hope-NYC, and then by tonight, everyone will be here to start the hunt for Tommy.

Chapter Fifty-Five

NATALIE

ROSE SLEPT WELL, THANKFULLY, AND IS BEAMING WITH smiles today. I was apprehensive when the therapy team first discussed bringing her in for this program. Rose is sensitive to the emotions of others, and I didn't want her to be traumatized by unforeseen problems. The staff assured me they wouldn't introduce Rose to anyone until they were confident it would be a positive environment for both Rose and the women involved. Viktor and I discussed it at length and eventually decided it would benefit everyone.

Jelena's Hope NYC has already had several women and even young girls come to us, either already aware they were pregnant or found out soon after arriving. Our goal is to provide each individual, regardless of age, with all available options and offer the counseling and support necessary to live with their decision. What they've already lived through has been pure hell. Their recovery alone is difficult. Adding an often-unwanted pregnancy only complicates things.

Our unique program offers a multifaceted and highly person-

218

alized approach. We focus on treating each woman with respect and ensuring she receives full support, regardless of her decision. Several women have requested to spend time with Rose and me to get a sense of what it's like to have a child. When Rose was taken out of the room, some voiced their desire to terminate their pregnancy. Knowing it wasn't an easy decision, I held them and cried with them.

Two women chose to carry their babies to term and give them up for adoption. I was present in the delivery room with both of them, supporting them through labor and the birth of their child. One did not wish to see her newborn, knowing it would only cause her to relive the brutal rapes she'd suffered. We ensured the adopted parents were present to begin bonding with the baby immediately.

The second woman took an active role in contacting the adoptive family and included them in her pregnancy. She requested that the adoptive mother be present in the delivery room. Together, they welcomed the child into the world surrounded by love and affection. She held her newborn for some time and made peace with her decision. Then, she lovingly placed her baby into the arms of the woman she trusted to show her child a life of love. These women often refer to themselves as weak, but I correct them each time and remind them that they are some of the strongest and bravest women I have ever met.

Today, I am having a one-on-one session with Margarite, a nineteen-year-old who is seven months pregnant and has chosen to keep her baby. Over the past month, she and I have had several sessions with Rose. In today's session, I'm focusing on the importance of relaxing and having playtime on the floor. It sounds simple, but the woman sitting across from me has been conditioned to always be on guard. Allowing herself to relax takes effort.

While we chat, Rose pulls herself up and holds onto a chair. She wobbles back and forth as she concentrates intensely on reaching for a toy. She's starting to get frustrated at not being able to coordinate her movements, but her determination is admirable.

"What do I do?" Margarite asks.

"Nothing yet. If we rescue her every time she gets a little frustrated, she'll never learn." Margarite plays with her fingers nervously. "I know. It's hard not to jump in and help her."

"It makes me feel helpless," she says quietly.

"I understand," I reassure her. "But hear me out."

She nods but doesn't lift her head.

"You're watching her and making sure she's safe. You'll encourage her, which will eventually help her take that first step. And when she falls, because she will, you'll be there to pick her up. Then you can give her the hugs and kisses she needs and set her back on her feet to try again," I explain. "By being here and remaining present, you're proving you're far from helpless."

Margarite lifts her eyes to meet mine and smiles. A second later, Rose bobbles and falls over. She's not hurt, but she pushes out her bottom lip.

"What should I do?"

"What do you think you should do? Trust what you feel."

Margarite grabs Rose's stuffed elephant. "This is her favorite," she says, placing it in front of Rose, who reaches out and takes the stuffed animal. Her pouty lip that was there moments ago has now been replaced with a big smile.

"Look at that. You did great."

We sit and talk while Rose chews on the ear of her elephant.

Margarite was with the first group of women who came to us the day after we opened. She'd been recovered several months earlier and was in another treatment center we network with. Since it's not the norm for a woman to choose to keep her baby, the other center had no program to support her. They were excited to hear about our Mothers-to-Be Program.

With her consent, Margarite was transferred to us. She and I clicked right away. Margarite was recovered from a particularly violent ring of traffickers. During one of her sessions, she described how she was violently raped by different groups of men daily. She has no idea which man is the biological father of her child.

"What if I don't love my baby when he or she is born?"

Margarite's question hits me like a ton of bricks. The pain and fear in her eyes are palpable, and my heart aches for her. How can I possibly find the right words to comfort her when her situation is so vastly different from mine? Rose was conceived in love, but Margarite's baby was conceived during a cruel and abusive act. She'll never be able to tell her child about their father, and the thought of that breaks my heart. I think about the stories and pictures I have to share with Rose, and it only deepens my empathy for Margarite.

As I struggle to respond, I take a deep breath and try to convey as much emotion as possible. "What you've survived is unimaginable. No one should ever have to endure what you have. But you are so incredibly strong. Despite everything, you have so much love to give. I see it when you look at Rose. I wish I could promise you that when you look at your child for the first time, you'll see and feel unconditional love, but I can't do that."

Margarite's eyes widen, but she says nothing. "I can promise you that you're not alone. We'll all be here to support you every step of the way."

"She's easy to love." Margarite glances downward. "I'm terrified of looking at my child and recognizing the face of the man who raped me. Of knowing who her father is," she confesses. "It's something I don't want to know."

Her question makes me question my ability as a therapist to handle this situation. It's not a topic that can be found in any textbook, and I feel ill-equipped. I'm overwhelmed, and there's no one to turn to for help. "Honestly, Margarite, that's a genuine fear, and I'm not sure how to approach it," I admit, feeling unsure.

"I can promise you this—you won't have to go through this alone. No matter what happens, you'll have a support system to assist you." Hoping my words offer comfort, I examine her face closely.

"Thank you, Natalie."

"There's nothing to thank me for. I don't feel like I did anything helpful." I shrug. "Actually, if I'm being honest, I feel totally ill-equipped right now."

She moves to sit next to me. "You're always honest with me. You're not afraid to tell me that you don't have all the answers," she says. "I know you're hurting too. It's not the same hurt I feel, and it doesn't have to be, but maybe it's sharing the hurt that helps the most."

My eyes fill with tears. This young girl is wise beyond her years. "Honesty is something I can always promise you."

In a very uncharacteristic move for Margarite, she hugs me. For the moment, we're just two women who cry together over the precious things we've lost. What was supposed to be a low-key play session has become an emotional and cathartic moment for us both. A knock on the door interrupts our session.

"Come in," I call and quickly wipe my eyes.

Margarite protectively grabs Rose.

Viktor peeks his head in. "I'm sorry to interrupt, but I just got the call. We need to head out."

"I'll be there in a minute." He nods and shuts the door quietly.

"Is everything okay?"

"We have some friends coming in from out of town. Their plane must've landed." I stand, and she passes Rose to me. With my free hand, I help Margarite off the floor. "Are you okay with going back to your residence, or would you like me to call your therapist?"

"I think I'm okay right now." She leans over and kisses Rose's chubby cheek. "I'll see you soon, Miss Rose."

We exit the therapy room together. When Margarite sees

Viktor standing across the room, she quickly drops her gaze. She still has a long road ahead of her, but I'm confident she'll eventually be okay.

"Ready?" Viktor pushes himself off the wall and makes his way across the room. "If we leave now, we should get back home before everyone gets there."

Chapter Fifty-Six

VIKTOR

We're home for about a half-hour when the elevator dings, signaling our guests' arrival. I meet them in the foyer.

"Didn't think we'd be crossing paths again," Michael says as he shakes my hand.

"Hoped we wouldn't have to."

"Where's Natalie?"

"She just went to put the baby down for a nap. She'll be out in a few minutes." I motion toward the kitchen. "I figured you'd all be hungry, so I had pizza delivered. Come on in."

The men follow me into the kitchen, where several boxes of takeout pizza are sitting on the counter. "Help yourselves."

They descend on the pizza like they haven't eaten in a week.

"I hope you guys planned on saving me a piece," Natalie says as she enters the kitchen.

"There she is." Michael puts his pizza down and wraps Natalie in a hug.

I realize I don't have a claim to her, but my muscles tighten seeing her in another man's arms. He whispers something to her that I can't hear before letting her go. She smiles and then turns to Timur.

"I sure have missed you." She reaches out and hugs him. He returns her affections with an awkward pat on her back. Maxim's men aren't used to so much emotion.

I elbow him.

"All right, that's enough of all this ooey-gooey stuff," I joke. "Let's eat, and then we'll go downstairs and get to work."

"Downstairs?" Natalie asks, shocked.

"Yes. We have to get a plan together—"

"I'm well aware of what needs to be done." She crosses her arms over her chest, her signature move. And once again, I know I'm in trouble. "And I plan on being a part of it."

"No."

"No?" The men all shift uncomfortably.

"You heard me. You'll be nowhere near any of this."

"I most certainly will." She looks between everyone—each man tries to avoid direct eye contact with her. "You want to lure Tommy out of the shadows? I'm the easiest way to do it."

"Viktor is right, Nat," Michael interrupts.

"It's too dangerous. We're not risking your safety," I say.

"I didn't ask your opinion."

"That's obvious," I mutter, earning me a disapproving glare from Natalie.

"It's me, Tommy wants. So, the most logical thing to do is to use me as bait." She hops onto a stool next to the kitchen island and grabs a piece of pizza, taking a bite.

Timur holds up his hands in defeat. Misha continues eating, pretending to ignore what's going on around him. Michael's men are smart enough to stay quiet. Dimitri snickers from where he leans in the doorway.

"You will have no part in this." I lean close to her. "That's final."

She rolls her eyes. Actually, rolls her eyes at me.

The elevator dings again.

"Who the hell is that?"

"It's Brandon." She smiles. "I invited him. We'll need someone to stay with Rose."

"You're fucking kidding me right now." I take her by the arm. "Come with me."

"My pizza," she protests.

I grab her plate off the counter and take it with us. "One of you tell Brandon to go home."

"Don't you dare," Natalie calls out over her shoulder. I drag her down the hall to the office and pull her inside before slamming the door shut. "Are you done manhandling me now?" She's pissed. But so am I.

"What the hell was that out there?" I put the plate with her pizza on the desk.

"I'm a part of this more than any of you." She pokes her finger into my chest. "You are not leaving me out of this. If you want Tommy, I'm the way to get him."

"I will not put you in danger. If anything were to happen to you." I put my hands on her arms and quiet my voice. "I wouldn't be able to live with myself."

"You'd never let anything happen to me." She looks at me. Her green eyes are still full of fight.

I can't help myself. I pull her to me and kiss her. It's not tender or sweet. It's full of all the anger I'm feeling right now. She kisses me back, her passion equaling mine, before pushing me away.

"You don't get to kiss me like that." She walks over to the window, turning her back to me. "I'm mad at you right now."

I come up behind her and tentatively put my arms around her. At first, she resists, but I don't let go. Eventually, she relaxes and rests her head against my chest. "I'm sorry you're mad at me."

"Sorry enough to let me help?" she asks.

"Absolutely not," I say, standing my ground.

"You're being a stubborn ass right now," she argues.

I spin her around to face me. She tries to escape, but I pin her against the window, caging her in with my arms. "You and I are just starting to figure things out between us. I can't risk losing you, not like this."

"What do you mean, not like this?"

"I won't allow you to risk your safety to leave me like that. It's one thing for you to decide you don't love me—"

"Don't talk like that."

"You need to hear it. I'm completely and totally in love with you, Natalie." I rest my forehead against hers. "If you decide not to love me back, if you choose someone else and leave me, that's one thing. I'll still be in your life. None of that will change. But if anything were to happen to you, I'd never forgive myself."

"Viktor, you know I care about you. You're the only man I'd ever open my heart to again." Her words fill me with hope for the future. "But we were discussing something else." She ducks under my arm and sidesteps me. The fire has returned to her eyes. "You will not be leaving me out of your little war plans."

My head is spinning. How did she manage to go from one extreme to the other in under thirty seconds?

With her hands on her hips, she's poised for a fight. But this time, I'm ready for her. I move so close to her that she's forced to look up to see me.

"I'm going to say this one last time. The answer is no. You can finish your pizza in here, or if you can control your temper, you can join us before we go downstairs." I turn and walk toward the door.

"Oh my God, you're impossible." She swipes her plate off the desk as she pushes past me and quickly hurries back to the kitchen.

"I'm impossible?" I mutter to myself as I make my way out of the office.

"Wassup. wassup." I hear Rose's sweet little voice and roll my eyes. When I poke my head into our bedroom, Brandon's standing there, a wide-awake Rose in his arms. "I guess they didn't send you home?"

"Timur tried, but it didn't work." Brandon chuckles. "I had to see my niece."

"If only you taught her to call you Uncle Brandon instead of *wassup wassup*."

"Are you jealous, *Fikr*?"

It's my turn to roll my eyes.

"Come on, get some pizza before it's gone. You can stay with Natalie while we get some work done."

"From what I just overheard, that's not going to go over well."

Chapter Fifty-Seven

∞

NATALIE

Despite my protests, the men pile into the elevator and go downstairs to Viktor's office. Brandon stays back to keep Rose and me company. He feeds her bananas and cereal while I tidy up the mess they created in the kitchen.

"Have you heard from Lana?" I ask while I load the dishwasher.

"She called me two weeks ago and asked to be released."

I spin around, shocked. "She did what? You didn't say yes, did you?"

"I can't force her to stay if she wants to be let go."

"She doesn't mean that. Lana's confused right now."

Brandon twirls the spoon in circles while Rose opens her mouth wide. "We don't want the same things anymore," he says sadly. "So, I released her."

I pull out the chair next to Brandon. "This can't be the end?"

"She just needs more time."

"People grow and change, so we agreed we'd review our contract at the one-year mark."

"So, what happened?"

"Svetlana wants clubs, public scenes, and other men. I've done all that and don't want that life again." Brandon looks at me. "I fell in love with her and thought she loved me." He shrugs. "I was wrong. She made it clear that she has no intention of getting married, and she certainly doesn't want a family."

"I've been so preoccupied with my own life. Maybe if I talk to her—"

Brandon places his hand over mine. "It's over, Natalie."

My heart aches for both of my friends. I can only hope that somehow, with time, they'll find their way back to each other. Brandon gets up to put Rose's empty bowl in the dishwasher and grabs a washcloth to clean her face.

"How are things going between you and Viktor?"

"He's in love with me."

Brandon stops and turns to me. "Are you in love with him?"

"I don't know." I stand up to finish cleaning off the counters. "We're trying. We're getting closer. He kissed me in the office before. It was different from the other kiss we've shared. But I stopped him."

"Why?" he asks while he resumes washing the baby's face.

"It's too soon."

"According to whom?"

I lean against the counters. "What do you mean?"

"Who said it's too soon?" Brandon lifts Rose from her high chair and puts her on the living room floor with some toys. I join him on the couch. "Who sets the rules for this kind of thing? Alex gave you both permission to move on with each other, right?"

"Yes."

"Then what's stopping you?"

I sink into the pillows on the couch, my heart heavy with emotion. Every word feels like a stab in my chest as I confess, "It feels like I'm betraying my vows with Alex." The memory of taking off my wedding rings right before Christmas floods my mind, and the pain of it all resurfaces with a vengeance. My trembling hand moves to the lock on my collar, the one thing I haven't been able to bring myself to remove. It's my last link to Alex.

"Natalie," Brandon takes my hand. "Alex is gone."

"I know."

"It's time to take his collar off."

I shoot up from the couch. "No, I can't do that." I go to the window and look out over the water. The city lights reflect like a mirror.

Brandon follows, putting his arm around me. "I have the key."

"How did you get it?"

"Viktor gave it to me. He knew I'd be the one to know when you were ready."

"Well, I'm not ready."

"I don't know that you'll ever think you're ready. But it's time."

Tears well up in my eyes, threatening to spill over at any moment. I know deep down that he's right, that I have to let go, but the thought of admitting it out loud is too painful to bear. The collar represents the last tangible piece of Alex that I have left. The mere thought of taking it off feels like the final nail in the coffin, making everything real and irreversible.

As I struggle to hold myself together, Brandon takes my hand and leads me to the couch, where we sit down together. At that moment, his warmth and support are the only things keeping me from falling apart completely.

"You know, after he heard about the police incident, he fought me about going to the club that night. He didn't want to babysit a whiny young college girl." I try to force a smile despite the tears cascading down my cheeks. "To be honest, I wasn't sure he'd show up."

"That bad, huh?" I wipe my eyes.

"Once he saw you and then that whole flogger episode—"

"He told you?" I gasp.

"Yep. You didn't know?" I shake my head. "He didn't stand a

chance after that. When you left that night, he told me he was going to marry you."

"I had no idea."

"You were his whole world, Natalie." Brandon's eyes fill with tears. "He loved you so much. And when he found out you were going to have a baby, he was over the moon. Then he came close to losing you both." He swipes at the tears dripping from his eyes.

"And here we are today, without him."

"We'll always have him here." He puts his hand on my heart. "But it's time for you to stop living in the past—in what might have been. There's a man downstairs who loves you just about as much as Alex did. Alex knew it, and that's why he set this up."

"Some days, I hate him for asking this of us."

"He knew exactly what he was doing." Brandon reaches out and takes my lock in his hand. My body shudders with sobs. "And now I'm giving you the permission I think you need to move forward."

The lock clicks open, and Brandon carefully removes the collar. My hand goes to my neck. I feel naked without it.

And alone, so very alone.

Brandon opens his arms, and I fall into his embrace as tears stream down my face. I'm unable to stop the grief pouring from deep within me. Rose sees our interaction and begins to cry.

"Do you need a hug from Uncle Brandon, too?" I ask her as I lift her from the floor and bring her to the couch. Brandon wraps us both in his arms as I continue to cry until I'm too tired and my eyes begin to close. I feel the weight of Rose being lifted from my lap before I lose the battle and fall into a deep sleep.

Chapter Fifty-Eight

TOMMY

The small café across from Natalie's building has become my home away from home. They encourage people to linger by offering free internet to their customers. All I have to do is dress the part in khakis, a polo shirt, and a man bun. Pair that with a laptop, and I look like all the other yuppies, all pretending they've got life figured out. The only difference between them and me is that I do have it all figured out. I know just what I want—who I want.

And I'm prepared to do whatever it takes to get it.

I caught a glimpse of Natalie earlier. She and *Vlad,* my pet name for the guy she's shacked up with, pulled into the parking garage. They usually go for a walk in the evening, but not today. Reaching into my pocket, I grab a pill and swallow it with my last mouthful of coffee before I throw a few dollars on the table and walk out.

If she's not coming out tonight, I need to get moving. I've double-crossed some dangerous people, and if I'm not careful, I'll be in a shitload of trouble. Using a different name has bought me some time, but these people are smart. If they haven't figured out who I am yet, they will soon. And I don't want to be around when they do. I need to get Natalie and get out of here.

There are eyes all over this city. I keep to the shadows until I get to a subway entrance, where I put my hat on and pull it low, so any security cameras don't catch my face. While I ride the train, my mind drifts back to last year. I might've strayed from the original plan, but with Montgomery right there, it was too good to pass up. Setting up that explosion was a lot of trouble, but it'll be worth it.

Very soon, I'll get my girl and bring her back home where she belongs. Not *Vlad* or the Scartelli family will be able to stop me.

It'll be just her and me, like it was always meant to be.

Chapter Fifty-Nine

∞

VIKTOR

WHAT THE HELL WAS SHE THINKING? I CAN'T BELIEVE she challenged me like that. I know she only sees the soft side of these men, but make no mistake, each is a ruthless killer. And yet she chooses to argue with me in front of them. Her spunk is part of what I love about her, but I need to make her understand what the consequences of her behavior could mean for me.

My job is dangerous, and that won't change anytime soon. And I'll be damned if I allow her to be involved in my work, no matter how much she pouts. Natalie needs to control her temper, especially in front of the men I work with.

"Viktor, are you with us?" Timur nudges my arm.

"Yeah, sorry." I adjust my position and sit up straighter. Realizing I didn't hear a word of what was said, I ask, "Can you repeat that, please?"

"I have to ask," Michael interrupts. "What's going on with you and Natalie? That looked like a lover's quarrel up there."

I didn't want to have this conversation. However, these men have risked their lives to save her once and are about to put their necks on the line again. They deserve to know the truth. No one makes a sound as I fill them in on Alex's request of me and the letter he left for Natalie.

"It's been hard, but we're figuring things out."

"Are you sure you want a girl who has a kid?" Dimitri chimes in.

"I'm sure," I bite out my response. His question irritates me. Just because he's remained unattached, choosing to fuck his way through St. Petersburg, doesn't mean that's what everyone strives for in life.

"Just checking." He raises his hands in mock surrender. "I mean, she's hot, but a kid too—"

I jump from my seat and grab him by his collar, my hand pulled back in a fist, ready to strike. "Don't ever talk about Natalie like that again. Do you understand?"

"Relax." Misha grabs me from behind, pulling me off Dimitri. "There will be no fighting between us. We need to stay focused on our goal." He looks between Dimitri and me. "You two good now?"

"Fine." I sit back down.

Dimitri adjusts his shirt, an arrogant smile on his face, before returning to his seat.

"Let's go back over what we know about Moore," Timur says, trying to get us back on track.

Despite poring over all the information we've collected, including the security footage from our building, we're still at a loss when it comes to finding a pattern. I'm seething with frustration. Moore has been right under our noses this whole time, and I missed it. It only fuels my anger, knowing he's been watching Natalie and the baby from across the street.

Moore seems to be smart enough to keep his routine unpredictable. He comes and goes at different times without any predictable routine. One of our main challenges is that the security camera at our building can only capture so much. Once he's out of view, he might as well be invisible.

"How the fuck does he just disappear?" I get up and start pacing.

"He may not be very smart, but there's no doubt he's savvy," Misha says. "Not many people could manage a vanishing act in this city."

Michael leans forward. "I hate to say this, but I think Natalie might be right?"

Raising my eyebrows, I ask. "How so?"

"It's closing in on a year since Alex was killed. This guy has managed to outsmart a lot of people. I know you don't want to hear it, but she may be the only way to draw him out."

"No. Absolutely not." I retake my seat. "We'll figure out another way. We'll wait for him to make a mistake."

"Viktor," Timur says. "Michael's right. He's not slipping up anytime soon. How much longer are you willing to let this go on? Natalie needs closure." He stops talking, giving me a moment to digest his words before he continues, "Our best chance is to put her out there and see if he takes the bait."

I can't believe what I'm hearing. I'm ready to explode. "And how do you propose we do this?"

"When we know he's in the café, we have to let her go out alone," Timur explains. "Or at least make it look like she's alone. Then, we hope he follows her."

"You and Natalie take the baby for a walk to the park every day. We don't want her to change the route in case Moore is familiar with it. The only thing that'll be different is her going alone with Rose. It shouldn't raise too many red flags. My snipers will be in place, and you and I will be on the ground," Michael says. "We've been in more dangerous situations with her before. You know we won't let anything happen to her."

I know every man in this room would give their life to protect Natalie. I can't argue with that—and Michael's right. The situation we faced with them at Moreno's compound was next to impossible. But we pulled that off without any significant issues.

These men are the best of the best. Compared to Mexico, this should be nothing.

I rub my hand across my forehead, trying to find a hole in their plan. Anything that could give me footing to say no, but I see no legitimate argument. "We can move forward with using Natalie." I look each man dead in the eye. "But Rose will not be part of this, or the deal is off."

"Fine," Michael agrees. "We'll get a lookalike doll instead."

"Not a hair on Natalie's head better be harmed, or I swear—"

"We know what she means to you." Timur puts his hand on my shoulder. "We'll keep her safe."

It started when we spent all those weeks together at that dump of a motel back in Missouri—bringing her to work every morning and home every night to have dinner together. Some nights, we'd play cards. Others we'd watch a movie. My head knew it was just another assignment, but somewhere inside me, I guess some would call it my heart, started to pretend it was real. It felt like we were a family—a couple. I developed feelings for her. I fell in love with her, but knew it could never be. She belonged to Alex, and that was something I would never interfere with. I was grateful for our friendship. It was enough to keep everything in check.

Then Alex asked me to promise him that I'd step in should anything ever happen to him. He knew how I felt about her, and he wasn't threatened by it. He trusted me to remain professional, and I did. I would never have betrayed him.

Natalie losing her husband wasn't something I wished for. Alex's death didn't make me happy because it meant Natalie had lost the man she was in love with. Her world shattered around her. I would've preferred to live the rest of my life without having her in my arms if it meant she didn't have to experience the heart-break she's lived through.

Alex's death shattered Natalie's world and left her drowning in a sea of grief. Watching her mourn the loss of her husband, the father of her baby, and the man she was supposed to spend the rest of her life with has been nothing short of gut-wrenching. It's a job that's tested me to my limits, and on countless occasions, I've questioned whether I'm strong enough to handle it.

I've come to accept that I'll always be her second choice, forever living in the shadow of Alex's memory. But that doesn't make it any easier. My heart aches with every reminder of him whenever she talks about him or mentions his name. I love her, and I know that in her own way, she loves me too. But it's hard not to feel like I'm competing with a ghost. A piece of her heart will always belong to Alex, and it's something I have to live with.

"So, we're a go?" Michael asks.

"I guess." I shrug, still not thrilled with this plan.

"Then let's go back upstairs and go over this with her." Michael gathers his things. "I'm sure she'll have her own thoughts on how we should handle this."

He laughs, and the other men join him.

I grab my things and roll my eyes, trying to keep a straight face, but end up laughing instead. Because Michael's right, my little firecracker is sure to have a plan of her very own.

Chapter Sixty

NATALIE

THE MEN HAVE BEEN DOWNSTAIRS FOR HOURS. I WISH I knew what they were plotting and planning, but Viktor clearly said that I was to be no part of it. Sometimes, he makes me want to scream—he can be so infuriating.

About thirty minutes ago, Brandon tucked Rose into bed and then came into the kitchen to join me for a glass of wine. That's where we are when Viktor and his posse stride out of the elevator and head directly toward us.

"Are you okay?" Viktor asks.

"I guess."

"You've been crying."

"Can we talk about it later?" I'm not ready to rehash what happened tonight, especially not in front of everyone.

He sits on the stool next to me. "We can."

Brandon drinks his last mouthful of wine and starts to stand. "I think I'll head out now."

"Sit," Viktor orders. "We need to talk."

"Alrighty, then." Brandon lowers himself back onto the stool, a curious look on his face.

Testosterone oozes from every corner of the room as the men file into the kitchen. Looking around, I get the distinct feeling something's amiss. "What's going on?"

"Were you serious when you volunteered to help?" Timur asks.

Now, he's got my attention. "Yes."

As Timur explains the proposed plan, I feel a sense of vindication, and my earlier irritation towards Viktor disappears.

Despite Viktor's hand resting on my thigh, I can sense the tension building in his body as Timur continues to speak. I shift my gaze toward the island and notice the disapproving expression written all over Brandon's face, as well.

Too bad, boys.

"Brandon, we'll need you after all," Viktor says.

"You need help from little 'ole me?" He brings his hand to his chest, feigning surprise.

I can't resist rolling my eyes as I listen to the playful banter between them.

Viktor leans in close and whispers in my ear, "That eye roll is going to get you in trouble one of these days."

A mischievous grin spreads across my face as I respond, "I'd like to see you try." I intertwine my fingers with his, feeling a thrill of excitement shoot through me. Viktor seems to be in a particularly flirty mood tonight. He brings my hand to his lips and softly kisses it, sending shivers down my spine.

"You're going to stay here with Rose. Misha will be here as security." Viktor informs Brandon.

"Would you be willing to babysit your niece?" Brandon asks mockingly. "Sure, Viktor. That shouldn't be a problem."

The room falls silent, all eyes darting back and forth between Viktor and Brandon. I can almost hear Viktor's blood boiling. Brandon doesn't realize he's pushing too far right now.

"Thank you. It'll make me feel better knowing you're here with Rose." I squeeze Viktor's hand, hoping to distract him. "When will all this happen?"

"There are a few things we need to get in place. Mostly, it depends on when Tommy's at the café," Dimitri says. "But we're hoping to be ready to go by the end of the week."

We move into the living room and talk well into the night until I lean against Viktor and yawn.

"Are you tired?" Viktor whispers.

"Mhm."

"Okay, guys." Viktor abruptly stops the conversation. "It's time to call it a night."

The men grab their things. They'll be staying downstairs while they're here. Viktor walks them to the elevator while I say goodnight to Brandon.

"Are you sure about this, Nat?" Brandon asks. "No offense, but your ex is batshit crazy. I don't like the sound of this."

"Tommy killed my husband. I want to make sure he suffers even just a fraction of what I've gone through the past ten months. What I have to live with the rest of my life." I look over his shoulder at the men standing with Viktor. "Those guys will never let anything happen to me."

"As long as you're sure you have my full support."

"Thank you." I hug him. "I'm sure we'll be in touch."

"Night." Brandon heads to the elevator and calls out, "Hold that door."

As I sit alone on the sofa in the dark, Viktor returns and sits beside me. The tension between us is palpable, and I can't stand it. "Viktor," I begin, hoping to clear the air.

But before I can say anything more, his sharp tone cuts me off. "Don't, Natalie," he snaps. "What you did in front of them is not okay. They're dangerous men, and you need to learn how to control your temper around them."

A sense of confusion washes over me at his warning. "They wouldn't hurt me."

"Of course, they'd never lay a finger on you. But when you confront me in front of them, it undermines my authority and makes me appear weak. If they sense you don't respect me or that I can't keep you in line, how can they trust me during a dangerous job?" Viktor explains, his tone serious.

I look down at my hands. I didn't consider that he had to work with those guys and how I made him look. "I'm sorry. I won't let it happen again."

Viktor's gaze lowers to my neck. "Where's your collar?"

I bring my hand to my now bare neck. "Brandon took it off."

"Is that why you were crying earlier?" I nod. "Come here." Viktor pulls me onto his lap.

I'm thankful for the warmth and safety he offers me, but I also feel what my being in this position is doing to him, and I try to pull away.

Please stay. "Viktor's voice is low and filled with need. I shift my position so I'm straddling him. His gray eyes bore into mine with such intensity that it feels like he sees deep into my soul. He leans in to kiss me with such tenderness it takes my breath away. His hands slide my shirt up my body, and I raise my arms, allowing him to remove it. Then, he pulls his T-shirt over his head.

His eyes fixate on my black lace bra as he unhooks it, sliding it off my arms and freeing my breasts. Viktor inhales sharply as he lowers his head, capturing one of my nipples in his mouth. While he teases my breast with his tongue, his hands explore my body. My heart rate quickens, and desire ignites within me.

Lifting me off his lap, he lays me on the sofa. I don't break eye contact as he opens the button on his jeans, sliding them off and standing before me completely naked. Viktor's body is lean and sculpted. His muscles appear as if they've been carved out of stone. Dropping my gaze lower, I take in his visible erection, which reveals the depths of his desire.

Reverently, he grasps my leggings and slides them off. He does the same with my panties, kissing his way back up my thigh before lowering himself over my body. "You're so fucking beautiful," he says before his lips meet mine. My mouth opens, welcoming him. He kisses me deeply as his hips move, rubbing his hard cock against my bare pussy.

I shut my eyes tightly, struggling to maintain my composure and remain present. The sensation of Viktor's touch is exquisite, each movement sending shivers down my spine. His fingers are delicately exploring uncharted territory, leaving a trail of electric energy in their wake.

His touch is familiar yet foreign, and my mind starts to wander to a distant memory, a different time and place, where I was with another man. The emotions that flood my heart are almost too much to bear.

"Viktor." I place my hands on his chest. This man is so caring, so selfless. When I look at his face, it's nearly my undoing. I almost give in and let him take me. A tear escapes. "I want to be with you, and I thought I was ready. I'm so sorry."

"You don't need to apologize or explain." Viktor gently wipes the tear from my cheek. "It's been a difficult night." He hands me his shirt, and I slip it over my head. "When we're together for the first time, I want it to be perfect. I want to be able to take my time with you and know you're only thinking about me."

"Viktor—"

"Shh." He kisses me gently. "It's not time yet, and that's okay. I'm not going anywhere. I'll wait forever for you."

I wear his T-shirt to bed tonight and tell myself that once this mess with Tommy is behind us, I'll have the closure I need to focus on my relationship with Viktor. That my heart and mind will be his and his alone.

Then, like every night, he holds me while I lie on his chest and let the rhythmic beat of his heart lull me to sleep.

Chapter Sixty-One

∞

VIKTOR

NATALIE'S LYING NEXT TO ME, WEARING MY SHIRT. Though we've been sleeping together for months, tonight feels more intimate than ever before. Earlier this evening, I was able to touch her and appreciate her beauty. Her nipples hardened under my touch. The feeling of her skin against mine was heaven. We came so close to taking our relationship to the next level until a shadow of memory passed over her, and she pulled away.

As difficult as it was, I was honest when I said I'd wait for her as long as she needed. I don't know what else to do. I can't compete with her husband's ghost. I have to hope that one day, when I'm making love to her, and she closes her eyes, I'll be the only man she sees.

"Alex," she calls in her sleep. "I've missed you so much. I need you." She runs her hand up my bare chest. "Make love to me, please."

"Natalie." I take her hand in mine.

Her eyes blink open. "Viktor?"

"It's me, sweetheart, not Alex."

She drifts into a restless sleep. I hold her tight throughout the night while she cries out from nightmares, but never fully wakes. Although I do my best to reassure her I'm here, it does little to calm her.

I'm woken from my light sleep when I hear Rose's sweet little voice babbling to herself in her playpen. I don't want her to wake Natalie now that she's finally resting peacefully. Carefully, I untangle myself from her body and get out of bed to get the baby.

"*Dobroye utro, printessa.*" I lift her into my arms, kissing her rosy cheeks.

Her chubby little hands reach out and grab my face. "Fikr," she says between baby kisses.

I've always believed a man in my line of work shouldn't have a wife or children—they're a liability. So, I never allowed myself to desire a family. But right now, holding this precious baby in my arms, everything's changed. I've never experienced this kind of all-consuming, unconditional love and had it returned.

Now, I can't imagine my life without this little girl who, although she doesn't share my biology, is very much my daughter. I look forward to a future where Natalie shares my name and carries a child we make together—a brother or sister for Rose. The feel of little teeth biting my nose snaps me back into the present.

"*Vy progolodalis*?" I ask if she's hungry.

"*Da,*" she responds.

For the past ten months, I've been speaking Russian to Rose, doing my best to facilitate her learning the language. I'm amazed each time she understands what I say, and she answers in my native tongue. I hope to teach her Ukrainian, too. It's my second language, the language of my mama's family.

"Let's get you something to eat." I bop her little nose, and she giggles. "Mama and I have friends we want you to meet today."

After a quick diaper change, we make our way to the kitchen. I know the guys are there. I hear their deep voices murmuring and smell food cooking. But when I step into the doorway with a baby in my arms, all conversation comes to a dead stop, and heads whip in my direction.

"Good morning," I say brightly. "I'd like you all to meet Rose."

Timur, who has several children of his own, is the first to get up. "*Dobroye utro,*" he says, kissing Rose's cheeks, making her giggle. "It's a pleasure to meet you, little lady."

"Rose, this is your Uncle Timur," I explain. "And that's your Uncle Michael." I point to the man sitting at the island, nursing a cup of coffee.

"Hey, kid. Nice to meet you." Michael lifts his mug in a toast-like manner.

"This ugly Russian right here is Uncle Dimitri." My comment earns a glare from my friend. "He can be a bit grumpy some-times," I say quietly.

"Don't listen to him, Miss Rose," Dimitri smirks. "Your Uncle Viktor is the grumpy one."

"Fikr. Fikr," Rose says, grabbing my face.

The men in the room laugh when they hear Rose's interpreta-tion of my name. "Not a word from any one of you," I issue a warning.

"I feel bad for the kid," Misha chimes in. "When she's older, she's never going to get a date with all these crazy Russian uncles." His comment elicits more laughter.

My protective instincts rise when I think of Rose dating. "That's fine with me. She won't be allowed to date until she's thir-ty." I grin as I get Rose buckled into her highchair. While I make her breakfast, the guys keep her entertained. I never thought this group of highly trained mercenaries would turn into mush the moment a baby entered the room.

Chapter Sixty-Two

NATALIE

It's been a tense week as Dimitri has been monitoring Tommy's movements at the café while the others finalize their preparations. Despite Viktor's reluctance to use me as bait and his suggestions of alternative solutions, such as hiring a body double, I'm not backing down. Using myself as bait is our best opportunity to lure Tommy out and get rid of him for good.

The mere thought of it sends chills down my spine as I wonder when I became the kind of person who's willing to take another's life. I know the exact moment - the day Tommy turned me into a widow.

I'm informed that today is the day, and everyone is in position. Apparently, Tommy has been at the café for an hour, sitting at his regular table with his laptop in front of him. As I try to apply my makeup, my hands tremble with a mixture of fear and rage. Suddenly, Viktor's reflection appears in the mirror. He stands behind me, leaning against the doorframe. His demeanor emits menacing energy in pulsating waves. After putting my lipstick on, I turn around but can't move. All I can do is observe the storm brewing in his eyes, turning them a deep shade of gray that I've never seen before.

"For the past few years, it's been my job to protect you." He pushes off the doorway and walks toward me. "Today, I'm willingly allowing you to walk into danger, and I hate it." He leans over me, placing his hands on my makeup table, caging me in place. "What I want to do is forbid you to go. Lock you in here and keep you safe."

"I understand, but we both know this will be the easiest way." I reach out and take his face in my hands, pulling him to me. "I'm not afraid because I know you'll be there."

"I'll do everything in my power to keep you safe."

He holds me against him. Although my body relaxes in his arms, there are other arms I still long to feel around me—even if just for the chance to say goodbye. Alex was taken from me without warning, but today is the day I finally get to take back the power and control.

"Are we ready?"

"Everyone's in place."

"Is Brandon here?"

"He's in the other room with Rose."

Standing on my tiptoes, I place a kiss on his lips. "Let's do this."

"You sure about this, Nat?" Brandon asks when he sees me come into the room.

"I'm sure." I get down on my knees. "Now, let me say goodbye to my little girl." I lift Rose from the floor. She squirms in my arms as I pepper her face with kisses. "You be a good girl for Uncle Brandon. Mommy and Viktor will be back in a little while." I squeeze her tight and then set her back down with her toys.

"Be careful," Brandon says, hugging me. "It's not too late to change your mind."

"I'll see you in a bit." I smile, trying to hide my nerves.

Viktor meets me at the elevator with the baby carriage. It's in the lying back position with a doll that looks way too much like a real baby tucked in, just like I do for Rose. From a distance, no one will be able to tell the difference.

"Is he still at the cafe?"

"Yes. Michael is on the ground and has a visual on him. When you get outside, don't look over there. Act as naturally as possible. Dimitri is monitoring the snipers, who are outfitted with cameras and are in position. Even though you won't see anyone, I'll be right behind you. I'm confident that once Tommy sees you alone, he'll follow you. Once you get to the bench, Michael and I will make our presence known."

"Okay." My heart races.

"It's not too late to back out."

"I have to do this."

"I have something for you," Viktor says, reaching into his pocket and pulling out a diamond heart on a silver chain. "It's a tracking necklace," he explains. "I'm not taking any chances."

I turn around and lift my hair so Viktor can easily fasten the necklace.

"Thank you," I whisper, my voice cracking. I have to go now, or I may back out. "Let's do this." I push the carriage into the elevator. The last thing I see is Viktor's worried expression before the doors close and the elevator descends to the ground floor.

The doorman opens the door, allowing me easy passage to the outdoors. Before walking, I look into the stroller and adjust the blanket on the doll, like I always do for Rose. Then, I turn right and head toward the park. The plan is to follow the path to the bench. Hopefully, Tommy thinks I'm alone and follows me. Thankfully, the park is usually quiet at this time of day. We want the guys to apprehend him with as little threat to the public as possible.

As I walk, my cell rings right on schedule. Touching the green connect button, I answer the call. "Hello?"

"It's me," Viktor says.

"Hey, Lana. What's up?"

"That's my girl." I can hear Viktor's smile through the phone. "Tommy's on the move. He's about a half-block behind you."

"Have you decided to come back yet? Brandon's a mess without you."

"Michael's already in place at the park."

"I miss my best friend too."

"I'm behind Moore. He hasn't even looked back. He's solely focused on you."

"I really do hope you reconsider."

"Moore's picking up speed and getting closer." Stay calm. I remind myself. "He's within hearing distance of our phone call."

"Can I call you back in a bit? I snuck out with Rose," I pause and pretend to laugh. "I sent Viktor on an errand to the other side of Manhattan. He needs to learn that he can't boss me around."

"Cheeky little thing." Viktor chuckles. "I'm right behind both of you. Just keep doing what you're doing."

"I'll talk to you later. I love you."

It takes him a second to respond. "I love you, Natalie."

With shaking hands, I disconnect the call. I didn't plan to say those words. They came out on their own. "Please forgive me, Alex," I whisper as I slide my cell into my pocket.

When I get to the park, I stop and look around. A few children run around on the playground. Their moms sit on nearby benches. "Next summer, you'll be big enough to play there," I tell the doll. "Let's go to our bench and watch the boats, okay?" I take the path around the park's edge, away from the playing children and their parents. Away from people walking their dogs. To the spot Alex and I first discovered, where a tree stands tall, its leaves just beginning to change color.

Viktor and I come here almost every day. And if our plan works, Tommy will follow me today. Then Viktor and Michael will apprehend him and get him into the car waiting on the other side of the building.

When I round the corner, I'm relieved to see no one's here. I sit on the bench and position the stroller so Tommy can't see in it when he approaches. Then, I pull my cell phone out of my pocket and send Viktor a quick text.

Me: I'm in position.

Viktor: Stay aware. He'll be rounding the corner any second.

My heart pounds, and for a moment, I second-guess whether this was a good idea. Quickly, I push that thought out of my head and let the pain and anger I feel every day without my husband take its place.

I pretend to scroll on my phone while pushing the stroller back and forth with my foot like I'm rocking Rose to sleep when I hear footsteps hitting the concrete path. People walking by are normal, and even though I'm sure it's not just any person heading in my direction, I don't look. I need to keep up the act of a typical afternoon. Everyone's safety depends on it.

Heavy footsteps stop a few feet from my right.

"Well, aren't you a sight for sore eyes," Tommy's voice croons.

I look up, startled, a reaction I don't have to fake. "What are you doing here? Aren't you supposed to be in prison?" I get a good look at him. He's thin and pale. His hair is blond now and much longer than usual. It's matted and greasy, like he hasn't showered in several days.

"They let me out early." He smiles. "Good behavior and all."

"What are you doing in New York City?" I stand.

"I heard about your husband's untimely demise." He steps toward me. "So, I came to find you."

I look around nervously, wondering where Viktor and Michael are. "Well, you found me, and as you can see, I'm just fine. So, you can leave now."

"I'm not going anywhere without you."

"What do you mean?" Now it's my hands that are shaking.

"I've waited a long time for this, baby. With Montgomery gone, you're free to come back to me."

His eyes meet mine, and I know something's very wrong. His pupils are constricted, and the whites of his eyes are bloodshot. His long sleeves are pushed up a little. When I look at his arms, I see the marks. He's using drugs again, and I'm pretty sure he's high right now.

"Tommy," I say softly, not wanting to agitate him. "Even though Alex is gone, we're not getting back together."

"That's where you're wrong, sweetheart." He steps even closer.

I pull the stroller behind me, my protective instincts taking over despite the fact that it's just a doll.

"Don't take another step, Moore," Viktor says from behind Tommy.

A twisted grin spreads on Tommy's face. "It seems we have company."

"Step away from Natalie," Michael instructs.

Everything happens so quickly. One second, Tommy's standing in front of me. The next, he's behind me, one arm wrapped around my waist, the other holding a gun to the side of my head.

"Let me go." I struggle to get out of his hold.

"Hold still bitch," Tommy warns. "Before you make me hurt you."

"Let her go, Moore," Viktor's baritone voice booms through the air. "Our snipers are trained on you and won't hesitate to shoot."

A maniacal laugh erupts from deep within Tommy's chest. "Go ahead. I dare you," he spits, then leans in close and whispers in my ear, "If they kill me, you'll never find him."

My heart stops. What does Tommy mean, we'll never find *him?*

"Alex?" The words from my mouth are barely a whisper. "Is Alex alive?"

"You'll have to come with me to find out." He nips at my ear, making my stomach turn. "Call off your henchman."

"Michael. Viktor," I say, looking the men dead in the eyes. "Put your weapons down. I've changed my mind. I want to go with Tommy."

"You're not going anywhere with him," Viktor argues.

"Take care of Rose for me," I plead. I hear the safety click off Viktor's gun. "Please, Viktor." Tears stream down my face. "Don't shoot. I want to be with him."

"Are you sure this is what you want?" Michael calls.

"I'm positive. I want to give us another chance." The lie drips from my lips, but Viktor doesn't budge from his stance until Michael puts his hand on top of the gun, forcing him to lower it.

"Good choice," Tommy yells to them. "Now, step out of the way. Natalie and I are leaving." He nudges my arm. "Drop your cell phone. We don't want anyone following us, do we?"

My fingers open, allowing my phone to fall to the concrete below. With the gun still held to my head, we walk past Michael and Viktor. My eyes lock with Viktor, silently pleading with him not to make a move. Tommy slides the gun lower against my back, so we don't draw unnecessary attention as we walk past the people in the park. We approach a waiting car, and Tommy slides the gun into his pocket.

I look over my shoulder. Michael is physically holding Viktor back. His hands are balled in fists, his face red with fury. I know he doesn't understand why I'm doing this, but if there's a chance Alex is alive, I have to take it.

I know that no matter what happens, Viktor will find me.

Chapter Sixty-Three

TOMMY

With a tight grip on Natalie's arm, I lead her to a waiting car. The other day, an old friend stopped by to let me know he's no longer working with Scartelli. He was hoping we could hook up and find some side jobs. It just so happened I was in need of a car and driver, and Jinx fit the bill perfectly.

"Get in." I open the car door and push Natalie onto the seat.

"Where are we going?"

"Home."

"Is Alex alive?"

"Shut up bitch." My hand connects with her face, hoping to silence her. Her hand flies to the red mark left behind, but at least she's stopped talking.

The ride back to my apartment is hell, as usual, but it gives me time to replay the past few months and how all my planning has finally paid off.

Setting it up was child's play. As soon as I found out the boss was asking Montgomery to come in for a final walk-through, I knew that was my cue. That night, I got myself a body. One would think acquiring a body would be a difficult task, but actually, it was quite easy.

Behind my apartment is a dumpster-lined alley where homeless people tend to linger after dark, looking for scraps left behind. I've been hanging out there for the past several weeks, pretending to be one of them. I made friends with Joe, a guy who once had it all—a good job, a house, a wife, and kids. He even had a fucking dog. But he got involved with the wrong crowd and made some bad business decisions. The schmuck lost his job and started drinking.

His wife didn't want to put up with him, so she kicked him out. Poor Joe found himself alone and in my alley. He didn't realize that he was pouring his heart out to the wrong person and became my perfect target. All I had to do was keep showing up to learn his pattern. My man Joe wasn't very street-smart, so it took no effort at all. Like so many nights before, Joe strolled down the alley and sat next to me. What he didn't know was that this night would be his last.

We often shared a bottle of vodka, so he was none the wiser when I passed him an already-open bottle.

Except this time, we weren't sharing.

The pill-laced liquor was meant only for him. After a few slugs, he passed out cold. Jinx was there to help me drag his limp body into his car. Once we got him in the trunk, I gave him a shot of heroin large enough to kill a horse. Bye-bye, Joe.

When I got to work the next morning, I stopped by to see my friend, Leon, who was now indebted to me for helping his dear wife get out of pain. His job was to cut the live security feed when Montgomery was leaving, replacing it with some older taped footage. That would give me the cover I needed for the next phase of my plan. Leon started to ask me why, but dangling some more product for his wife was all the incentive he needed to keep his mouth shut—done.

The last step was patience, something I've become very good at. I had to stay out of the way while Montgomery took his tour and wait for him to leave. That's when things really started to get fun.

The elevator stopped a few floors down, and a well-dressed businessman entered. Who was that man? It was none other than Jinx. The guy doesn't clean up half bad. Just as Alex was about to step out of the elevator to go to his car, Jinx stuck him with a syringe full of Special K. Montgomery didn't know what hit him. In less than thirty seconds, he was unconscious on the ground.

Jinx stripped Montgomery of his personal belongings. Then we made the switch. The dearly departed Joe was placed in Montgomery's car with all his personal effects, and Montgomery came with me. Then we got the hell out of there just before the vehicle exploded. And just as I suspected, no one questioned the identity of the person who perished in such an unfortunate accident.

See, I never intended to kill Montgomery, at least not right then. No, Montgomery deserved to suffer. He took something from me that was never his to take. Now, it's time for him to have a taste of his own medicine. It's his turn to see how it feels to have his girl stolen right out from under him while he watches helplessly from the sidelines. All I had to do was mention the possibility of Montgomery being alive, and Natalie was putty in my hands.

Luck has been on my side from day one. Inside the apartment I'm renting, I found a secret room, a bomb shelter that must've been a leftover from the Cold War era. It's been the ideal guestroom for Montgomery. He gets to stay chained to the wall, where he watches streaming videos of Natalie and *Vlad* playing house with the kid. I let the stream play over and over for hours at a time. He's watched his daughter's first ten months of life with another man being her daddy. The best part is the dreadful look on his face when he sees his grieving widow happy and smiling in *Vlad's* arms. I've loved every fucking second.

Finally, Jinx slows to a stop at my apartment.

"Welcome home, Natalie."

Chapter Sixty-Four

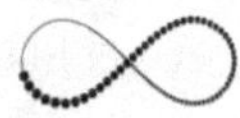

NATALIE

I try to rub away the sting left from where Tommy hit me. I'm terrified of being anywhere near him while he's in such a deranged state. And whoever this guy is driving doesn't seem to care either. But I had no other choice. If there's even a possibility of Alex being alive, I have to take my chances and find out—find him.

Tommy's quiet the whole ride, seemingly lost in his thoughts, and that's fine with me. While he's quiet, I look out the window, trying to keep track of where we're going. I'm good for a while until we get to a part of the city I'm unfamiliar with, and then I lose my bearings. Eventually, we turn into an alley and stop behind a dilapidated building.

"Welcome home, Natalie." Tommy grins. "Now, you're going to be a good little girl and come with me quietly, so I don't have to drug you, right?"

He grabs my wrist and pulls me across the sticky leather seat. As soon as we're out of the car, the driver races away. Tommy's hand never leaves my wrist as he unlocks the door.

"Let's go," he says, and we start walking down a set of steps.

"Is Alex alive?" As soon as the words leave my mouth, I realize my mistake, but it's too late. Tommy spins around on the step, nearly causing me to fall.

He grabs my shoulders and squeezes. "I don't want to hear his name, do you understand?"

I nod in response.

At the bottom of the steps is another door. Tommy puts the key in the lock, and with a click, it opens. He steps aside, motioning for me to go ahead of him. "You're home now." Tommy flips a switch, and the lights come on. We're in a dingy apartment. The air is stagnant and musty. There are several small windows in the cracked concrete walls, but they don't look like they open. The place is sparsely furnished with only an old, torn sofa and a coffee table. No television. The kitchen is small and hasn't been cleaned in weeks. Flies circle a stack of dirty dishes, no doubt feeding on the rotting food.

"Are you hungry?" Tommy asks, his demeanor now calm.

"Not really." The stench alone is enough to make me lose my appetite.

"I know it's not much." Tommy looks around nervously. "This city is too damn expensive. We won't be here long, though."

"What do you mean? Where are we going?"

"We're going back to Northmeadow." Tommy flops on the sofa and picks up a plastic pill bottle from the table in front of him. He dumps two pills in his hand and swallows them.

"You're back on drugs?"

He appears annoyed by my comment. "Medicine. For my back pain."

I don't want to deal with an angry Tommy, so instead of being hostile, I take a different approach. "I didn't realize it still bothered you. Is there anything I can do to help?"

He ignores my question, lost in his own train of thought.

"Like I said, we're going back to Northmeadow as soon as I tie up one more loose end." He pats the sofa next to him. "Come sit with me. I've missed you."

Hesitantly, I start walking over to the couch when a cockroach crawls out from under it and crosses my path. I scream and jump back, afraid of the giant bug.

Tommy laughs. "Don't worry about them. They won't hurt you."

"I don't like it here, Tommy," I say as I sit next to him.

He puts his arm around me, pulling me close to him. "I know, sweetheart. You deserve better than this." He runs his fingers through my hair. "But it's only for tonight. Unless you'd rather leave now?" Tommy sits up suddenly. "Yes. Let's get this over with and get out of here tonight."

"What do we have to do before we leave?" As much as I don't want to be here, I have to stall him long enough for Viktor to catch up with us.

"We have to kill Montgomery."

Chapter Sixty-Five

ALEX

AFTER ALL THIS TIME, I STILL CAN'T FIGURE OUT WHAT happened. I remember leaving Jelena's Hope and getting into the elevator. It stopped a few floors down, and another man, I assumed an employee from a lower floor, stepped in.

Then, I go blank.

The next thing I remember is waking up in this stuffy, concrete room stripped down to my boxers. My wrist is connected to the wall by a chain. Next to me was a water bottle, a bowl of rice, and a bucket—my bathroom facilities. The ceiling has old-style fluorescent lighting that's turned off and on at regular intervals.

The only other thing in the room is a TV mounted on the wall across from me. I remember thinking that was an odd addition to this space. It was days before the large door creaked open, and my captor made his identity known. Standing in the dim light was none other than Thomas Moore.

"What the hell's going on, Moore? Why aren't you in jail?"

"You thought you won when you had me locked up. But it looks like the tables have turned," he sneers.

With the click of a button, the TV came to life. On it are images of Natalie and my daughter. At first, I was concerned. It was too early for Rose to be born, but she looked healthy. And Viktor was right by Natalie's side.

"They all think you're dead." He laughs. "And your little whore didn't even wait to move on with Vlad. I bet she's been fucking him behind your back the entire time." He stoops down next to me. "You were nothing to her, Montgomery. Just someone to warm her bed until the next thing came along."

"And you think you mean something to her?"

Tommy's fist lands across my face. "Shut the fuck up."

"What's your plan now? How long do you think you can hold me hostage?"

"You're going to watch your widow with her new man until I decide it's time for me to take her. When I bring her back here, I'm going to make you watch as I fuck her sweet little cunt. Then, she and I are going back to Northmeadow together." Tommy turns to walk out of the room. "Oh yeah, and right before we leave, I'm going to kill you."

Bile rises in the back of my throat when I think of him laying a finger on Natalie.

The monitor turns on daily and shows me videos and picture collages of Natalie, Rose, and Viktor. Rose has grown so much, and she's beautiful like her mama. Natalie is finally starting to smile again. She and Viktor look happy together. Watching my wife in another man's arms is hard, but they're both doing just as I asked. Knowing that Natalie's not alone brings me peace.

Moore thinks he's torturing me by showing me these scenes. So I show him the rage and disgust he expects while I try to figure out how I can try to get out of here alive. And if I don't, if he kills me, I'll die knowing my girls are safe and loved.

But Thomas Moore is playing a game he can't win. He might get rid of me, but Viktor will never allow him to get anywhere near Natalie and Rose.

Chapter Sixty-Six

VIKTOR

"Why the hell didn't you let me kill the bastard?" I yell in Michael's face.

"Didn't you see the look on Natalie's face after he whispered in her ear? Her entire demeanor changed."

"Who cares?" I grab Rose's stroller with the baby doll and pull out my cell phone, hitting Dimitri's contact. "You just made our job more difficult."

"What happened?" Dimitri answers.

"Moore has her. Are you tracking her?"

"I am. They're moving south."

"Don't lose them. I'm on my way back to grab supplies." I glance over my shoulder at Michael. "Then I'm going after them."

Next, I call Maxim.

He answers on the first ring. "Do you have him?"

"No. But Moore has Natalie."

"What the hell went wrong?"

"I'm not sure." I shove the stroller out of my way. It's only slowing me down. "Moore said something to her. Then she insisted we let her go with him. Something's not right."

"Is she wearing the necklace?"

"Yes. Dimitri's tracking her. They're on the move. I'm heading back to the apartment. Then I'm going after Moore."

"I am calling Scartelli. Do not do anything until you hear back from me." The phone disconnects.

Once I'm back at our apartment, I repeatedly hit the elevator call button. It isn't moving fast enough.

"The only thing you're going to do is break it," Michael says.

"I don't want to hear your voice." I point my finger at his face. "If it weren't for you, we wouldn't be in this situation."

"There's more to this, Viktor. We need to take a minute and regroup. Try to figure out what's going on."

"If he hurts her. I'll kill you."

"I'll hold you to that," Michael replies.

The elevator ride is quiet. When the doors finally open, I rush out and head straight to the office.

"What's going on?" Brandon asks.

"Moore has Natalie." I don't stop as I bark out the words.

"What the hell happened?" Brandon yells.

Rose startles and begins crying. I freeze mid-step and then go back to pick her up. "Don't cry, *printessa*. Viktor's going to get your mama back." My cell phone rings. "What did you find out?"

"I spoke to Scartelli. He sent one of his guys, someone named Jinx, out looking for Moore last week. Moore was finally tracked down at a joint he frequents. Jinx told Moore that Scartelli cut him loose, and he needed a job," Maxim explains. "Jinx called Scartelli a short time ago. Said Tommy's high as a kite. He has been carrying on all day about having to tie up loose ends after he picked up his girl."

"Loose ends?"

"Apparently, Jinx gave Moore some assistance the day of the explosion. Told Scartelli he helped Moore switch bodies, some homeless guy for his intended target. Jinx did not know who the guy was or what he did with him until today. He has been holding Alex hostage in an apartment in the city this whole time."

"What the hell?" I raise my voice, making Rose cry again. "I'm sorry, sweetheart." I pass her back to Brandon and storm off toward the office with Michael on my heels.

"Jinx informed Scartelli that he dropped off Moore and a pretty blonde about twenty minutes ago. He gave Scartelli the address. Then Scartelli doled out Jinx's punishment for his role in this mess. He will not be a problem anymore."

"That bastard. He wanted everyone to believe Alex died in the explosion. None of us even questioned the identity of the body."

"We had no reason to." Maxim's voice is strained. He's barely hanging onto control. "All this time, Alex has been alive."

"Fuck," I yell as I throw open the door to the weapons safe.

"Dimitri's sending the address now," Michael says. "They're in Hell's Kitchen."

"Viktor." Maxim's voice is serious. "Moore has a syringe containing a lethal dose of heroin. He plans to use it to kill Alexander."

"We're wasting time on the phone. I'll get them back." I disconnect the call and stick my cell back in my pocket.

Michael's on a conference call with his team, giving them the address so they can meet us there while he loads up with extra ammo. I finish getting my weapons and then grab the Narcan. I thought Alex was crazy insisting we keep some on hand, but I'm incredibly thankful right now.

"Ready?" I ask Michael.

"Let's roll."

Chapter Sixty-Seven

NATALIE

Whatever Tommy's taking has him wired, and he can't stop moving. I need him to trust me, so I choose my words carefully. Somehow, I have to buy myself some time. If Tommy's to be believed, Alex is not only here somewhere, he's still alive. I have to find him before it's too late.

"I think we should eat before we leave, don't you?"

"You're hungry. See, I still know you." Tommy looks proud of himself.

"Yes, you do." I run my knuckles down his face. "How about I cook us some dinner?"

"Yeah, that's a good idea. I'm starving."

"Okay. I'm going to go to the kitchen." I stand slowly, not wanting to spook him. "And I'll see what you have that I can make."

Tommy nods.

I walk over to the kitchen and open the fridge. There are several cans of beer and a bottle of ketchup. Nothing useful. In the freezer, I find a few frozen dinners. Pulling two out, I read the directions and throw them in the microwave.

"Do the dishes while you're over there," Tommy calls from the couch.

"No problem, babe."

While the food cooks, I start sorting the dishes to clean them. To think, if I married him, this would've been my life. I shiver at the thought. I need to stay focused on my goal.

Looking over my shoulder, I see Tommy's head has fallen back. His eyes are closed. He's either asleep or passed out—either way works for me. I leave the water running while I look around for something to use as a weapon. That's when I see his gun hanging out of his pants pocket. I move as slowly and quietly as possible. This is my only chance, and I don't want to know what'll happen if I fail.

Carefully, I wrap my fingers around the handle and slide the gun from his pocket. Tommy doesn't move. Then I tuck it against my side in the waistband of my leggings. My long, loose shirt is perfect for concealing the weapon.

"Aren't you supposed to be doing dishes?" Tommy wakes up abruptly.

"I was just coming to check on you, babe." I force my lips to touch his.

"That's my girl. I knew you'd see things my way once you were away from him." He takes my hand in his. "You know we were always meant to be together."

"I'm sorry I didn't realize it sooner."

He pulls me into him. "I forgive you. That's all in the past now." Then, recognition sweeps across his face. "I almost forgot. We have something important to do. Come with me."

"I made dinner." I try to pull him toward the kitchen. "I thought we were going to eat."

"This is more important," he insists. "We'll eat after." He grabs my wrist and leads me down a narrow, dark hall and through a doorway that's missing its door. We're standing in what must be his bedroom. Tommy looks between the bed and me. "I can't wait to sink my cock inside your tight cunt." He leans in and kisses me. I try to pull away, but he holds tight.

His tongue pushes its way between my unwilling lips as his hands roam down to my ass. "And then I'm going to take you here just like I've always wanted to. I'm going to fuck you until you forget you've had anyone else but me." He pulls back, his glazed-over eyes roam up and down my body. "But first, I have a surprise for you."

He pushes a small table out of the way, revealing a door hidden in the wall. Then, he unlatches a lock and pulls a handle that opens a large door. "Come on." He motions for me to follow him.

When I step into the room, my heart stops. There, huddled in the corner, chained to the wall, is Alex. He's deathly thin, and his complexion is nearly translucent, but his chest slowly rises and falls. "Oh my God, Alex. You're alive."

Tommy cackles. "Barely." He kicks Alex in the side. "Get up, Montgomery. You have company."

"Alex, it's me. I'm here."

Alex groans as he lifts his head and slowly opens his eyes. "Natalie?" he asks, his voice hoarse. "Is that really you?"

Tommy grabs me and pulls me to his side. "It's really her, and she's here with me." He leans over and attacks my mouth. I struggle against him. "You like it rough now? That fucking turns me." He grabs my hand and puts it over his erection.

"Get away from her, you sick bastard," Alex says weakly. He tries to stand but falls to his knees.

"Alex." I try to go to him, but Tommy grabs me.

"Where do you think you're going? You're staying right here. Montgomery's going to watch me fuck you." Tommy pulls a set of handcuffs from his pocket and, grabbing my hand, snaps them over my wrist, attaching the other side to a clip on the wall. "This will keep you right where I want you while I take care of him." Tommy pulls a syringe from his pocket. "You'll live just long enough to watch me sink my cock deep into your wife."

While Tommy's back is turned, I use my free hand to pull out the gun. "Don't move, or I'll shoot you."

"What the hell?" Tommy spins around, shocked, but quickly composes himself. "You'll never pull the trigger on me, baby." He takes another step toward Alex.

My hands shake as I click the safety off and fire. The bullet hits Tommy's leg.

"You fucking bitch," he yells.

Everything moves in slow motion.

Tommy lunges at Alex, piercing him with the needle. "No," I scream as I fire a second shot, this time hitting Tommy in the chest. He falls to the floor and turns his head to face me.

"You think you saved him by killing me, bitch." Tommy's words are gurgled as blood drips from the corner of his mouth. "But Montgomery's going to die, too."

Then, Tommy takes his final breath.

I killed him.

"Alex," I scream, but he doesn't respond. I tug my hand, but the cuff's too tight.

Alex slumps lifeless next to Tommy's dead body.

"Alex, please stay with me. You can't leave me."

Chapter Sixty-Eight

VIKTOR

We arrive at Moore's apartment at the same time as a black Mercedes with opaque windows. Its driver steps out, opening the rear door. Luciano Scartelli emerges from the vehicle. However, before he can utter a word, gunfire erupts from inside the building.

"Fuck." I don't waste time on introductions. I immediately pull out my weapon, test the door, and discover it isn't locked. Rushing inside, I take the steps two at a time and end up stopped at another door—this one's locked. Determined to gain entry, I kick the door down.

"Natalie. Are you here?"

"Viktor?"

"Where are you?"

"Down the hall," she cries. "Please, hurry."

I race down the narrow hallway in the direction of her voice. When I finally get to her, I find her handcuffed to a wall. "Are you okay? Did he hurt you?"

"You have to help Alex." She pushes me with her free hand. "Tommy had a syringe. I think he overdosed him on something."

I spin around and see Tommy's body lying in a pool of blood. Next to him, Alex lies lifeless on the floor.

"What the hell?" Michael asks as he runs into the room behind me.

I'm already on my knees administering a dose of Narcan to Alex. "Get her out of those damn cuffs," I yell.

As soon as she's free, she rushes to Alex's side. "Is he alive?"

I've given the medication, hoping it's the right antidote, but Alex still isn't responding, so I start CPR. "Michael, call 911."

"The ambulance is already en route," Scartelli says. "Get the girl out of here."

"I'm not going anywhere." She clings to Alex's hand as tears pour down her face. "Alex, please wake up. You can't leave me."

"She needs to be gone before the cops get here," Scartelli instructs. "My men will take care of this." He motions to the bloody scene where one of his men is already cleaning the prints off the gun.

"I'm not leaving him."

I continue chest compressions while the debate goes on around me. I am torn between staying to work on Alex and ensuring Natalie's interrogated by the police or turning over Alex's care to Michael and getting her out of here as quickly as possible.

"I'll take over." Michael pushes me out of the way and continues CPR. "Go with Natalie."

As the wailing of sirens grows louder, I clasp Natalie's arm in a tight grip. "We need to leave now." She tries to resist, but I grab her around the waist and pull her away from Alex. I turn to Scartelli. "You'd better make sure this doesn't come back to her."

Chapter Sixty-Nine

NATALIE

"Alex, please wake up. You can't leave me," I beg, but Alex remains unresponsive.

The sound of sirens grows closer with each passing second. I'm sure the ambulance, as well as the NYPD, are on their way.

"She needs to be gone before the cops get here," a well-dressed older man instructs. There will be questions about the man lying on the ground with a bullet hole through his chest, but I don't care. I feel no remorse and would do it again if it meant saving Alex.

Viktor takes my arm. "We need to leave now." I kick and scream, fighting against his hold, but it's useless. His strong arm wraps around my waist, dragging me away from Alex. He stops in the doorway and warns the man. "You'd better make sure this doesn't come back to her."

"You have my word. I'll be in touch with the hospital information," he assures Viktor. "Now get her out of here."

Viktor takes the steps two at a time, carrying me as if I weigh nothing. We exit through the back door, and he sets me down next. "Get in the car."

I look at the door to the apartment, considering trying to make a run for it.

"Natalie, now. We need to be gone before the cops get here," Viktor pleads, but I don't move. "Dammit, Natalie." He opens the door and pushes me into the car. Then, he rounds the front and jumps in the driver's seat. The tires squeal as he pulls away quickly.

"Is he going to make it?" I ask through my tears.

"They'll do everything they can," he reassures me.

"Who was that guy?"

Viktor's phone rings. He pulls it out and tosses it on my lap.

"Put it on speaker."

"He'll be at New York Presbyterian," an unfamiliar voice says. "Take the girl home to shower and get rid of her clothes."

"Who is this?" I ask.

"Natalie, stop," Viktor warns.

"Wait for a call." The line goes dead.

"Was that the same man who was at Tommy's? Who is he?" I've never seen him before, so I'm sure he isn't one of Maxim's men.

"Someone you don't want to cross."

"Why was he there?"

"He was looking for Tommy."

"Why?"

"Natalie, please. Not now."

I take as many side streets as I can to avoid traffic. Natalie needs to be as far away from that place as possible. And I have to trust Scartelli will keep his word. Finally, we're pulling back into the parking garage.

"We're going to my apartment, where you'll shower, and we'll wait for a call."

My heart is racing, my mind consumed by a single thought—I need to get to the hospital. I don't give a damn about taking a shower. "I want to go to Alex."

"We can't. Not yet," Viktor replies.

Desperation washes over me as we walk into Viktor's apartment. But instead of rushing to the hospital, I'm led to the primary bathroom. My nerves are shot as Viktor barks out his orders, "Take your clothes off and get into the shower." I comply, but I notice his eyes avoiding my body.

"Viktor—"

"I'll explain everything when you're done." He grabs the pile of clothes. "I'll be back in a few minutes." Every second feels like an eternity as I wash away the evidence of my crime.

After finishing my shower, I reach for one of Viktor's dark gray towels and head to his bedroom to change into fresh clothes.

I walk into the kitchen and find Viktor sitting on a bench at his kitchen island, his head buried in his hands. Walking up to him, I place my hands on his shoulders, and his muscles tense under my touch.

"Will you tell me what's going on now?"

"Have a seat." He gestures for me to sit next to him and slides a bottle of water to me. "While Dimitri was searching for Moore's whereabouts, he uncovered Tommy's involvement with the Scartelli Family."

Viktor explains that Tommy double-crossed them, and they were out for blood, but arrived too late. "Scartelli will make sure none of what happened is ever traced back to you."

I take a drink of the cool liquid, trying to wrap my head around the events that occurred in the past few hours.

"I need to ask you something."

"Anything."

"What happened? Why did you go with him?"

"Tommy told me if you or Michael shot him, we'd never find *him*. I knew he had to be talking about Alex." I take Viktor's hand in mine. "I had to go. I needed to see if Alex was still alive."

My cell rings, but I don't recognize the number. I look to Viktor for direction.

"Answer it, but don't let on you know anything."

"Hello?"

"Is this Mrs. Montgomery?"

"It is."

"Ma'am, this is Detective Walters. We met shortly after your husband's accident."

I put the phone on speaker so Viktor can hear, too. "Yes, I remember."

"I'm not sure how to say this." He stumbles over his words. "Your husband was found alive tonight."

"Excuse me. Can you repeat that?" I don't have to pretend. His words are a shock because they mean Alex didn't die in that room after we left. My tears fall like rain.

"Your husband is alive, ma'am." Detective Walters repeats the words I never thought I'd hear.

"How? Where is he? Is he okay?" I fire off rapid questions.

"A short time ago, Mr. Montgomery was brought to New York Presbyterian Hospital. He's in the ICU in serious condition," Detective Walters explains. "The rest is a complicated story that's best told in person."

"I understand," I reply. "But right now, my priority is getting to my husband."

I hang up the phone and look at Viktor. "Will you please take me to him?"

The car ride to the hospital is silent, the weight of fear and uncertainty heavy in the air. My mind is racing with thoughts of Alex. He's alive. How is that even possible? What does this mean for Viktor and me?

It takes entirely too long before we pull up outside the hospital. Viktor hands the keys to the valet. I hurry inside, adrenaline coursing through my veins. The elevator ride feels like it takes forever, each passing floor causing my anxiety to rise.

Finally, we reach the ICU floor and are met in the waiting room by Detective Walters. Tears well up in my eyes when I see the concern etched on his face, and I can't help but wonder what kind of news he has for us.

"Mrs. Montgomery, may I have a moment of your time?"

"I'd prefer to go to my husband."

"I just have a few quick questions."

"Can't this wait? As you can imagine, Mrs. Montgomery is shocked to learn her husband is alive after all this time and wants to go directly to him," Viktor says.

"Unfortunately, this can't wait. It'll only take a few minutes."

"Make it fast." Viktor's tone is edgy.

"Are you familiar with a Thomas Moore?"

"Yes, I am. We dated in high school back in Missouri. Last year, he shot my father in an attempted robbery for which he went to prison."

"Well, ma'am. It seems Mr. Moore was released early and had been living in the city under an assumed name."

"What does this have to do with Alex?"

"We found evidence in Mr. Moore's apartment that connects him to the explosion we thought killed your husband." The detective cracks his knuckles nervously. "It appears Mr. Moore has been holding your husband hostage ever since."

"Holding him hostage?" Although I was there and saw it for myself, it's easy to be shocked. All of this sounds like a movie plot rather than real life. "Where's Tommy now? I'm assuming you've apprehended him?"

"He was shot and killed tonight, ma'am."

"Oh, my God."

"One of his neighbors heard a gunshot in Mr. Moore's apartment and phoned the authorities. When the officers arrived, it was clear there was a break-in," he explains. "Upon further investigation, we uncovered a hidden room in Mr. Moore's apartment. That's where we found Mr. Montgomery and Mr. Moore."

A doctor enters the waiting area, interrupting the detective. "Mrs. Montgomery?"

"Yes."

"I'm Dr. Stevens. I've been caring for your husband since he was brought in earlier."

"How is he? Can I see him?"

"Let's have a seat." I don't want to *have a* seat. I want to see my husband. Viktor must sense my apprehension and guides me to a chair where he stands at my side. "Your husband's a very lucky man. He was injected with a large dose of heroin. If that good Samaritan didn't administer the Narcan when they did, Mr. Montgomery wouldn't be with us."

"Good Samaritan?" I ask.

"We don't know who it was. They were gone by the time my officers arrived," Detective Walters adds.

"Is Alex going to be okay?"

"He's malnourished and suffering from multiple injuries. None of which appears to be life-threatening. Although he's still unconscious, his vitals are strong. I expect he'll wake soon, and I'll be able to assess more then."

"Do you have any more questions for me, Detective? If not, I'd like to go to my husband now."

"That's everything, ma'am. I hope your husband has a speedy recovery." Detective Walters leaves us with the doctor.

"Can you take us to Alex, Doctor?"

My heart races as Viktor and I follow the doctor down the hall. Dread fills me as the all-too-familiar smell of antiseptic permeates the air, reminding me of the night my father was shot. I can feel the weight of the past settling on my shoulders like a heavy blanket. The constant beeping of the monitors is a stark reminder of the precariousness of life, and it sends shivers down my spine.

But this time, when we stop outside a room, it's not my father lying in the bed—it's Alex. His eyes are closed, and he looks too peaceful, too still. Tubes and wires are attached to his body. The steady rhythm of the monitor is the only sound in the room.

As I take in the scene before me, tears stream down my face uncontrollably. I try to wipe them away, but they keep coming, blurring my vision. Seeing Alex in this condition is almost unbearable. Sensing my pain, Viktor puts his arm around me, and I find comfort in his embrace.

"I know it's difficult to see a loved one in this condition. The good news is he's breathing on his own. Mr. Montgomery's body has been through a lot and needs rest. But I'm confident he'll be okay," the doctor reassures me. "Go in and talk to him."

Viktor leads me to a chair by Alex's bed. "I'll give you some time with him," he says quietly before leaving the room.

"I'm here, Alex." I take his hand in mine, relieved to feel its warmth. "Please open your eyes." Alex doesn't stir. Doesn't wake.

Chapter Seventy

ALEX

My body feels like it was hit by a train. Muscles I
didn't know existed hurt, and my head is throbbing. I open my
eyes, and the room slowly comes into focus. I'm in a hospital. But
how did I get here?

Natalie. She's next to me, her head resting on my bed. She's
holding my hand—she's sleeping. Is this another dream? I don't
move or speak, afraid she'll disappear if I do.

Eventually, she stirs and lifts her head.

"Hi, baby girl." My throat is dry, and my voice cracks when I
speak.

"You're awake." She sits up quickly. "I need to call the nurse."

"Wait." I hold her hand. "I just want to be with you for a
minute."

"You're alive." She begins to cry. "All this time, I thought you
were dead."

"It's okay." I wipe a tear from her cheek. "I'm here now."

She looks at my chest, covered in bruises, some old, some new.
"What did he do to you?"

"It's just a few bruises. They'll heal."

"You're so thin." She gently runs her hand down my cheek.

"Feeding me wasn't Tommy's top priority."

"There's so much to tell you. You need to meet your daughter." Natalie grabs her phone.

"No, not here."

The door creaks open, and a doctor walks in, interrupting us. "Welcome back, Mr. Montgomery. I'm Dr. Stevens."

"It's good to be here, and please call me Alex."

"How are you feeling, Alex?"

"My head's throbbing."

"That's to be expected. In addition to being severely dehydrated, you had quite the concoction of heroin and Narcan. I'll make sure you get something for the pain. But first, I'd like to examine you." He takes a few minutes to study the readouts from the machines. "Your heart rate is steady, and your blood pressure has stabilized. I think we can get rid of these." He begins to remove some of the wires and the oxygen tubes before doing a physical exam. "You've lost muscle tone and will need physical therapy so we can get you walking again."

"He can't walk?" My heart sinks.

"Due to the lack of nutrition and being restrained, Alex's muscles have become too weak. But I suspect he'll be up and around in no time."

"How long do I have to stay here?"

"I'd like to keep you at least overnight for observation."

"Overnight, I can do. But I'm going home with my wife tomorrow." I squeeze Natalie's hand. "I have a private gym where I can do my physical therapy. Just let me know if there's anything special needed, and I'll make sure to get it."

"Is he always this bossy, Mrs. Montgomery?"

"You have no idea." She laughs.

Dr. Stevens chuckles. "I think that can be arranged. You've been away from your family long enough. I'll see that you're provided a list of any supplies you'll need for rehab."

Shortly after the doctor leaves, Viktor comes into the room. "Welcome back, boss."

"Good to be back."

"I'm not staying. They told me you were awake, and I wanted to see it for myself." Viktor turns to leave. "I'll be in the waiting room if you need anything."

"Can you call Brandon and have him bring Rose down?"

"No," I interrupt.

"Don't you want to see her?"

"I don't want her to see me like this. It'll scare her," I explain.

"Do you need anything else?" Viktor asks.

I shake my head and wait until he's out of the room, and I'm alone with my wife. Carefully, I slide over and make room for her next to me. "Come here. Let me hold you."

"I don't want to hurt you."

"You won't hurt me. It's been too long. I need to feel you in my arms."

Natalie slips off her shoes and slides into bed next to me. She feels like heaven in my arms. Despite my current state, my body responds to having her close.

"What did he do to you?"

I try to answer her truthfully without telling her the details she doesn't need to know.

"Mostly, he tried to play mind games with me by showing me videos of you and Viktor with the baby. He thought he was torturing me, and I let him believe that, but in reality, it gave me peace seeing that you and Rose were safe."

"We're going to need to talk about that letter you left," she says. "What you asked us to do—"

"But for once, you obeyed," I chuckle. "I thought I was going to die. But knowing you were happy and moving on with Viktor got me through."

"I feel so guilty. Like I betrayed you."

"baby girl, I don't want to hear you talk like that again."

This time, a nurse enters, interrupting our conversation. "I have some medicine for your headache. It's probably going to make you a bit drowsy." She hands me the pills and a glass of cold water. "If you need anything, just hit the red button."

As much as I don't want to let her out of my sight, Natalie's been through a lot today. She killed to save me. That's a lot to deal with. I know that firsthand.

"You should go home and get some rest. I'm sure Rose misses her mama."

"I'm not leaving you." She grabs my hand. "Brandon's with her, and we'll be home tomorrow."

I don't want my daughter to meet me while I'm useless. I can barely stand on my own, and my arms can't hold her. When I see Rose for the first time, I intend to be healthy and strong. If I know my wife, she's going to fight me on this, but that's a bridge we'll cross after I'm home.

"Have you eaten?" I ask, changing the subject.

"No, Sir."

"I need to speak to Viktor. Can you get him?"

"Sure." Natalie disappears down the hall and returns with Viktor by her side.

"What's up, boss?"

"Natalie needs to eat, and I need to speak with you."

"Michael is in the waiting room. I'll send him with Natalie if that's okay?"

"That'll work." Michael more than proved himself in Mexico. I trust him with my life, and that of my wife's as well.

"Can I bring you anything?" Natalie asks.

"No, thank you, baby girl."

Viktor escorts Natalie to Michael before returning to the room and closing the door behind him. We spend some time debriefing everything that's happened over the past twenty-four hours. I feel the drowsiness from the medication, but I fight it. I'm not ready to sleep.

While we're talking, another nurse comes in and hands me a list of the equipment I'll need for my physical therapy program.

The first item on the list is a wheelchair. Knowing that I'll be leaving this place tomorrow, unable to walk on my own, is a difficult pill to swallow. Now, I understand what Stanley went through all those months when he was stuck in a wheelchair.

"I'll be staying in your apartment until I'm back to myself."

"What do you mean?"

"I refuse to meet Rose like this," I explain. "I'll stay in your apartment, so I'm close, but until I can walk, I will not rejoin my family in our home."

"Rose isn't going to care if you can walk or not," Viktor argues.

"I care." I hand him the list. "Can you make sure everything on here gets delivered to the apartment?"

"Yes, boss."

"Wait," I say as he stands to leave. "Thank you for honoring my wishes and caring for my girls while I was gone."

"It's what I promised." He turns and leaves the room.

Viktor was distant, almost cold. His feelings for Natalie are very real. I'm sure my coming back from the dead isn't going to be easy for him.

What kind of mess did I create?

Chapter Seventy-One

VIKTOR

WITH A HEAVY HEART, I SLOWLY MAKE MY WAY OUT OF Alex's room. I fumble with the list, and with shaking hands, I quickly look at it before texting it to Dimitri. He can get started on ordering everything Alex will need.

My mind is racing with a million thoughts, each more painful than the last. As I step into the ICU waiting room, I'm struck by the silence surrounding me. The emptiness of the room mirrors the emptiness in my heart, and I feel myself crumbling under the weight of it all. I slump into one of the chairs, and with tears threatening to spill from my eyes, I put my head in my hands.

The world around me seems to fade away, leaving me alone with my thoughts. I can't help but think about Natalie, the love of my life, and the plans I had for our future. The ring burning a hole in my pocket serves as a painful reminder of what could have been. I was going to propose to her after Moore was taken care of. We were supposed to have forever, but now it feels like nothing but a distant dream.

But that's not all. There's Rose, the precious little girl who, like her mama, owns a piece of my heart. For the past year, I've been the father in her life. Hell, I've been there for her since the day she was born. I cut the cord that connected mother and daughter. The thought of losing Natalie and Rose is almost too much to bear.

I'm lost, confused, and heartbroken. I don't know where to go from here, but one thing is sure—everything has changed, and nothing will ever be the same again.

"You okay?" Michael's voice cuts through my thoughts.

"Where's Natalie?"

"I delivered her safely back to her husband." He sits in the chair next to me. "You look like shit. What's going on?"

Do I tell him? Do I want him to know what a selfish bastard I'm being right now? "Just trying to process all this." I give him the short, uncomplicated answer.

"You mean, you're trying to figure out how to give Natalie back to her husband?"

"Exactly. I feel like shit because I know I should be happy for her instead of wishing Alex was still gone."

"But a part of you does wish that." Michael looks me dead in the eye.

"What kind of person does that make me?"

"A man. One who's in love with a woman he thought he'd get to spend his life with. But then life threw a huge curveball and brought back the man she's supposed to be with."

"I can't do this. There's no way I can go back to just being her bodyguard. I can't just stop loving her."

"That's a lot to process." Michael puts his hand on my shoulder for support.

"I won't stand in the way of Natalie and Alex reuniting, but I also can't stand by and watch it happen. I don't know what to do."

"You don't have to have all the answers tonight," Michael reassures me. "Give yourself some time to process everything. You'll find your way."

The waiting room walls are suffocating me, crushing my chest with each passing second. I feel like I'm trapped in a box, and the mere thought of staying here for another minute makes me want to scream. I can't take it anymore. I need to get out.

I jump to my feet. "I have some calls to make," I say, my voice shaking with emotion. I hurry out of the room, my legs moving faster than my mind can process. I rush to the stairwell, my breath coming in short, sharp gasps. I don't stop until I'm outside, the cool air hitting me like a punch in the gut, and I gasp to take a deep breath.

I know I'm not a good guy. I've killed more people than I can count—all in the name of exacting justice. But just this once, I thought maybe I'd have something good in my life. Natalie was the light in my dark world, the one person who made me believe I could be more than just a killer. I thought I had something good in my life, and now it's all slipping away.

Tears prick at the corners of my eyes as I realize what I have to do. I have to let Natalie go back to her husband, the man she belongs to. It's the right thing to do, I know that. But it hurts, oh God, it hurts so much. It's like a knife in my heart, a reminder that my past sins can never be washed away. I'll never be able to atone for all the lives I've taken, all the pain I've caused. I'll never deserve anything or anyone good in my life.

Once I regain my composure, I look for a quiet place to call Maxim. My hands shake as I dial his number, my mind racing with everything I need to say. But for now, all I can manage is a simple plea.

"Help me, Max," I whisper into the phone. "Please, just help me."

Chapter Seventy-Two

ALEX

"What do you mean you're moving into Viktor's apartment? Would you please tell him he's crazy?" Viktor, who's driving us home, shrugs his shoulders, refusing to get involved. He's barely spoken two words to either of us all day. Something's not right, and I'm sure it has to do with his feelings for Natalie. That's something we're going to have to confront. But right now, I need my wife to accept my plans.

"I won't meet my daughter until I'm healthy and able to walk," I insist.

"This is crazy." She crosses her arms, ready for a fight.

"Natalie, I need you to understand. This is important to me."

It takes a few minutes, but finally, her features soften. "Yes, Sir. I hate that more time is going to pass that Rose won't get to know her daddy."

"It won't be for long. Then we have forever together."

"Forever." She rests her head on my shoulder. "I like the sound of that."

The rest of the car ride home is in silence. I'm certain Viktor and Natalie's thoughts are as heavy as mine. So much has happened while I was gone. This transition isn't going to be easy for any of us.

We pull into the parking garage, and I'm filled with a sense of calm.

Viktor takes my wheelchair from the trunk before opening my door and helping me into it. Despite my protests, Natalie insists on pushing. When we exit the elevator, the feeling of being in familiar surroundings is surreal.

"Dimitri installed a few cameras upstairs so you can see and hear Rose." Viktor turns the TV on, and the screen comes to life. "You can watch all the feeds or choose one to see up close." He chooses a camera that's in Rose's nursery. Brandon's giving her a bottle, rocking her to sleep.

"This is perfect. Please tell him how much I appreciate it." I stare in awe at my daughter.

"I'll be upstairs if you need me." Viktor leaves quietly.

Natalie watches him. Sadness reflects in her eyes.

"He's in love with you."

"I know," she says softly.

"And I think you're in love with him too."

Natalie looks at me. "Alex, I—"

"Shh." I take her hands. "It's okay. I was dead. What happened between you two was exactly what I orchestrated."

"I don't know how to make this easier for him."

"We'll figure it out together."

"Frikr." A sweet little voice comes through the TV, stopping my heart. She holds her little arms out to him.

"There goes her nap," Brandon says with a smile as he passes Rose to Viktor. "Uncle Brandon needs a nap now."

"Can you say bye-bye to Uncle Brandon?"

"Bye-bye, wassup." She opens and closes her chubby little hand.

"Wassup?" I ask, confused.

Natalie laughs. "Ever since she was born, and Brandon would visit, he says *wassup*. Now, that's what she calls him.

No matter how hard we try to get her to call him Uncle Brandon."

"I bet he loves that." I chuckle.

"She can do no wrong in his eyes."

It's only a few minutes before the elevator dings, signaling someone is coming.

"And he can even rise from the dead," Brandon says as he comes into the apartment.

"Brandon." Natalie slaps his shoulder. "So not funny."

"It's all good, baby girl."

Brandon leans down and hugs me. "Seriously, I'm glad you're back."

"So am I."

A soft male voice singing plays through the speakers, and I shift my attention back to the TV. I'm transfixed by the image on the screen. Viktor's sitting in the rocking chair, snuggling Rose. Her tiny hand touches his lips as he sings softly to her.

"He loves that little girl," Brandon says.

I have no words to answer him. My heart's being shredded into pieces watching the two of them together. Viktor and Natalie are in love, and he loves my daughter as if she's his. It's clear Rose loves him just as much. In her eyes, Viktor is her father.

This mess is all my fault. No one ever imagined I'd come back from the dead, and they moved on without me. I'm left wondering if I still have a place in their lives.

"Well, I just wanted to stop and say welcome home," Brandon says. "I'm going to head out."

Natalie reaches out and embraces him. "Thank you so much for taking care of her."

"Anytime."

Natalie's phone rings, and she steps away to answer it.

Once we're alone, Brandon reaches into his pocket and hands me a box. "It's her collar. I took it off, but I've been carrying it with me, not quite sure what to do with it. Now I know why. This belongs to you."

I take the box from him. The absence of her collar and wedding rings suddenly dawns on me, hitting me hard.

After she finishes her call, Natalie walks Brandon to the elevator while I wheel myself into the living room and over to the windows. I'm trying to process what everyone has gone through all these months while they believed I was dead. The heartache my wife must've felt giving birth to our child without me by her side. The pain of waking up every day without each other. I know because I experienced those things, too.

"What's on your mind?"

"Come here," I take her hand and lead her around the chair to sit on my lap. "I'm so sorry I left you."

"Alex." She cups my cheek with her palm. "You don't have to apologize."

"I feel like I do. You've been living, thinking I was dead. I can't imagine how difficult that was."

She closes her eyes. "My world was dark. I was lost." When she opens them, she looks at me with her piercing green stare. "If it wasn't for the baby, I don't know if I would've been able to continue. Rose saved me."

The anguish in her voice cuts deep into my soul.

"I can't imagine what you endured. My psycho ex-boyfriend chained you up in an old panic room. He hurt you. Forced you to watch us live."

"I felt helpless." For the first time since being rescued, I allow myself to feel the emotions I've been holding back. Tears fill my eyes. "While we were being held with Moreno, things looked bleak, but I never gave up hope. But this, I wasn't certain I was going to make it out of there. Every day, Tommy reminded me that he planned to kill me."

Natalie leans forward, her lips meeting mine. "You're back now and never leaving me again," she says between kisses.

Chapter Seventy-Three

∞

NATALIE

LEAVING ALEX BEHIND IS DIFFICULT, BUT I HAVE TO GO upstairs to feed the baby before putting her to bed. Viktor's been transitioning Rose to her crib overnight, but this is the first time since her birth that I've been in the nursery. I know Alex is watching the camera as Rose latches onto my breast. She brings her tiny hand to my mouth, and I shower it with affectionate kisses.

"Your daddy's home, sweet girl," I tell her. "As soon as he's better, you'll meet him." She smiles as though she understands what I'm saying, and milk drips from the corner of her mouth. "He loves you so much."

I look up and see Viktor standing in the doorway. "You can come in, you know." He doesn't move. "Please, Viktor."

Silently, he makes his way into the room. "I was surprised to find you in here."

"Me too. But it feels right."

"My little *printessa,*" Viktor whispers as he gently brushes his hand over Rose's brown curls. His gray eyes fill with tears.

"Nothing needs to change." I place my hand on his.

"Everything's already changed." He pulls away. "I no longer have a place in yours or Rose's life."

"Don't say that." My voice cracks. "You'll always have a place in our lives."

Viktor looks toward the camera mounted on the wall. "Not anymore," he declares with a voice thick with emotion before walking out of the room, leaving behind a trail of heartache and despair.

Tears stream down my face while Rose finishes nursing and drifts into a peaceful slumber. Trembling with emotion, I carefully lift her and lay her down. It's the first time I've placed her in her crib. She looks so tiny.

Me: I'm going to shower and put on pajamas. I'll be down soon.

Alex: Take your time.

After a hot shower, I go in search of Viktor, but he's nowhere to be found. Instead, Dimitri's sitting at the kitchen island, his laptop open.

"Where's Viktor?"

"He left a while ago."

"Left? Where did he go?"

"No idea. He didn't say."

I head back to my bedroom and grab my phone.

Me: Where are you?

Viktor: I'm out.

Me: We need to talk.

Viktor: Not tonight.

Me: Please don't shut me out.

Viktor: I need some space. Dimitri said he'll stay with Rose until I get back. Go to your husband.

I take a deep breath, knowing how badly Viktor's hurting right now because I'm hurting too. No matter how wrong it may be, I'm in love with two men and don't know what to do. How do I keep them both in my life? Because I don't want to lose either of them.

I'm packing an overnight bag to bring some clean pajamas and clothes to Alex. While I'm in our bedroom, I also grab our wedding rings. As I slide mine back onto my finger, a broken piece of me mends back together. I put Alex's ring on my thumb to return it to him.

Before I leave, stop in the kitchen to talk to Dimitri. "Viktor said you'll be here until he gets back?"

"Yes."

"I have the baby monitor app on my phone. If she wakes, I'll be right up."

"No problem," he answers, not taking his eyes from his computer screen.

"Alrighty then. Good night."

"Mhm."

I roll my eyes as I walk away. It's no wonder he's single. No girl can compete with his electronics.

Walking into the downstairs apartment, I hear Alex's deep voice coming from down the hall. It sounds like he's in the office. On the way, I put his clothes and wedding band on the dresser in the guest room.

When he sees me in the doorway, his face lights up. I missed seeing his blue eyes, the same ones his daughter has. After all this time, he still gives me butterflies. Then he hits a button, putting the phone on speaker.

"She just walked in."

"How are you holding up?" Sam asks.

"I think I'm still in shock." I walk over to Alex. "It's truly a miracle."

"Yes, it is. Alex told me what happened. Are you okay?"

He's referring to the fact that I killed Tommy. Something no one's mentioned since Viktor carried me out of the apartment.

While I sat in Alex's hospital room, waiting for him to wake up, the stillness of the room allowed me to relive the moment repeatedly in my mind. I chose to end someone's life, someone I knew and once cared about.

I'm sure I should feel remorse, but no matter how deep I looked for it, I found none. If I were to face the same situation again, I'd make the same decision to pull the trigger.

"I'm okay," I say, knowing I mean the words with all my heart. "Alex is back. That's all that matters."

"Luna and I would like to come in. I want to see you, son."

"Really, Dad?" Alex rolls his eyes.

"Yes, really. I thought you were dead. I need to see for myself that this is real."

"I assure you it is."

"You and Luna are welcome to come as soon as you'd like," I interrupt. "Don't mind my husband. He's being a bit stubborn right now."

That comment earns me a stern look from Alex, but I ignore it and place a kiss on his cheek.

"I'll book a flight and let you know when we'll be arriving. Talk to you soon."

"I don't want them to see—"

I put my finger over his lips, stopping his next words. "No one cares that you're in a wheelchair. It's only temporary while you recover. Your father thought he had lost you. Let him come see you."

"I guess you're right," Alex says and looks down. "I just hate this." He motions to the chair.

Chapter Seventy-Four

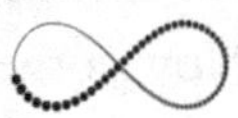

ALEX

Natalie helps wheel me into the bedroom. "I brought some pajamas. I thought you'd appreciate getting cleaned up and into your own clothes."

"That sounds wonderful."

Between the two of us, I'm able to transfer myself from the chair into bed.

"Wait here," Natalie says and disappears into the bathroom. A few minutes later, she comes out with a washcloth, a towel, and a bowl of warm water.

Carefully, she strips my clothes off and begins washing me. It's been so long since I've felt her touch. I'm hard as a rock, desperate for more. Pulling her close, I kiss her. "I need you."

She puts her hand on my chest. "I don't think that's a good idea. The doctor said you need to rest."

"Does it look like I need rest?"

She looks at my dick. It's hard and dripping with precum. "Well, no. But I don't want to hurt you."

"baby girl, you could never hurt me." I try to pull her over my body, but with my limited strength, I'm not successful. She steps away from the bed. "Where are you going?"

"I'm going to give my husband a show," she says as she slowly pulls her nightgown up her legs. Slowly, she exposes her midsection, then her breasts, before removing it entirely and tossing it on the floor.

"You're gorgeous." I'm in awe of my wife.

"I'm afraid my body isn't quite back to where I'd like it."

"Hush. You're perfect. Now come here."

Natalie climbs onto the bed and straddles me. I pull her to me, pressing her breasts against my chest as I kiss her. She rocks against my erection, coating it in her excitement before she pushes herself up. Taking my cock in her hand, she lines it up with her entrance as she slowly lowers herself. I close my eyes and moan as her body envelops mine, inch by inch.

"Don't move, baby girl."

"Am I hurting you?"

"No. But if you move, I'm going to come right now, and I don't want this to end yet."

She smiles seductively and places her palms on my chest. I reach up and take her breasts in my hands, rolling her hard nipples between my fingers. "I've missed you so much."

Natalie moves slowly, lifting and lowering herself onto my hard length. I watch with rapt attention, savoring every second. Having sex with my wife is something I didn't think I'd ever have the chance to enjoy again. She drags her hand down my chest and between her legs. I watch as she plays with her clit and groan in appreciation.

"I'm so close, baby," I growl and grab her hips, taking control of the speed.

I'm a desperate man starving for my wife, aching to climax inside her. It only takes a few thrusts before Natalie throws her head back in ecstasy, her inner muscles squeezing my cock. It's enough to send me over the edge. My orgasm is so intense, I see black at the edge of my vision. I pull her against me as we ride out the waves of our climaxes together. She remains on my chest as we come down from our shared high.

I've used up every ounce of my energy, but don't care. There was no way I would not be inside my wife tonight.

Gently, she pushes herself up. "Are you okay?"

"I've never been better." A yawn escapes, and Natalie slides off me. I immediately miss the warmth of her body.

"Let me finish washing you, and then you need to rest."

"I need you." I reach for her.

"I'm not going anywhere. But physical therapy starts tomorrow. You need some sleep to be ready to work."

As much as I want to take her again, she's right. I'm spent and need to sleep so I can regain my muscle strength. There's a little girl upstairs I'm dying to meet.

Chapter Seventy-Five

NATALIE

I finish Alex's sponge bath and get him into his pajamas.

"You put your rings back on."

"I did," I say and hold up his wedding band.

"How did you get it?"

"The police brought it to me with the rest of your belongings after the explosion."

"Will you put it on for me?" He lifts his hand, and I slide it back onto his finger. Then I crawl into bed next to him. Alex wraps me in his embrace, and we fall asleep, clinging to one another.

My sleep is interrupted all night. Each time I wake up, I'm afraid to open my eyes and find this is just another dream. But it isn't. Every time I check, Alex is still next to me, sleeping soundly.

Rose babbling away on the baby monitor app wakes me. I hate leaving Alex, but I need to feed her. Carefully, I slide out of bed and leave the door cracked open.

"Good morning," Timur says, coffee cup in hand.

"I didn't know you were here."

"I knew you'd need to tend to the baby, and Alex would need help to get dressed and fed. And I'm the best cook among us." He chuckles.

"I appreciate it." I sigh deeply. "I wish Alex would just come home—to *our* home."

"He's a proud man."

"He's being hard-headed."

"Natalie, Alex has been through a terrible ordeal. One he didn't think he'd survive." Timur's tone is patient. "He needs time to process everything."

"I understand, but Rose needs her daddy."

"And she'll have him—forever. Right now, you need to give him a little time. Don't rush him."

"I'll try." Rose's babbles turn into whimpers. I hold up the phone. "Miss Rose is beckoning me. I have to go. Please tell Alex I'll be down at naptime."

"Will do."

When the elevator opens to our apartment, I feel like I've entered Grand Central Station. Michael and his team are in the kitchen, no doubt discussing everything that's happened over the past few days.

"Good morning," Michael says. "Can I get you a coffee?"

"I'd love one, but I have to feed the baby first."

"I'll bring one down to you."

As I get close to the nursery, I hear Viktor's deep timbre as he talks to Rose. I stand just out of sight, listening to him.

"I'm not going to be here much longer, *printessa*. You and your mama don't need me anymore. Your papa's home now. There's no room for me."

"There's always room for you." I make my presence known.

"Mama," Rose squeals.

"Good morning, sweet girl." Viktor passes her to me. "Don't listen to Viktor. He's not going anywhere."

"Natalie, we need to talk." Viktor's tone is serious.

"Pull up a seat," I say as I get comfortable in the rocker to nurse Rose.

"Not here. Not now." Viktor moves toward the door. "Take your time with the baby. We'll talk later."

He disappears before I can say anything. "Men," I say, and look down at Rose. "I don't understand them at all."

Rose rewards me with a smile. Now that she's eating more solid food, she's only nursing first thing in the morning and before bed. Pretty soon, she'll have outgrown this part of her infancy. I savor this time we have together, just her and me.

After she finishes eating, I get dressed for the day, and we join the guys in the kitchen. This time, Viktor's with them, and I hear Maxim's voice coming through the cell phone on speaker in the center of the table.

"Say hi to *Dedushka,* Rose."

"Is that *moya vnuchka?*"

Rose squeals and kicks her legs when she hears Max's voice.

"Yes, it is."

"How are you today?"

"I feel like I'm living in a dream, Max. I'm still afraid to believe it's real."

"It is not a dream, Natalia. You and Alexander deserve your happy ending." Maxim pauses. "We were just discussing relocating Timur's family to New York City."

"I didn't realize Timur was planning to stay here," I say.

"I'll be taking Viktor's place," Timur interjects.

"Why is he taking your place? Where are you going?" I look to Viktor, who's standing off to the side, arms crossed over his chest, but he refuses to look at me. "Where's Viktor going?" No one answers me. "Would someone please tell me what's going on?"

Dimitri picks up the phone and takes it off speaker. He switches to Russian as he talks to Max.

"Viktor?" More silence. "Viktor, please say something."

"Let me take Rose while you two talk." Timur reaches out, and Rose gladly goes with him.

"Can we talk alone?" he asks.

Chapter Seventy-Six

VIKTOR

I lead Natalie to the bedroom we've shared for the past ten months. The room where I've held her every night. To the bed we shared.

"Sit," I instruct her.

She perches on the edge of the bed, her shoulders tight, fingers twisting in the blanket. I drag the armchair closer and sink into it, close enough to see the flicker of panic in her eyes. Natalie stares at me as though searching for the answer I can't give, as though she might pry it out if she looks hard enough. My throat tightens. I don't know how to say this—how to walk away from her when every part of me wants to stay. The silence stretches, heavy, suffocating.

"I don't want you to leave," she whispers, her voice breaking on the words.

"I can't stay," I murmur, forcing the admission past the ache in my chest.

Her breath catches, her eyes wide and shining. "Why not?" she demands, too quickly, as if sheer urgency might change my mind. "Nothing has to change." Her voice climbs, edged with desperation.

I drop my head into my hands, her words echoing in my chest. *Nothing has to change.*

If only she understood—everything already has. The ground shifted the moment I let her in, and nothing will ever be the same again.

Slowly, I lift my head, forcing myself to meet her gaze.

"The day we thought Alex died was the day I started to fulfill Alex's request of me. It was the day I took all my feelings for you, the ones I kept locked away, and allowed myself to love you for the first time. But Alex isn't dead anymore, and you aren't mine to love."

"But—"

"Let me finish," I cut her off. "Your eyes sparkle again, something I haven't seen since Alex left. I can't compete with that, and I'd never ask you to choose between us. He's your forever." I reach out and wipe a tear from Natalie's face. "I can't stay because I can't stop loving you."

"I know I'm being selfish asking you to stay, but I can't help it. I love you too and don't want to lose you."

"You'll never lose me. If you ever need me, I'll be there. But I can't be here every day and watch you in Alex's arms—even if that's where you belong."

"You promised me you'd never leave. That you'd always be here," she cries. "Was that a lie?"

"No, sweetheart. It wasn't a lie." I reach into my pocket and pull out the ring I've been carrying with me. "I bought this for you. I was planning to ask you to marry me after we took care of Moore."

"It's beautiful," she says through her tears.

"I was going to promise you forever. But it wasn't meant to be." I put the ring back into my pocket. Taking Natalie's hand in mine, I stand and pull her to her feet. "For ten months, I was the luckiest man on earth. I had the honor of loving you and having your love in return. I'll never forget what we had. I love you, Natalie. I always will." I lower my face, my lips meeting hers. Tears spill from my eyes as she grants me a final kiss.

"I love you, Viktor." She holds my face in her hands. "There's a piece of my heart that will forever be yours."

Her words sear into my heart, and I have to hurry from the room while I still have some sense of composure. I close the door and hear her crying on the other side.

It takes everything I have in me to walk away from her. Maxim's jet is waiting at JFK to take me back to Russia, but I need to talk to Alex before I leave.

Chapter Seventy-Seven

NATALIE

"I LOVE YOU, NATALIE. I ALWAYS WILL."

Viktor's words will forever be etched in my heart. My trembling hand touches my lips where he just kissed me. The depth of his love and heartache was palpable, seeping into every fiber of my being. Viktor is an incredible man who's selfless and caring. His love was the very glue that held me together. His arms were the safety I clung to.

But now, as I stand at the crossroads of my heart, I am forced to confront a harsh reality. Each time I tried to take the next step in our relationship, something held me back—that something was Alex. Even though I love them both, I know in my heart that I can't have them both. It's a selfish thought to wish for, and the harsh truth is that I must choose between them.

My heart is heavy with the weight of this decision, and I know that whatever I choose will shatter one man's heart. Yet, despite the pain, I know I'll always choose Alex. He is my true love, my soulmate, and the one who has always held the key to my heart. It's a choice that breaks me, but I know it's the right one.

I take a shower, allowing myself to purge all these overwhelming emotions. After I've dried and dressed, I feel a bit better. When I go into the living room, I find Timur playing with Rose.

"Where did everyone go?"

"They've left for the airport." Timur looks at me, compassion in his gaze. "Are you okay?"

"I don't know." I sink onto the couch, willing the tears not to fall again.

"He'll be okay. He needs time." Timur moves from the floor to sit beside me on the sofa.

"I want them both in my life. I don't want him to leave." Rose toddles over, holding her arms out to me. "The pain in his eyes when he said goodbye physically hurt. I never meant for any of this to happen. Viktor doesn't deserve to have his heart broken. He's a good man, but Alex is my husband. I—"

"Viktor would never ask you to choose him over Alex," Timur interrupts me mid-sentence. "He loves you. Enough to set you free to return to the man you belong with. Somewhere out there is a woman who'll return all the love Viktor has to give. When the time is right, he'll meet her."

I snuggle Rose and kiss the top of her head. "Please don't misunderstand. Alex coming back to me is a miracle, something I never imagined. But Viktor's leaving is a huge loss." I look to Timur. "Viktor's been an important part of my life. We've shared so much together. I love Viktor, but not in the same way I love Alex. At the same time, I don't know how to move forward without him."

"One step at a time. That's all anyone expects." Timur offers me a kind smile. "Alex is certain to have hurdles to overcome, and he's going to need you. He's been through quite an ordeal. You and he need time to get reacquainted with each other." Timur reaches out and takes Rose's tiny hand in his. "And there's this little princess. She still has to meet her daddy and form a bond with him."

"Right now, everything feels so overwhelming. What do I do first? How do I move past this?"

"I hope I'm not overstepping with my next statement," Timur says cautiously. "But have you spoken with your therapist?"

"No. Not since Alex came back," I admit. "She's tried calling, but I didn't answer."

"May I suggest you take a few minutes to connect with her before you go to Alex? I'll keep Rose this afternoon. You need to take some time to care for yourself."

"Are you sure?"

Timur scoops Rose from my lap. "I have four *mladensty* of my own. I think I can handle one little one for a day."

I lean over and give Timur a peck on the cheek. "Thank you for talking with me."

I think about his words while I go to Alex's office to call Yekaterina. First, I owe her an apology for ignoring her, and then I'm hoping she'll be able to help me sort through this crazy mess of emotions.

Chapter Seventy-Eight

VIKTOR

After I say goodbye to Natalie, I take a few minutes to compose myself before heading downstairs to Alex. Before I leave, we need to talk. I have to be honest with him about everything that's happened between Natalie and me before I leave.

I've known Alex for many years. He's more than just my boss. He's my friend. And as brutal as this will be, it's something I must do. I hope my relationship with his wife hasn't screwed our friendship up for good.

When I get to the apartment, I find him and Misha eating a late breakfast at the kitchen table.

"Care to join us?" Alex asks. "Timur made enough for an army."

"No thanks. I only have a few minutes." I look around nervously. "I was hoping we could talk."

Misha grabs his plate. "I have some work to do. I'll be in the office if you need me."

I wait until I hear the door close before sitting across from Alex. "You look much better today." His color's coming back, and he already looks stronger.

"A good night's sleep and some food will do that." He studies me for a minute. "But I don't think you came to talk about how good I look."

"No. I didn't. I—"

"Before you say anything," Alex interrupts. "While Tommy was holding me, he tried torturing me by showing me pictures and videos of you and Natalie together." I remain quiet, not sure how to respond. Alex continues, "What he didn't realize was that showing me those videos was what got me through. It meant you were both doing what I asked. Natalie and Rose were safe and loved."

"I don't know what to say." Words usually come easily to me, but now they're gone, scattered like ash. How do I tell a man that being given the chance to love his wife has been the greatest gift of my life?

"I know how much you love her. I see it every time you look at her. And I know my coming back has complicated everything." Alex exhales, the weight of it heavy in his voice. "Sometimes I wonder if coming back into her life was a mistake. She loves you. Rose is bonded with you. Maybe... Maybe they'd be better off without me."

"You're wrong. Natalie loves me, yes, but I'm her second choice. She'll never love me the way she does you. I don't want to leave her. I want to make her mine and keep her forever," I confess. "But I can't do that. You're her heart. Her whole world. When she thought you were dead—"

My mind drifts back to the day we got the news of the explosion. The light in her eyes went out. I genuinely believe that if it wasn't for Rose, she might have tried to end it then. But once Rose came, Natalie had a purpose to get up every day.

There was still an empty place in her heart that I could never fill, no matter how much love I gave her. That place was never meant for me. Sure, she loved me, and we were good together. But I know she'll never look at me the same way she looks at Alex. He's her destiny—her forever.

"I need to tell you everything that happened between Natalie and me. The things you didn't see on Tommy's camera."

Talking to another man and telling him the intimate moments you've shared with his wife is the hardest conversation I've ever had. While I speak, I try to avoid looking Alex in the eye because the pain I see there is too much. Alex remains calm throughout everything I have to tell him. When I'm done, he says nothing for a few tense minutes.

"I know that wasn't easy for you to say, and it was equally difficult to hear, but I am grateful for your honesty," Alex says. "That's exactly why I chose you. You're a good man, Viktor. I'll never forget what you've done for my family and me."

How do I respond to that? Do I thank him? No response feels appropriate. "I wanted to know everything before I leave."

"You're leaving?"

"I have to." I look him in the eye, willing to accept whatever punishment he might give. "Alex, I'm in love with your wife. I can't and don't want to stop loving her."

"Does Natalie know?"

"Yes."

"And?"

"She begged me to stay, but I can't. There isn't room for both of us, and she belongs with you. Timur will be staying on in my place."

"I see." Alex's eyes fill with tears. "Words can't express my gratitude for how much love you showed them both in my absence."

"There were days I hated you for asking that of us," I confess, my throat tightening around the words. "But I can't deny what it gave me. I'd never known what it was to be in a relationship. I'd never felt the love of a woman. And then I had ten months with her. Ten months of loving her and feeling her love in return. That was the greatest honor of my life." My voice cracks, and I swallow hard before finishing. "She's extraordinary. And you're one hell of a lucky man."

. . .

I stand, my chest heavy.

"I'll never forget what you've done for me. For us." Alex's voice is steady, but the weight behind it is unmistakable. He extends his hand, and I clasp it firmly. His grip tightens, holding me in place a moment longer than expected.

"Promise me you'll keep in touch," he says quietly, his eyes searching mine.

"Will do, boss," I manage, forcing the words out even though I know they're a lie. Keeping in touch isn't an option. I need a clean break, no lingering ties.

The elevator ride feels endless and far too quick all at once, carrying me down to the underground parking garage for the last time. The black SUV waits, engine humming, Michael and the rest of the team already inside. I slide into the passenger seat, the leather cold against me.

"You good?" Michael asks, his voice low, searching.

I nod once, unable to trust my voice. The dam inside me trembles, dangerously close to breaking, and I know if I speak, everything I've been holding back will come pouring out.

As Michael drives us to the airport, I sit in silence, gazing out the window while the men in the back talk amongst themselves. None of them makes an effort to draw me into their discussion.

When we reach the tarmac, Maxim's plane is already waiting for us. Each man grabs their luggage and proceeds to board the plane, anxious to return home. Yet, I find myself frozen beside the SUV. I'm at a crossroads. I must choose between boarding the plane and flying to the other side of the globe, away from the woman I love and the little girl who has become my own, or returning to Natalie and begging her to choose me.

"What's going on?" Michael stands beside me.

"Just debating my options."

"You know she's meant to be with him. Your only option is to get on the plane and set her free. You need to give yourself permission to be free as well," Michael says as he walks away.

His words echo in my head. *Set her free.* She was never mine to keep. I close my eyes and take a deep breath before steeling my shoulders and walking to the jet. I climb the steps and resist the urge to turn around, fearing I won't get on the plane.

It isn't long before we're taxiing down the runway. Then, finally, the plane's wheels lift from the ground, and I'm on my way back to my home country.

Tears fall, knowing a piece of my heart will always belong to Natalie.

Chapter Seventy-Nine

NATALIE

"IT'S OKAY TO ADMIT YOU HAVE FEELINGS FOR HIM," Yekaterina says.

"Knowing Alex was alive all that time. Kat, I feel like I cheated on him. We slept together every night. I let myself fall in love with him," I confess. "We came very close to having sex."

"Natalie, this situation is far from what anyone would call normal. Nothing that happened between you and Viktor was wrong. Look at me," she instructs. I look up at the camera. "Be honest with Alex. He's a reasonable man."

Her comment makes me laugh through my tears. "Reasonable, usually. Possessive and dominant—always. I'm afraid of what Alex's reaction will be when I tell him everything."

"Remember, it was Alex's wish for you and Viktor to be together. No one could've envisioned the twist this situation would take."

She's right. My husband literally came back from the dead. That goes far beyond anything imaginable. What a complicated mess this is.

"Natalie," Yekaterina's tone turns serious. "Are you struggling because you want to be with Viktor?"

"I have no doubt that I want to be with my husband. I love Alex. He's my world. The fact that we have this second chance is nothing if not a miracle. And I know this is selfish, but I love Viktor, and I want him, too. I don't want him to leave."

"Because you care about him, that is why you must let him go. It's the only way you'll be able to reconnect and move forward with Alex. More importantly, it's the only way Viktor will be able to heal his broken heart and move on," she says sympathetically. "You have Alex and Rose. Viktor is alone. He'll be okay. But he needs distance and time."

"As hard as it is, I do know that. Hopefully, one day, we can continue our friendship."

"One step at a time, honey." She smiles. "Now, take a few deep breaths and go to your husband."

"Thank you for taking my call."

"We'll talk again in a day or two. But if you need me before then, don't hesitate to text."

I disconnect the video chat and take a few cleansing breaths before leaving the office.

Timur's just exiting Rose's nursery. "She's all fed and napping soundly."

"Thank you, Timur. I'm going downstairs with Alex. He should be finishing up his physical therapy session. If you need me, just text. I'll have my phone."

When I get downstairs, I hear noises from the gym. Alex must not be done with therapy yet. Not wanting to interrupt, I stand quietly in the doorway and watch. Alex is lying on a mat while his therapist rotates and stretches his leg.

"I can see you in the mirror," Alex says. "Come in."

"I didn't want to interrupt."

"Natalie, this is Craig. Craig, this is my wife, Natalie."

"Pleased to meet you," Craig says. "Alex hasn't stopped talking about you since I got here."

A blush creeps over my cheeks. "It's nice to meet you, too."

While he continues stretching Alex's legs, he explains what the recovery plan will look like.

"Alex is lucky he was in such good shape before all this. It means he hasn't lost too much muscle tone, and what was lost will come right back with exercise. The biggest issue we have to deal with is atrophy. These stretches will help with that," Craig explains. "It won't take long for him to walk independently, but he'll need to not overdo it. His muscles won't be completely back to normal for about six weeks."

"Is there anything I can do to help on the days you aren't here?"

"I'm leaving instructions with the stretches and exercises he'll need to do daily."

I take the papers Craig hands me and start flipping through them. While I'm reading, Craig helps Alex from the mat and onto a chair next to me.

"Alex is strong enough that I think we can get rid of the wheelchair. I brought a walker that he can use in the house. He can use the chair if he gets tired, but I'd like to see him up and moving as much as possible."

"I won't be using the chair," Alex interjects.

"Don't push yourself too hard, or you'll just set your recovery back."

Alex waves him off, and I giggle.

"Well, that's everything for today. You did well."

Alex grabs the walker and stands, holding onto it. We take a slow walk down the hall to see Craig out.

Chapter Eighty

ALEX

Once Craig leaves and we're alone, I turn to
Natalie. "You've been crying."

"It's that obvious?"

"We need to talk," Natalie says.

As we walk to the living room, I'm awkward and uncoordi-
nated, but I eventually settle onto the sofa independently. In the
silence of the room, Natalie fidgets with her fingers, and I can
sense that saying goodbye to Viktor was as hard for her as it was
for him. Although we need to address the situation, I don't want
to force her to speak about it. I'm hoping she'll open up to me of
her own accord.

"Viktor and I shared a bed every night for months. He held
me while we slept. I let him kiss me—touch me. We never had sex,
but we came very close. I fell in love with him," she confesses as
her tears fall.

Even though I already knew everything, hearing it from
Natalie is like another punch to the gut, and I have to force myself
not to react.

Since I spoke to Viktor earlier, I've been struggling to temper the jealous, possessive Dominant in me who wants to express the rage I feel knowing another man touched my wife. It's hard to hear, but I have no right to be angry. I'm the one who gave them permission to be together. They had no idea I was alive.

"When he said goodbye earlier, he kissed me. And I let him." Tears pour down her face. "I'm sorry. I feel so guilty for allowing it."

I pull her to me and hold her tight. She nestles her head on my chest. "Neither of you did anything wrong," I say quietly. "The circumstance we all found ourselves in was unimaginable."

"I feel like I cheated on you," she cries.

"I don't ever want to hear you say that. You did no such thing." Taking her by the shoulders, I pull her back to see her face. "What you and Viktor feel for one another, whatever happened between you, is okay. I understand."

"You do?"

"It was my doing that put you both in that situation. But I also have faith in us." I use my thumbs to wipe her tears. "We have a once-in-a-lifetime love that nothing and no one can come between."

"I kept dreaming about you. The dreams were so real I'd wake up expecting to find you next to me, but you weren't there. I'm so afraid this is a dream, and I'm going to wake up, and you'll be gone again."

"baby girl, this isn't a dream, and I'm not going anywhere."

The next couple of weeks are filled with intense physical therapy sessions. Each day, I work harder than I did before. I'm pushing all of my limits. Natalie's no longer allowed to help with my therapy because she gets too nervous seeing me struggle. Instead, Misha and Timur take turns working out with me. What makes me work so hard? My daughter lives one floor above me, and she doesn't even know I exist.

That's why today's a big day. I woke early and am watching the monitor. Rose just woke up Natalie. They're lying in bed while Natalie nurses her.

It's time.

The elevator doors open, and for the first time in almost a year, I'm finally home.

"Alex," Timur says when he sees me walk in.

"Shh. I want to surprise Natalie."

"It's good to see you home, boss." Timur gives me a quick hug. "I was just about to leave for the airport. My wife and kids will be here in a few hours."

"Go, spend the day with your family. I plan to do the same."

"Misha went out for an early morning run, but I expect him back any minute. I'll instruct him to stay downstairs."

As I near the bedroom, I hear Natalie talking to Rose. She's telling her what they're going to do today, including a walk to the park.

"I'd love to accompany you ladies," I say as I walk into the room.

"Alex," Natalie exclaims. "You're here, and you're walking on your own. Why didn't you tell me?"

"Because I wanted to see the look on your face."

Rose, who's still nursing, tries to look around without unlatching from Natalie's breast. I walk over to the bed and sit next to Natalie.

For the first time, I lay eyes on my daughter. She's so beautiful. She takes my breath away. Rose makes eye contact with me, and I see familiar dark blue eyes looking back. When she smiles, milk drips down her face. Natalie adjusts Rose's position, sitting her up. It's then that my world comes to a screeching halt.

"Dada," Rose says and reaches her arms out to me.

I take my daughter in my arms. Her tiny hands come to my face, and she places a wet kiss on my nose. I can't help the tears that fall down my face. When I look over at Natalie, she's also crying. "How does she know?" I ask.

"She heard your voice for months while she was inside me. Since she was born, I showed her your pictures and told her stories about you."

"Dada. Dada," Rose says again and giggles. Her laugh is perfect and fills my soul with a love I've never known.

"Yes, sweet girl. I'm your Daddy." I kiss her chubby cheeks. "And I love you very much."

Rose and I continue our Daddy/daughter time while Natalie showers. Although I've missed the first ten months of her life, right now, it doesn't feel as though I've missed a second. The magnitude of unconditional love I have for my daughter is indescribable.

"I promise Daddy will never leave you again."

Chapter Eighty-One

NATALIE

Misha stays a few steps behind, allowing us the space we need to bond as a family. His watchful gaze, constantly scanning the surroundings for any sign of danger, makes me feel secure and safe. It's a different feeling than when Viktor was with us. I can't help the tinge of sadness I still feel at losing him. It'll take some time, but I trust we'll adjust to our new normal.

My heart swells with emotion as I watch Rose and Alex play together on the swing set. I'm still in complete awe of how Rose immediately knew who Alex was and how strong their connection is. It fills me with indescribable joy. Alex pushes Rose gently in the baby swing. She giggles uncontrollably each time she gets near, and he tickles her little feet. I snap picture after picture, wanting to capture this moment and hold on to it forever.

As I sit on the bench basking in the warmth of my family's love, my cell phone buzzes in my hand. It's my mom. I haven't heard from her since they walked out of the cottage months ago, and I feel torn about whether to answer. I don't want anything to ruin this perfect moment. Something in me decides to take the call, and I answer with a shaky hand, bracing myself for whatever news may come my way.

Not knowing how this conversation is going to play out, I walk away from where Alex and Rose are playing so I don't interrupt them. "Hello?"

"Natalie, it's Mom." I don't speak. I have nothing to say to her. "I had to call you. I just hung up with Delia Laurel. She told me Tommy's dead."

I hear her sniffle. She's crying. How do I respond to that? Do I tell her the truth? That I'm the one who took Tommy's life, and I'm happy I did. That I'd do it all over again. I don't get a chance to respond because she continues talking.

"Oh, Natalie. I'm so sorry for how I behaved when you were here. I was out of line and had no right to judge you or Viktor."

I hear her apology, but that does little to lower my defenses. "No, you didn't."

"Dad and I have talked about it at great length. It's not up to us to tell you how to grieve your husband or how you should move forward. Or who you should move forward with."

She doesn't know Alex is alive. This is a genuine apology. But why? "I appreciate your support, but why the sudden change of heart?" I struggle to keep my icy tone under control.

"Talking to Delia brought back so many memories. So many of the emotions we experienced when your brother died. Delia loved Tommy as if he were her own child. She knows she made mistakes with him. Natalie, we made so many mistakes when Michael told us who he loved. If only we'd done things differently. Looked past our own prejudices and accepted how much Michael loved Evan. He'd still be with us." She pauses, trying to control her sobbing.

"We've been doing the same thing with you—making the same mistakes. It's taken another tragedy for us to realize that we don't want history to keep repeating itself. Dad and I know it's us who must change. We're going to do things differently from now on. We just hope it's not too late. We want to spend more time with you and Viktor."

I find the nearest bench, needing to sit. I hate that it's taken another tragedy for my parents to finally see reason, but I accept it, nonetheless. "Is Dad with you?"

"Yes, dear. He's right here."

"Can you put the phone on speaker and maybe sit down? I have something I need to tell you."

I hear the scuffle of her pulling out a kitchen chair and sitting down.

"You're on speaker."

I look up and see Alex walking toward me with Rose in his arms. I mouth *it's my parents* to him. Quietly, he sits next to me with Rose on his lap. She reaches for the phone.

"Fikr?"

"No, Rose, it's Grandma and Grandpa."

"Is that my little granddaughter?" Dad asks.

"It sure is. It's a beautiful day, and there won't be many more before it gets cold, so we came to the park to play."

"Gampa," Rose says, leaning into the phone.

"She said my name," Dad says proudly. "Did you hear that, Char?"

"I did. Rose, can you say Grandma?" Rose's attention has already moved on, and she's watching a group of children running by.

"I want you both to know I forgive you and that I, too, hope we can move forward and do better." I grab Alex's hand. "There's something else I need to tell you. Something that's kind of unbelievable and nothing short of a miracle."

"Go ahead," Dad says hesitantly.

I don't know how to say it, so I blurt it out. "Alex is alive."

"What did you say?" Mom asks.

"Alex is alive. He's sitting here next to me." There's no reaction from either of my parents. "Are you guys there?"

"We're here," Mom says. "But I don't understand."

"It's a complicated story, Charlotte," Alex adds.

"Alexander? Is that really you?"

"Alive and in the flesh." He laughs.

"How?"

"As Alex said, it's a complicated story. One I don't think we should discuss over the phone."

"Did Thomas Moore have something to do with this?" Dad asks.

I look to Alex, unsure how to answer Dad's question. "He did," Alex says. "Tommy got mixed up with the wrong crowd and then tried to take his revenge on me for marrying Natalie. Unfortunately, it's this situation that led to his death."

"Delia said he was shot. It was during a break-in, but she asked them not to tell her any more details," Dad explains. "Did you—"

"No, it wasn't me who shot him," Alex interrupts. "I have no idea who did it."

I look at Alex and shake my head. I don't want him to lie for me, but he puts his finger to my lips, silencing me.

"I'm sorry for whatever Tommy did, son. We're mighty glad you're still with us."

"Me too, sir."

"And Viktor?" Dad asks. "I know how much he cares for Natalie and the baby. How's he handling all this?"

"He's decided to return to Russia. I'm sure you understand," Alex explains. "We have new security in place."

"I still don't understand why you need security?" Mom questions.

"It's just a precaution. Being a successful business owner and now having the women's shelter can attract unwanted attention. Can't be too safe where Natalie and Rose are concerned."

"Well, that makes sense," Mom agrees.

"Rose is getting sleepy, so we need to head back home. We'll make plans to visit soon."

"Please do," Dad says. "And welcome home, son."

"That was unexpected," I say when we hang up.

"Everything has a way of working itself out." Alex leans over and kisses me.

Once he gets Rose buckled in her stroller, we begin walking back to our apartment.

The phone call and apology came as a complete surprise. But I'm grateful to have everything and everyone I love back in my life. This time, I hope it's for good.

Chapter Eighty-Two

ALEX

ONE YEAR EARLIER...

Brandon buzzes me into his apartment building. Today's our final online class with Master Kiyoshi. I get to his door and knock.

"You're late," he says as he pulls the door open.

I finish my text and look up. "What the hell?" Standing in front of me is my best friend, I think.

"A little birdy told me you preferred blondes," Brandon says as he fluffs a long blond wig. He steps aside, but I don't move to go in. "What are you waiting for, handsome?"

"What's wrong with you?" I take a few tentative steps into his apartment.

Brandon's wearing gym shorts and a woman's maternity shirt with a pillow stuffed under it. He's lost his ever-loving mind.

"We're practicing Shibari for your pregnant wife. How can we do that without you having someone pregnant to practice on?"

I can't hold it back, and I double over laughing. "You are one crazy son of a bitch, you know that?"

"Just devoted to the cause, brother."

As we walk to his office, Brandon puts his hand on his back, acting as if he's heavily pregnant. What he doesn't know is I'm recording him. He pulls out his desk chair and gives his best impression of a pregnant woman sitting down. I can't wait to see Master Kiyoshi's reaction to my insane friend.

Brandon pulls up the website and logs into our video meeting room. Master Kiyoshi joins us a few minutes later. His eyes grow wide when he sees a blond-haired Brandon.

Trying to maintain his composure, he greets us. "Good afternoon. Are you ready for our last class?"

"Yes, sir. I am."

"Let's start with the first binding. I'll give you any necessary corrections as you work." Brandon stands, and Master Kiyoshi gets the full view of his body. The always quiet and serious Shibari Master breaks into hysterical laughter. "Brandon, may I ask what you're doing dressed like that?"

"You must be mistaken. My name is Natalie," he says in a high-pitched voice.

"What is going on?" Master Kiyoshi asks, clearly confused.

"Alex needs to practice on a pregnant woman, and since we don't know any," He does a little twirl, "I've transformed into one."

Tears roll down Master Kiyoshi's face as he listens to Brandon's explanation. Brandon looks back at me and sees my cell out, taping this entire spectacle.

"Oh no, you don't." Brandon takes a swipe at the camera. "Shut that thing off."

"Natalie dear, don't get yourself all worked up. It's not good for the baby," I say, laughing. "We want to preserve these moments to show our little girl one day. Now stand still like a good girl and let your Dominant tie you up."

"Alex, stop recording right now," Brandon protests.

"Be a good little sub and stay quiet, or I'll have to gag you," I threaten my friend. "On second thought, keep talking. Gagging you will make this video even better."

Brandon pulls the pillow out from under his shirt and takes a swing at me.

Master Kiyoshi is clearly entertained by our banter. He hasn't stopped laughing.

It takes a while for Brandon and me to compose ourselves, but finally, Brandon ditches the wig and the woman's shirt, and we get to work.

In the end, the Shibari Master is pleased with my technique. This is going to be the perfect Christmas present.

Chapter Eighty-Three

ALEX

PRESENT DAY...

It's been nearly a month, but I've finally recovered to my post-almost-death health. I've held off on collaring Natalie until I felt strong enough physically and emotionally to be the Dominant she deserves.

She's just put Rose down to sleep for the night and is on her way back to our bedroom, where I'm waiting for her with her collar laid out on the bed. She gasps when she steps across the threshold to our room.

"Close the door behind you and strip, baby girl."

"Yes, Sir."

She shuts the door quietly and begins a sexy striptease for me, starting with my favorite pair of gray leggings that hug her curves. Slowly, she slides them down her legs before she kicks them out of the way. Then she grabs the hem of her light pink T-shirt and slides it up her abdomen and over her lace-covered breasts. Her shirt soon joins her pants in a pile on the floor. She bites her lip and turns around. I'm treated to a sexy view of Natalie's ass in a black thong. My erection strains against my zipper, aching to sink into her. Then, with a quick look over her shoulder, she unhooks her bra, letting it fall to the ground.

I can't wait any longer and come behind her, wrapping my arms around her, my hands going straight for her breasts. She rests her head back on my chest as she moans quietly. I slide one hand down her taut abdomen and into her panties. Feeling impatient, I grab the side of the fabric and tug, tearing it and tossing it to the side.

"They were one of my favorites," she pouts.

"I'll buy you new ones." My mouth descends on her neck, sucking and biting my way down while I tease her clit with my finger. "Tonight's a night we've both been waiting for. I'm going to put my collar back around your neck where it belongs."

Natalie smiles. "I've waited for this moment, Sir."

"Kneel," I command. Natalie turns to face me and lowers herself to the floor, her legs slightly open and her gaze down. My beautiful submissive. I lift her collar from the bed and hold it in my hand. "Look at me."

She lifts her face. I'm in awe that this woman is mine. That, against all odds, I've made it back to her once more.

With trembling hands and a heart full of emotion, I begin speaking, "Just a few weeks ago, I didn't think I'd ever see you again. I thought all hope was lost. But fate, or perhaps the universe itself, has granted me a precious gift, a chance to hold you again and feel your presence by my side." My emotions are overwhelming, and I struggle to find the right words.

"Now, I stand before you, ready to offer myself to you once again. To be your husband, your protector, and your Dominant. I'm asking for your trust and your submission. I'm offering you a symbol of our bond. With it comes my solemn promise of unwavering devotion, unconditional love, and steadfast support. And so, I ask, would you do me the incredible honor of accepting my collar and gifting me with your submission?"

"I would love nothing more, Sir."

I place the collar around her neck and connect the two ends of the chain with a lock, then I kneel before her—a Dominant, a man, humbled by the love of this woman. "Everything I have, everything I am, and everything I will be, is yours."

With her collar back in place, she's never looked more radiant.

"I have a gift for you," I say as I get to my feet. "Wait here." Making my way into our closet, I grab the box Brandon brought over earlier and the bouquet of white roses I hid in here. When I return, I set the box, wrapped in Christmas paper, on the bed and lay the roses next to it before helping Natalie to her feet.

"What is it?" she asks.

"This was supposed to be your gift from me last Christmas. Brandon's been holding onto it all this time. Open it."

Natalie grabs the box and tears at the paper. Excitement sparkles in her emerald eyes. She removes the lid and begins pulling out the contents—ropes of varying shades of pink and my camera. "What's all this for?"

"I read that women in their final trimester of pregnancy often don't see their beauty. I planned a Shibari photoshoot to highlight how incredibly beautiful you were carrying our child."

"I had no idea." Sadness washes over her face. "That would've been incredible."

"You may not be pregnant now, but tonight's a special night for us. We're reconnecting as a Dominant and his submissive. Will you allow me to use you as my canvas?"

"It would be my honor, Sir."

With a couple of touches on my phone, soft music plays through the speakers in our bedroom, setting the mood. I begin by braiding Natalie's long blonde curls and weaving a rope into them. Then, I place three pieces of thin rope around her neck, like a necklace, being careful not to catch her collar. I braid the ropes between her breasts and down over her abdomen. Had she still been carrying my child, I would have split the rope around her tummy. Tonight, I continue to her waist, bringing it around her body to create a harness.

I caress her skin, ensuring an intimate connection with my submissive as I wrap the rope around her breasts. Her nipples harden with each pass. I finish by connecting this to the harness at her waist. Because she's no longer pregnant, I'm free to alter my design. "I need you to turn around and put your arms behind your back," I instruct.

Then, with the same braiding technique, I wrap her upper arms in rope and work down to her wrists. This rope is woven in and out of the ties going down her back, restraining her arms behind her. I pause to look over my work and check in with my submissive. "What's your color?"

"Green, Sir."

"You may stop me at any time if anything is uncomfortable," I remind her.

"Yes, Sir. I understand.

After securing her arms, I use a heavier rope as a harness around her waist, leaving a long tail. "This will be for the suspension."

"How did Master Kyoshi teach you suspension over video lessons?"

"I had a willing volunteer to practice on."

As soon as the words leave my mouth, I see the jealousy on her face. "A volunteer?"

"Well, a semi-willing volunteer." I grin. "Don't get yourself all upset. It was only Brandon."

"Brandon? There must be a story behind that."

"He put his all into it—I have the video to prove it. We'll watch it another day. But, for now, no more talking."

She nods, letting me know she understands.

I help her lie down on the floor so I can work on her legs. Taking her left leg, I bend it at the knee and use the same braided design to hold it in place. With her leg secure, I slide a rope beneath the restraint. It will also be used to connect to the suspension ropes.

"Are you ready?"

"I can't wait."

Carefully, I attach the ends of her rope harness to a pulley system connected to the heavy-duty clip that's permanently fixed on our ceiling. Then, ever so slowly, I pull the ropes, and her body rises off the floor.

"Color?"

"Yellow. Can you adjust the suspension ropes around my waist?"

I spread the ropes out, so the pressure is more even.

"That's much better, Sir. Thank you."

I lean in to kiss her. "Almost done."

The final rope is braided around her right ankle. I pull on the rope gently, drawing her foot back, and attach it to the rope that's entwined in her braid. Then, I pull her body up the rest of the way.

Hanging nearly inverted, her legs bend and spread slightly. Her back arches, so her breasts push out—she's the picture of grace and beauty.

The last thing I do is take the white roses I had dethorned and slide them through the braided rope in the middle of her breasts.

"Do you know how incredibly gorgeous you look right now?"

She rewards me with a contented smile.

Grabbing my camera, I begin snapping pictures. I plan to capture her from every angle to avoid missing anything. The longer her body remains weightless, the more she relaxes until she's floating in subspace.

After finishing my photographs, I step back to admire her for a few moments longer.

"Natalie," I whisper, pulling her from her bliss. "I'm going to bring you down now."

"Mhm," she says softly.

Once she's back on the floor, I begin untying her with the same love and care I put into the initial ties.

During my absence, I felt so far from Natalie. Our connection was broken and desperately missed. But right now, our breaths are in sync as I allow my fingers to caress her skin while I remove the ropes.

Shibari's an incredibly sensual and intimate process, which is why I chose it for our first scene. I knew it would provide the sexual connection we crave and the emotional connection that makes our relationship so very special.

I lift her from the floor and cradle her against me as I carry her to the bed. Then, gently, I set her on top of the white comforter. Her eyes never leave mine while I remove my pants and boxers.

I've been hard for her from the moment she walked into the room. It's taken every ounce of my self-control not to rush this evening. Kneeling beside her, I explore her body with my hands and mouth—reacquainting myself with every inch of her.

We've been together since I've been back. But tonight, we're no longer just husband and wife, but also Dominant and submissive—our relationship whole once again.

I lower myself over her, kissing her lips, my tongue meeting no resistance. She opens her legs, allowing me entrance into her body. Once fully sheathed, I pause, memorizing the feeling of being inside her.

"I need You, Sir," she whispers between kisses.

"You have all of me, baby girl. Every heartbeat, every breath is for you."

Slow and sensual. I make love to Natalie. Each touch, each kiss meant to erase the terror of the past, replacing it with sweet promises of our future.

From that very first time I saw her across the room at Fire and Ice, I knew we were destined for each other. We were both terrified and tried to fight it, but destiny cannot be stopped.

Natalie Montgomery, my wife and submissive, is the happily ever after I never knew I wanted, but she's exactly what I needed."

Every beat of my heart belongs to her.

She owns every part of me.

My heart is overflowing with love and adoration for Natalie. I promise to cherish and honor her. To spend the rest of my life ensuring that this beautiful and selfless woman, who not only challenges me but also gifts me with her submission, experiences nothing but the happily ever after she deserves.

Epilogue

TWO YEARS LATER...

It's the early morning hours of June eleventh. A short time ago, Natalie and I arrived at the hospital, her contractions already in full force. We've decided not to find out the sex of the baby, although we both have our guesses. I think we're having another little girl. Natalie disagrees.

Once again, Natalie insisted on not using any medication to dull the pain of her contractions. After a particularly difficult one, I'm ready to beg.

"Please let them give you something." I can't stand seeing her in agony.

"No," she says, still breathless from the last contraction.

"Do it for me." I'm desperate to see her out of pain.

"If I can do it, so can you."

And she thinks I'm stubborn.

The contractions are coming in quick succession, and Natalie's face contorts in pain.

"Look at me, baby girl. You've got this." I help her breathe through the worst of it. "It's going to start going away now," I say as I watch the printout on the monitor go down.

"Call Esperanza. I need to push."

My heart rate spikes. "You can't push. No one's in here."

"That's why I asked you to call her. Now, Alex. This baby's ready to come."

Instead of pressing the red button and waiting for someone to answer, I open the door. Luckily, Dr. Young is writing in a chart at the nurses' station.

"Doc, we need you," I call down the hall. "The baby's coming." Dr. Young finishes what he's doing before he and Esperanza begin walking down the hall. "Hurry, please." They're moving far too slowly for my liking.

Finally, they get to Natalie's room just as another contraction causes my wife more agony. She scrunches her face, struggling to breathe through it. I rush over to her, grabbing her hand. "I'm here. Breathe with me."

She mimics the short, quick breaths we learned in our childbirth class. I missed the final weeks of Natalie's pregnancy and Rose's birth. This time, I made sure to be there for everything.

Dr. Young finishes checking Natalie, and Esperanza is readjusting the bed like it's a transformer toy.

"She's ten centimeters," Dr. Young informs me. "Looks like you'll be sharing your birthday with your new baby, Alex."

Esperanza instructs me on how to hold Natalie's leg right as the next contraction hits. Then, Natalie bears down and pushes with all her might. We continue this process over and over until Dr. Young tells me the baby's head is crowning. That's when I switch positions, taking my spot next to the doctor to help bring my baby into the world.

"One more push, baby girl. You can do it."

When the contraction hits, my strong, brave wife pushes, and our baby's head appears.

"Ease up on the next push, Natalie," Dr. Young instructs.

With his hands over mine, he helps me maneuver our baby from Natalie's body into the world.

"It's a boy," I say reverently and lay our son on Natalie's chest.

Tears pour down my face. I'm overwhelmed at the sight of my child, who just moments ago was nestled inside Natalie's body.

"Are you ready to cut the cord?"

"I think so."

I take the offered scissors and cut where the doctor shows me. I've officially severed the cord between our son and his mother. Then, I return to my place next to my wife, tucking a stray curl behind her ear.

"You are amazing."

"I'm so glad you're here, Alex." She looks up at me, tears streaming down her face. "Happy Birthday."

"This is the most incredible present you could ever give me, baby girl." I lean over and kiss my wife. "I love you so very much."

"And I love you."

Esperanza takes our son from Natalie to finish cleaning him and get his measurements. I stand over her shoulder, watching like the nervous father I am.

"You're even worse than Viktor was," Esperanza jokes.

When we made our birthing plan with Dr. Young, Natalie insisted on explaining everything to Esperanza. Then she asked the older woman to be her labor and delivery nurse again. Esperanza was so moved by our story that she readily agreed.

"He's tiny," she says. "Five pounds three ounces and sixteen inches."

"Is he okay?" I ask, concerned.

"He's perfect." With the ease of a practiced nurse, she swaddles our son tightly in a blanket. "Does he have a name yet?" Esperanza asks as she passes the baby back to Natalie.

Natalie looks at me, and I nod. "His name is Michael Alexander Montgomery," she says.

Our son's name is a tribute to two extraordinary men. Michael, the uncle who will always be his guardian angel, and

Michael, the man who saved our lives. I'm honored for my son carries their name.

Esperanza writes it on his crib card, and then she and the doctor leave the room.

"Would you like to hold your son?"

I sit on the bed next to my wife as she passes me the tiny bundle. Cradling him in my arms, I'm moved beyond words as I gaze at the most perfect baby I've ever seen, except for his sister.

There's a knock on our door a second before it opens. Dr. Young has Rose in his arms. "Someone wanted to meet her little brother." The doctor sets her on the bed beside me before he leaves us again.

"Rose, this is your baby brother, Michael."

Rose looks curiously at the sleeping baby before she reaches out to touch him. Natalie reminds her to use gentle touches.

"Mikel," Rose says as she touches his cheek.

Natalie and I both laugh.

"It's clear she spends a lot of time with her Russian family."

Michael starts to fuss. I hand him back to Natalie, who helps him latch onto her breast for his first meal. Rose crawls onto my lap and watches.

"Mikel hunry," she says.

"Yes, Rose. Michael is hungry." I kiss her head.

Then, I watch as my newborn son suckles from his mother's breast while I hold our toddler on my lap.

This is my family. That realization is overwhelming.

"We're finally complete," Natalie says, looking up at me.

She's right. Baby Michael is the missing piece. The heartbeat we didn't know our family needed until he was here. With him in our arms, everything feels complete, like all the broken parts of us have finally fit together.

My chest tightens as I pull out my phone, the screen blurring for a moment through the sting of tears. With one arm, I guide Rose closer to Natalie, pressing us all together, unwilling to let go. I lift the phone and capture the first picture of us—our family, imperfect and scarred, but ours. Perfect in a way only we could understand.

It's true. We've been through hell. We've lived through moments that could have torn us apart, that should have broken us beyond repair. But instead of falling, we held on. Instead of crumbling, we rose from the wreckage. What we share now isn't fragile. It's love forged in fire, unbreakable and eternal.

I turn to the woman beside me, the woman who has been my anchor, my storm, and my salvation. My throat closes as the words come, raw and certain.

She is my yesterday.

My today.

My forever.

The End

Viktor is leaving New York with a shattered heart and nothing left to fight for.

The woman he wanted was never his to love.

Now he's going back to Ukraine with nothing except a heart barely holding together.

But he's about to learn rock bottom has no mercy.

Continue the Fire & Ice series in *His Melody*.

Find Tara's Books Here

About Tara

Bestselling author Tara Conrad writes where passion meets peril, crafting dark, spellbinding romances that blur the line between devotion and destruction.

Inspired by the haunting brilliance of Edgar Allan Poe, her stories reimagine Gothic tales with modern sensuality and power.

Within her pages, heroines rise unbroken, villains fall beautifully, and the darkness always tells the truth.

When she isn't writing, Tara travels with her husband, meeting readers who have found pieces of themselves in her worlds.

She believes love isn't always light. Sometimes, it's found in the dark. 🖤

Acknowledgments

First, I have to thank my husband, George. Alex and Natalie's story wouldn't be what it is today if it weren't for your help. I thought it was a lot of work getting these books out the first time, but getting them out for their re-release has been a whole new experience. There's no one else I'd want to do this with. You're the brains behind the operation. You're my plot twist generator. You are the most patient man, listening to me read and re-read each book until you could recite them from memory. And then there's research—the best part of this gig. You are my yesterday, my today, and my tomorrow. i love You!

To my children (and you, too, Jonathan): thank you for all of your patience. I know there are many days I stay locked away in the office or sit with my headphones on in the living room. I appreciate your patience and support. The five of you are my biggest cheering section. Your encouragement keeps me going on days when I want to give up. You give me ideas for what to post on social media. And you're always ready to go to all my signings. I love you all very much.

Thank you to my beta readers: You ladies are speed readers! I appreciate and value your honesty. You aren't afraid to tell me when something needs to be corrected. You've helped make these stories better and this experience much more fun.

To all my new readers: Wow! It's been quite the journey with Alex and Natalie. I've loved getting to know each of you and am so very thankful for the love and support you've shown me. I have many more adventures planned, and I hope you'll be there for all of them.

National Human Trafficking Resource Center 1-888-373-7888
TTY 711
Text HELP to 233733

ONLINE RESOURCES

www.dhs.gov/bluecampaign

polarisproject.org

humantraffickinghotline.org